## CODE NAME: NANNY

"Delightful and memorable . . . another sizzling adventure romance." —*Romance*

"A fun story blending romance with intrigue. The characters are hot, and so is the book." —*Hawthorne Press Tribune*

## HOT PURSUIT

"Sky has hit her stride with this delightful Navy SEAL romance. . . . A compelling story; endearing, well-developed primary characters . . . and sizzling, sensual sex scenes make Skye's latest a romance not to be missed." —*Booklist* (starred review)

"Skye writes briskly and well. The story hums right along . . . and Skye's descriptions of the California shoreline are marvelously evocative." —*Pittsburgh Post-Gazette*

"Entertaining, engrossing and jam-packed with action and fun, *Hot Pursuit* is sure to please fans of romantic suspense." —*Romance Reviews Today*

# code name :Princess

## CHRISTINA SKYE

A Dell Book

CODE NAME: PRINCESS
A Dell Book / October 2004

Published by
Bantam Dell
A Division of Random House, Inc.
New York, New York

ISBN 0–440–23761–0

Manufactured in the United States of America
Published simultaneously in Canada

OPM 10 9 8 7 6 5 4 3 2 1

*For Christine Helmer*

code
name 'Princess

# prologue

---

**S**omething was wrong.

The woman stood unmoving, trying to shake a bad case of the jitters. Closing her eyes, she worked back through every step of her day.

No clear threats. No signs of pursuit or surveillance. But the uneasiness continued. Cold, like nagging fingers that wouldn't let go.

She checked the nearby playpen. No problems there.

Maybe the weirdness factor of this job was finally getting to her.

Frowning, she pulled out her cell phone and punched in a number. With the movement, a silver badge gleamed briefly beneath her blazer.

"Yeah, it's Agent Harrison. I just ran a perimeter check and the package is safe. Estimated departure time tomorrow is 0500 hours. Maintain full security at the dock until then." When her instructions were complete, she ended the call, glancing into the playpen set up near the end of the bed.

The face she saw there made her smile, even though she wasn't remotely maternal or nurturing, which meant this job was *definitely* getting to her.

She was about to kick off her shoes, when she heard a knock at the door.

"Portland P.D., ma'am."

She didn't answer, moving away from the window, her mind already racing through defensive options.

"Ms. Harrison, are you in there?"

The agent took a deep breath and checked the peephole, frowning. "Give me your name and ID number."

There was a pause. "John Wilson, ma'am. Badge number 21109. Feel free to check with the station."

*You bet I will.* Agent Harrison pulled the playpen closer. As she did, the blanket slipped off the small, sleeping form beneath it.

Smoothing the blanket protectively, she hit the speed dial of her cell phone and spoke quietly. "Izzy? Right, I'm here at the safe house in Portland, right behind the Sunrise Suites. The package is fine, but something is damn strange, because I've got Portland P.D. banging on my front door."

There was another knock, and it was harder this time. "Ma'am, I'm afraid we need you to step outside."

"Izzy, check the Portland roster for a John Wilson, ID number 21109. Sure, I'll hold on. The door's got a dead bolt and I rigged a few additions of my own, but don't take too much time. Princess will be waking up soon." The agent glanced at the playpen. The pink baby blanket shifted and a furry face looked back at her.

Big expressive eyes, fresh from sleep. Round dark ears.

"Shhh, honey." The FBI field agent smiled crookedly. "Aunt Moira is right here and everything's fine. I'll get your bottle in a minute." She heard a burst of static, and then Izzy Teague, one of the finest security operatives she knew, cut back onto the line.

"No go, Harrison. The name's real, but Wilson's on sick leave today. Your man's a fake, and two green vans just pulled up in the back alley. Five people are currently in place, and I've got a SEAL team en route, so stay low and do not open the door. I repeat, *do not open your door* unless the code word is given."

"Copy that, Izzy."

The doorknob shook. Something big slammed against the wood, shaking the whole wall.

"Better get a move on those SEALs. My visitors are getting nasty."

Cool after years of training, the agent checked her field weapon and then lifted a silver-white koala bear out of the playpen, tucking the world's rarest mammal into a padded Kevlar baby carrier at her chest. As she headed for the stairs to the fortified attic, two bullets hammered the lock on the front door.

"Teague, I'm under attack. Get me that SEAL team pronto."

She was halfway up the stairs when the window behind her exploded in a shower of glass. Automatic weapons spit angrily from the parking lot, the front door slammed open, and the agent fell backward, her precious cargo cradled at her chest.

Her fingers were struggling with empty air as the room went dark around her.

# chapter 1

*Ten hours later*
*Washington State, near*
*the Canadian border*

The wind hit him like an ice pick from hell.

It was a nasty night in a week of nasty nights, but Hawk Mackenzie barely noticed. After twelve years as a Navy SEAL, bad nights were his specialty.

He studied the rugged terrain around him. Layered tracks led across the cliffs and then turned sharply, looping back to the road.

*They'd stopped here for a break.*

As Hawk maneuvered his powerful off-road motorcycle through ankle-high mud, his encrypted cell phone began to beep.

"Mackenzie here."

"This is Teague. What have you got?"

"Motorcycle tracks. Probably a dozen or so, but only three sets look fresh. Hold on." Hawk smiled grimly. "Someone's been through here recently, Izzy. Thanks to the rain, most of the detail is gone, but I'd say we're talking three dirt bikes." He ran a flashlight over the wet, freshly gouged earth. "The tracks heading back to the road appear to be deeper, too. Before they turned around, they picked up more weight."

Since the man on the other end of the line was one of the government's finest security operatives, Hawk knew every word between them was being recorded. After the call was complete, every detail would be tracked and analyzed.

"You're sure they had more weight when they left?"

"No doubt about it." Hawk pulled out a digital camera and powered up the flash. "I'm running some shots for you now. Maybe you can pull details from the tire tracks. Off the cuff I'd say there are three or four usable footprints here, too, probably from boots."

Ishmael Teague was silent for a long moment. "I need a field assessment, Mackenzie. Where are they headed?"

The Navy SEAL squinted into the icy rain sheeting down the cliff face. "They know the terrain, Izzy. If I hadn't been right on top of these tracks, I never would have found them. The tracks appear to be running north, so the obvious answer would be Canada."

Keys tapped quickly at a computer. "But—?"

"But I don't buy it. I think they'll stay local." Hawk studied the mud, frowning. "They'll go to ground and try to wait us out."

Hawk had been teamed with Izzy Teague before, involved in covert missions that required brains, guts and seat-of-the-pants planning, and Hawk trusted the man without reservation.

And trust was something Hawk didn't give easily.

"So you advise that we scratch our surveillance team in Portland?"

"Roger that." The SEAL hunched his shoulders against the driving rain, reading the terrain for subtle clues he might have missed. "Put a skeleton force in place for insurance. Meanwhile, I'll stay up here. Call it a bad ache in my bones, but I think something's out here."

Izzy bit back a curse. "I don't need to remind you that careers—and a hell of a lot of lives—are riding on this mission."

"No, you don't have to remind me." As he spoke, Hawk left his bike and walked in a careful circle, trying to piece together what had happened here.

*Three off-road bikes, traveling fast.*

*Men with heavy boots, staying close to the granite edge so they'd leave few prints.*

As his flashlight swept the ground, Hawk frowned. There were no dropped cigarette butts, no water bottles, no candy wrappers. All he found were three partial foot-prints and several indistinct tire tracks.

Phone in hand, the SEAL squinted out at the gunmetal water below him. "They're pros, Izzy. This place is clean. If they go to ground and try to wait us out, the weather is on their side. There have to be a thousand coves and inlets where they can hide along the Sound or across the Strait."

"The weather's heading downhill, too. I just pulled up the latest satellite maps, and tonight's winds are expected to top forty miles per hour."

Hawk said a few choice words under his breath. More dark clouds were already shouldering their way toward the coast.

"It's your call." Izzy Teague sounded irritated. "If you think they'll stay local, maintain your search area. Check in every six hours, and record all information precisely. Heads are going to roll if we don't recover this package pronto."

"No need for reminders." Hawk knew exactly what this mission entailed. As a SEAL, he was used to mantras about national security, but warnings about *a scientific debacle* and *grave medical consequences* indicated a whole new threat level. "I'll hang around here and see if I can find anything else before the rain scours the cliffs clean."

"Copy that." Izzy cleared his throat. "How are your ribs holding up?"

"What ribs?" Hawk picked his way slowly over the muddy ground. If he allowed himself to think about it, his pain was constant, despite the top-secret meds the Navy was testing on him.

"The ribs you broke two months ago, Mackenzie."

"They're no worse than they were yesterday."

Which wasn't saying a hell of a lot.

But Hawk Mackenzie knew this corner of Washington State better than anyone, and he didn't cave in to pain, so his tone was steady as he walked back to his mud-spattered bike. "Gotta go, Izzy. Wind's picking up."

"Keep your search short, and upload those images as soon as you get back to the hotel. If there's any speck of evidence left, I'll isolate it."

Hawk knew this was no idle boast. The man on the other end of the phone could geek one pixel out of a million until you knew names and dates—who, what and why.

"Roger that, Izzy. Signing off now."

"Keep your powder dry, Navy."

Hawk stared into the sheeting rain. Staying dry tonight was about as likely as getting laid.

Thirty minutes later more rain was hammering down the cliff, and the last hint of tracks was gone.

Cold and disgusted, Hawk packed up his flashlight and waterproof camera and kick-started his dirt bike. The pain at his side was angry and insistent, like a crowbar going in slowly under the bone, and the sooner he got inside, the better.

Izzy had arranged a suite at a swank hotel along the

coast, where Hawk could power up his laptop and upload his high-resolution digital images, then grab a short nap before he headed out again.

But first Hawk had a treacherous ride ahead of him.

A section of the cliff vanished in a brown slide of mud as he toed his bike into gear, all the while struck by the sense that he was being watched. When he finally made his way down the mountain, he was drenched to the skin and covered with mud, his ribs throbbing.

He tried to hide his exhaustion as he shouldered his backpack and strode through the lobby toward his room. Thanks to his carefully nurtured identity as a nature photographer on assignment for a respected travel magazine, there would be no questions about his odd hours or bedraggled appearance. The bored night manager nodded as he passed, and Hawk noticed that the waitress in the lounge off the lobby shot him a glance that suggested intimate possibilities.

But the SEAL's only concern was the fastest route to his room. All his thoughts were focused on his current assignment, recovering a top-secret donor mammal stolen from a secure location in Portland, leaving two agents dead and two more wounded.

Hawk's boots squished softly as he left the elevator and checked the hall. When he was certain no one was too close or too interested, he inserted his room key and waited impatiently for the green light to flash on the entrance pad.

Nothing happened.

*Damned electronics.* He swiped his key card again, controlling his impatience as icy water trickled down his neck. When the red light continued to flash, he inserted a small silver chip in the scanner. Within seconds the light flashed once, then changed to solid green.

Mission accomplished, thanks to Izzy's latest electronic wizardry.

After pocketing his priceless and highly illicit piece of technology, Hawk stepped inside, where he was immediately hit by the faint scent of perfume. A suitcase stood on the floor next to the closet, and a robe lay neatly folded across the end of the bed, covered by a red silk scarf.

He froze, focused on the off-key singing that drifted down the hall. Only two people knew that he was here and both of them had security clearance at the highest levels. It was impossible that either one would have betrayed his location.

Palming his field knife, he moved silently down the hall toward the shower. Steam drifted past as he put down his knapsack and glanced around the corner.

There was a woman in front of him.

A completely naked woman who was using his shower.

His first thought was that he'd opened the door to the wrong room. Since no electronic lock outside the Pentagon's E-wing was immune to Izzy's newest gadget, Hawk silently rechecked the number.

It was his number, and it was his room. What the hell was going on?

He moved back into the shadows, watching the woman lather shampoo into her hair and crank out a hip-gyrating, off-key Rolling Stones classic while hot water pounded over her shoulders. Hawk took a good look at the rest of her body, chin to toe. Even through the steam and the haze on the glass, that part of her looked just as interesting as what he had seen so far.

The woman had amazing legs. Her ass looked pretty damned nice, too, and while he waited for her to turn around, he felt a nudge of desire, which he ruthlessly suppressed.

When she started into a new song, he fingered his cell phone, inching back into the living room.

Izzy picked up on the second ring. "Joe's Pizza."

"There's a woman in my shower," Hawk whispered. "She looks to be five seven, maybe 140. Caucasian. Black hair." Bending down, he studied her suitcase. "Initials are E.G. Check the hotel database and see what you find."

As he waited, Hawk glanced through the closet.

A worn denim jacket. A pair of black jeans. A gray University of California sweatshirt. A pink silk suit with puffy sleeves and a short, tight skirt.

Somehow the jeans didn't track with the suit.

Hawk frowned. He was about to go for her purse when Izzy came back on the line.

"Hotel records show a new person registered in your room. Her name is Elena Grimaldi. No other information is available via the hotel computer."

"If *she's* here, where am I supposed to be?"

"You were moved to a different wing about two hours ago. It could be a computer error."

"Yeah, and I could be *Time* magazine's Man of the Year." Hawk cradled the phone, watching the hall to the shower. "What do you have on this Grimaldi woman? Is she a foreign national?"

Keys clicked rapidly on a keyboard. "No sign of any passport registered in that name entering the U.S. in the last six months." The keys clicked again. "The IRS has nothing available on that name either."

"So she's an illegal?"

"Looks like it. She's got no driver's license, no car or health insurance." More keys clicked. "*Whoa*—I just brought up a credit card. Only one. Strange that there's nothing else in that name."

A fake identity, Hawk thought grimly. Someone was

baiting a nice mousetrap for him with a wet, willing and very attractive female body.

The singing halted. A towel slid over the shower door and vanished. "Gotta go, Izzy. Keep on digging."

"Will do. Watch your back, pal."

Hawk broke the connection. The field knife was still hidden at his jacket sleeve when he sat down in the shadows, exhaustion forgotten. He'd give his intruder five seconds to start explaining who the hell she was and why she was in his room. If he didn't like what he heard, he'd start eliciting answers in the most direct way. Naked or not, gorgeous or not, the woman was a simple military objective as far as he was concerned.

Down the corridor, the shower door opened. Watching the mirror nearby, Hawk saw steam billow out into the airy bathroom. She worked at her tangled hair with a comb, mouthing an old Beach Boys tune, and with every movement her towel hitched up, offering him an excellent view of long legs and wet, gleaming skin.

A moment later she disappeared. Water ran in the sink, and bottles slid across the vanity. Hawk stood up, his back to the wall, as fabric rustled next door.

When she finally reappeared, a dry towel covered her damp body and her hair lay thick and dark on her shoulders. Big white cotton balls were stuck between her toes and she walked carefully, rubbing some kind of cream on her bare arms.

Certain that no weapons were visible, Hawk picked his moment and shot forward, spinning her hard. Her lips worked but she didn't make a sound. No protests or screams emerged. He felt her body tense, shock merging with panic.

And then her eyes went blank, almost as if she were

about to faint. The oldest dodge in the book, he thought grimly.

"Who are you?" she rasped.

He didn't answer.

She took a shuddering breath. "Are you from Kelleher's office?"

Hawk shook his head once.

"Did Isaacson send you?" Her voice was squeaky and tight.

He filed the names away in his memory on the slim chance she had revealed two of her contacts. He decided the greed angle would work best, and he was about to offer her triple what the others were paying, when he noticed a container leaning against the corner of the bed. Made of reinforced mesh with heavy black nylon straps, it resembled the carriers used for medium-size dogs.

Or for a priceless, genetically engineered government lab animal.

Hawk checked the floor. There was no sign of movement, but a smart operative would have hidden the animal immediately.

Outside in the night, lightning cracked and wind hurled itself against the small balcony. Hawk decided it was time for answers. "Where did you hide it?"

Her eyes widened. Then she dug her nails into his shoulders and began to scream.

Hawk cut her off with one hand clamped across her mouth. He was cold, wet and disgusted. His ribs hurt, his mood was getting nastier by the second and he wasn't inclined to be patient.

He turned her slowly so that he could check the whole floor behind the bed, conscious of his orders to guard the missing animal at all cost. As a SEAL, he was fully prepared to give his life to guarantee that safety. Anyone who got in his way would be immobilized, male or female.

Something stabbed him hard in his side, just below his ribs. He grunted at the sudden wave of pain burning from his old wound. His hand loosened slightly, and in a second she shot past him. She was struggling with the front door when Hawk spun her around and shoved her against the wall beside the open door.

"Where is it?" he growled.

She didn't answer, fighting furiously.

*"Where did you put it?"*

"Where did I put what? When I tell Isaacson about this, you'll be fired. I don't care about the deadline or any other instructions they gave you."

So she knew about the deadline to recover the animal?

But there was something too pat about the explanation.

Hawk scowled as she managed to wedge one bare foot in the open door. Down the hall two men emerged from the elevator, and any minute the damned female was going to create a scene, which was the last thing the government needed.

"Move your foot out of the doorway." His arm circled her throat to keep her from screaming. "Otherwise, I start breaking small bones."

She paid no attention. Her towel slipped as she fought back wildly, slamming him in the ribs with her fist.

So she'd been briefed on his weak points.

"Two can play dirty, honey." His arm tightened, cutting off her air while he held her in place with his body. But her foot was still wedged in the open door, and the two men were getting closer.

"I'm just—doing—what they pay me to do." The words were a hoarse whisper.

"So were the Nazi death squads, honey."

She was bordering on hysteria now, thrashing wildly. Hawk knew his options were dwindling fast.

That left him one choice.

His fingers feathered along her collarbone, fast and expert. They tightened sharply until she stopped fighting.

Five seconds later she was sliding down the wall into his arms, out cold.

# chapter 2

**H**awk opened the bedroom door silently. It was still early and Elena Grimaldi was out cold where he had left her on the bed. As a precaution he had clipped her wrist in a plastic hand restraint, which he attached to the head of the bed. No running away for this Mata Hari.

With his intruder immobilized, Hawk pulled a laptop from his backpack and set it up to download his digital photos from the cliffs. While the photographs loaded, he stripped off his muddy clothes and took a two-minute shower, alert for any noises from the bedroom. Not that it mattered, because the lady was going nowhere.

After his shower, he checked on her again, but Elena Grimaldi slept on, one foot dangling from the bed. Quickly he rebandaged his ribs and then inspected the closet. Three sweaters were neatly folded on an upper shelf next to a big leather purse. At the back of the highest shelf, he found a worn pair of red sneakers, contrasting sharply with the pink silk suit nearby. Why did he get the sense of MTV meets haute couture?

Curious, Hawk opened her purse and pulled out a well-worn notebook carrying pages full of times, dates and names, along with what looked like detailed descriptions of various hotels. Security assessments of civilian targets? In an inside pocket he found breath mints, dental floss and a half-used packet of birth control pills.

The lady got around, he thought wryly. Searching one of the dressers, he pulled out an old and well-used laptop. Hawk booted it up, waiting for a password query and security protocols.

He was surprised when none came. Files filled the screen, organized under neat directories by date, location and what appeared to be hotel names. Hawk took a closer look, puzzled to see precise evaluations of housekeeping, restaurant facilities, public areas and recreation staff. There were records of hygiene compliance and services performed by employees, including names and dates. Occasionally an employee's name was flagged in red, along with a note about unacceptable work or guest complaints.

Hawk sat back, staring at the computer. Her security was nonexistent, but the files could have been recorded in some kind of code. If so, it was different from any others he'd seen.

But guest complaints? Hygiene compliance?

He noticed the frayed bottom of her leather purse and the hole in her right shoe, lying on its side in the bottom of the closet. A sweater was folded neatly on the desk, and he saw careful stitches across one elbow, where it looked recently mended.

Who the hell *was* Elena Grimaldi?

The surf was coming in, murmuring lightly along the hot sand. There were no car payments to worry about, no pennies to pinch. Only the beach stretched before her, with no responsibilities, no schedules—

Abruptly Jess Mulcahey woke up. Her eyes snapped open as memories returned in a rush.

Had the hotel found out about her visit in advance? Was that why the man had broken into her room while she showered?

If only she'd managed to wrench the door open before he'd—

Before what?

Shivering, Jess looked down at the towel draped loosely around her body. The last thing she remembered, he'd done something with his hand, and then everything blurred.

And now she was locked to the bed by some kind of hard plastic cuff that made her whole arm burn.

In growing fright, she stared out the partially opened door. Was the crazy commando-type in the leather jacket still nearby?

A drawer closed outside in the little sitting area. She sprawled back on the bed, feigning sleep and trying to ignore the terrified hammering of her heart. Footsteps crossed the hall and approached the bed.

She could almost see him frowning down at her.

Somehow she managed not to flinch when his fingers touched her wrist, measuring her pulse beneath the plastic cuff. The blanket beside her shifted, and then the quiet footsteps moved back down the hall.

A chair creaked, and she heard him speaking on a phone.

She scowled at her wrist, which was burning savagely. Anger warred with panic as she scanned the room. Then her eyes narrowed on the bedside chest.

Twisting hard, she opened the drawer with her left hand crossed tight over her chest.

Telephone directory.

Blank postcards.

Laundry schedule.

Twisting, she looked on the other side of the bed. A bottle of bright pink nail polish lay on the edge of the bed, where she had left it just before her shower. But it was the thought of the tweezer and nail clippers in her carry-on bag that made her heart pound.

But the bag was on a chair at the far side of the bed. Grimacing, Jess stretched out her free arm, coming nowhere within reach. When her first effort failed, she wriggled down and dangled her foot as far as she could, ignoring the pain from the plastic band digging into her wrist.

Her toe nudged the bag, then curled, hooking one handle. Holding her breath, she pulled the bag back across the carpet until it rested at the edge of the bed.

In the room next door the man was pacing, snapping out quick questions. Jess heard him ask something about topo maps and satellite photos. What was he, a spy as well as a kidnapper?

She forced down her fear and concentrated on finding her nail trimmers. Her hands were slippery with sweat by the time she pulled them out and fit them over the plastic restraint.

Three times the clippers slipped free. Jess's fingers began to shake. Outside she heard the footsteps cross back and forth.

Desperate, she shoved the narrow blades over the ridged plastic, gripped hard and felt the plastic snap in two.

Outside the talking suddenly stopped. She heard the chair creak.

She dropped the nail trimmers, hiked up her towel and crept to the open door. He was facing away from her at the desk, glaring down at a digital camera hooked up to an expensive laptop.

"No, the woman's still asleep, but she should be coming

around before long." When he stood up to pace again, Jess inched behind the door so he wouldn't see her. "I checked her laptop and found files on hotel properties and staff performance. Beats the hell out of me what those could be used for." His voice hardened. "Possible hostage scenarios? A terrorist assessing civilian targets?"

He thought she was a *terrorist*? Furious, Jess reached for the door, determined to set the record straight.

Immediately common sense prevailed. The man outside was either crazy or a criminal—maybe both. And the woman who had registered as Elena Grimaldi wasn't a pampered princess, the offspring of an obscure branch of European royalty, the way she'd explained when she had registered. She wasn't wealthy or arrogant, and the expensive designer shoes and pink silk suit in her closet were simply part of a professional disguise. As Elena Grimaldi, Jess lived large, dispensing big tips and bigger bribes to see how many workers she could find to break hotel rules in return for personal gain. Well trained and efficient, Jess noted hotel strengths and weaknesses in detailed reports filed within hours of her visit. In the last month alone she had visited twenty-one different properties, finding serious problems in eighteen of them.

Just that morning, as Elena Grimaldi, Jess had slipped fifty dollars into a clerk's pocket and asked that a registered hotel guest be shifted so that she could have a better room location. The bribe had been successful.

Of course, she hadn't expected that a crazy man would ambush her on the way out of her shower or suspect that she was a terrorist. So, was her crazed mystery man some kind of security agent working for the hotel?

*Not your problem, Mulcahey. Get out fast, file your report, then forget all about it.*

A quick peek out the window revealed a narrow balcony

about eight feet above the ground. Difficult but not impossible, she decided.

Silently, she pulled a pair of sweatpants and a T-shirt out of the square mesh laundry bag beside her bed and changed quickly. Shoes would have been nice, but her assailant would definitely spot any move toward the closet. As she finished dressing, Jess heard him on the phone, asking questions about tire prints and weather predictions. She didn't understand any of it, but she certainly wasn't hanging around for clarification.

She slid open the bedroom window and climbed onto the balcony, shivering in the icy wind.

Her captor was just finishing on the phone. "I sent through all the digital shots from the cliff. See what you can do with those tire prints, Izzy. If they're expensive, we could locate dealers and subpoena sales records. Yeah, I'm in for the night, unless our carpetbagger causes more trouble. I'll find out what I can, then you can take her off my hands. After I catch a few hours of sleep, I'll head north and see if I can pick up their trail."

Jess barely heard, focusing on closing the window behind her. Gritting her teeth, she eased the frame down slowly, wishing she could go back for her purse.

"My suitcase? Yeah, it was in the new room. I called downstairs and was told everything had been switched while I was out." A few choice words followed. "Izzy, I have to go."

Cold rain hit Jess's face. Her bare feet slipped as she climbed over the icy railing and jumped to the ground.

She staggered, then stood up slowly.

No broken bones; always a positive sign.

Wincing, she ran across the wet grass, making mental notes shaping a report that would make heads roll, starting with her kidnapper's.

The hotel job had come at a time when she needed a change. Her sister had never understood her restlessness, but then, Summer was established in her career as an FBI field agent in Philadelphia. Meanwhile, Jess had been eager to stand on her own two feet, and when she revealed a flair for the dramatic, along with an intuitive skill at assessing people, her employment agency had recommended her for the job of hotel investigator.

Now she was on the road an average of twenty-five days per month, always careful to maintain her false identity and smile seductively while she probed for any secrets a hotel manager might prefer to hide.

And the current hotel manager was going to get a tongue-lashing he would never forget.

Hawk scanned the bedroom and swore. The woman was gone, her towel tossed on the floor. The nylon carrier lay open on top of the robe, next to the cut plastic restraint.

He felt a cold wind. Curtains fluttered through the crack in the window, which she hadn't closed completely behind her when she'd escaped. He crossed the room and looked out, cursing as he saw her run over the grass, bare feet flashing.

His face hardened. He closed the window and packed up all his gear. In minutes he was gone, leaving no trace.

# chapter 3

**B**ut he was there a minute ago. I heard him talking on the phone."

Jess stared at the uniformed hotel security guard in the doorway of her room. "He knocked me out and cuffed me to the bed."

The guard looked unconvinced. "Sorry, ma'am. All I know is that no one's here now. Check the other room for yourself if you don't believe me."

Jess stalked past him, throwing open the closet and the door to the bedroom. Both were empty, except for her shoes and jacket. To her surprise her purse was still where she'd left it, too.

Aware that the hotel guard was watching her curiously, Jess took a deep breath and assessed her situation. She had already decided to cut her investigation short and leave as soon as she collected her things. Before she'd taken this assignment, she'd heard warnings about this particular hotel, which had a reputation for harassing inspectors. But she had never expected a physical assault in her room.

First things first.

She decided to make a quick stop downstairs to stock up on coffee, fruit, and free pastries from the self-serve kitchen off the lobby. That way she would be stocked adequately for her drive home to San Diego.

Every penny helped.

The security guard was still waiting impatiently at the door. "Are you done here, ma'am?"

Jess summoned a smile. "Everything's fine now. Thanks for taking a look."

"No problem. I'll call in a report, ma'am." The guard headed back outside, fingering his walkie-talkie before the door had closed behind him.

After he left, Jess stood tensely in the middle of the room. The attack was like a horrible dream, after weeks of nonstop travel. Her shoulders sagged. She realized how much she wanted to be at home in her small apartment, where she'd always felt safe.

Jess closed her eyes, struggling beneath a wave of hopelessness as she remembered the clever way she had been suckered into a new hotel venture in Mexico with its "guaranteed" promise of ground-floor profits for the first ten investors.

At first the enterprise had been solid, banked by reputable American and Mexican firms. The profits had seemed like a sure thing until the owners had vanished in the night, leaving Jess and the other investors with useless contracts, broken promises and a pile of debts.

Now her shoes had holes and she had to squirrel away food at every hotel she visited. She felt powerless or humiliated when she thought of all she had lost, which happened to be almost every penny of her savings.

But there was no going back and no point in kicking herself for being naïve. If she wanted to be paid, she had a job to do. She'd finish her report and be on her way.

With any kind of luck, this whole nightmare would be nothing more than a bad memory in a few hours.

---

Hawk stared north, squinting into the wind.

Driftwood littered the beach around him, and low-lying clouds darkened the gray water stretching between Washington and Canada. He'd left the hotel and followed the road west, hugging the coast, stopping often to check for signs of motorcycle tracks. He wasn't overly disappointed when he found nothing, because the mountains hugged the coast here, making off-road travel next to impossible. Eventually, however, they would have pulled off for a break, and the isolated wildlife refuge where Hawk stood was a perfect spot to avoid prying eyes.

To the north, surf pounded the spit of land that curved out into the Strait of Juan de Fuca. Beneath a gunmetal sky, waterbirds nested on the tidal flats, oblivious to Hawk as he moved slowly along the beach. Turning inland, he searched for tire marks or footprints that had survived the rain. Patient and thorough, he covered the entire beach and all its gravel access roads. Finally, at the far side of the cove, protected from the numbing north wind, he found the sign he had been looking for.

The partial print of a metal-tipped motorcycle boot lay protected in a hollow between two rocks. The print was fresh, and Hawk quickly snapped six shots for Izzy. Following the beach for two hundred feet, he came across a second bootprint indented in a patch of moss. When Hawk bent down to capture the detail with his camera, he saw a tiny wedge of chewed gum nearby. With gloved fingers he slid the evidence into a plastic bag. Having a recent DNA sample to accompany the boot imprint would make the government's job easier.

To the north the San Juan Islands were hidden beneath a layer of clouds. Even as Hawk worked, Izzy was researching motorcycle travelers who had used the local ferries.

Private boat rentals would be harder to trace, but Izzy was making inroads there, too. Meanwhile, some instinct told Hawk that the men he was tracking hadn't left the peninsula. Between the rugged Olympic Mountains and the rain forests in the south, there were a thousand places where a well-provisioned and experienced outdoor team could vanish for weeks, taking a stolen animal with them.

Hawk's current orders were to track the attackers without alerting local residents. Privately, he suspected that telling the truth would have been easier and more effective, but sometimes telling the truth was dangerous—at least that's what the politicians and experts kept saying.

With the light fading fast, he slid his camera into his pack and studied the road that looped west. In a few hours he would be back, hoping for more sunlight and another glimpse of a motorcycle boot.

As rain struck his face, Hawk cursed softly, wet and cold, angry that he hadn't come up with more solid evidence. He wondered how far the woman in the shower had gotten and what kind of story she had told the hotel staff. She was unquestionably smart and resourceful, and he still railed at himself for not securing *both* of her hands.

Down the road a bus lumbered into view, its lights blurred by the heavy rain. Hawk realized his ribs were aching again.

So much for the Navy's latest experiment with tissue regrowth medications. Right now an elastic bandage and a dry towel would have been a hell of a lot more useful to him, and they'd be a damned sight cheaper.

Shouldering his backpack, he revved his motorcycle and headed back the way he had come.

It was done, Jess thought. Her report was finished, sent via e-mail, and she couldn't wait to hit the road.

She tossed her single suitcase into the back of her Jeep, shivering in the cold rain. Despite the storm, she meant to push south without a break until she reached Portland.

As she started her car, Jess glanced over her shoulder nervously. Inspectors had one ironclad rule in her occupation: check out and *then* file the report. Those who forgot the rule risked verbal harassment or physical retaliation. In her case, she figured the harassment had already begun. She was lucky she'd come away with no more than a few bruises.

Anxiety made her floor the Jeep down the hotel's main driveway. Her cell phone began to ring, but she ignored it, peering into the gray light as the road twisted through fingers of mist.

After a brief pause, the shrill peals began again.

Muttering, she dug into her purse for her phone. "I can't talk now," she snapped. "I just turned in a report."

"Did they pay you this time?" a dry female voice asked.

"I *always* get paid." It was a lie, she knew. Her checks usually arrived several months late, stretching her finances perilously thin. "I'm fine, I'm happy, and I'll call you in thirty minutes, Summer. I want to get away from the hotel. Especially *this* hotel."

"Why?" Jess's twin sister said sharply. "Did something happen to you?"

"Nothing's happened, but I have to go. The fog's getting worse."

"What fog?" Summer Mulcahey's voice changed, more worried than irritated. "Where the heck are you, Jess? You're breaking up."

"I just checked out of a hotel on the Olympic Peninsula. Sorry, Summer, but I've really got to go."

"Okay, call me, hear? Make it soon."

A few minutes after Jess cut the connection, lights flashed on a gravel road that wound down to the beach.

She had meant to explore the cove, but she never had. As usual, there had been too much work to do.

She shivered a little, bumping up the heat while the motor whined. She realized she needed to clean her carburetor and check the idle. Though she loved her Jeep, it had seen plenty of off-road miles and was in need of some major repairs, none of which she could currently afford.

One more consequence of being incredibly stupid and trusting people she barely knew.

Suddenly car lights cut across the highway. A commercial delivery van swerved from its lane and passed a farm truck, headed directly for her.

Braking hard, Jess turned onto the shoulder, her tires spinning in the mud. The van fishtailed, its lights leaving her temporarily blinded, and she swung hard to the right to avoid impact. Her Jeep took a half-circle through the mud and the van raced past her with inches to spare.

A black shape flashed through the trees on her left. Jess jerked the wheel hard, trying to maneuver out of the mud and back onto the road while the farm truck rumbled toward her, also on the left. Somewhere ahead of her came the powerful whine of a motorcycle traveling off-road.

In the Jeep's headlights Jess suddenly saw a black helmet, sleek chrome exhaust pipes and a driver in a black jacket. Because of the sharp curve and the farm truck blocking his view, Jess realized he wouldn't be able to see her until he was nearly on top of her.

As she churned through the mud, clouds drifted over the trees, veiling the road. When the rider took the turn without slowing, Jess wrenched the wheel sharply, trying to clear a path for him, but she spun out in the mud, struck a boulder and then fishtailed sideways.

The sickening *thump* she heard next was the sound of a body slamming against her front fender.

# chapter 4

Jess crouched in the rain, fighting panic. She'd struck a man with her car. Hit him hard, with almost no warning. Now he wasn't moving, and she was probably a murderer. Meanwhile, he was bleeding heavily.

Clamping down on her hysteria, Jess moved so she could check his face. She tried opening one of his eyes carefully with her finger, but he didn't react. When her hands slipped on something that felt like blood, she gave a start and sprawled back on the ground in the mud. Wincing, she pulled off one of the man's gloves and searched desperately for a pulse.

Yes. No.

*Maybe?*

But she was no doctor, and she couldn't tell if he had a pulse, especially with her hands shaking like Jell-O. Meanwhile, her victim still wasn't moving, wasn't making any noise, and neither seemed to be a good sign.

*Cold.*

Suddenly Jess remembered reading about heat loss in cases of shock and trauma. Dragging her coat out of the Jeep, she draped the heavy wool over his motionless body.

When her fingers brushed his neck, she felt the warm, sticky thing again and was certain it was blood.

She had to call the police or 911. She needed help *now*.

A shrill ringing broke through her panic. Not her cell phone, Jess realized, but his. The sound was coming from somewhere inside his leather jacket.

After a few fumbled tries, she managed to find a small silver flip phone. "Yes," she answered, gasping. "Who is this?"

She heard a little click, followed by silence.

"If you're there, answer me. I need help." Her voice broke. "Hello?" Shivering, she leaned over the man on the ground and continued to talk. "He's not moving. Dear God, he's not saying anything. I'm afraid that I killed him."

"Killed who?" The voice on the phone was male, cold and clipped.

"The man. The one you were calling. I found this phone in his jacket after he—he fell." Jess swallowed hard, trying to stay lucid. "He was on the motorcycle, but he couldn't see me at the curve. Then the farm truck swerved and he turned at the same time and I—I hit him."

"Take it easy, ma'am. Is he breathing?"

"I don't *know*. Just—just hurry. He needs help now."

"I'll send someone." The voice became brisk and precise. "Tell me exactly where you are and what happened."

"I *told* you, I came around the corner in the fog. I'd turned off the road to avoid that stupid van, but he couldn't see me, and then I—" Jess took a deep breath. "Then I hit him. Now he's here on the ground, not moving. I've covered him with my coat, but there's something on my hands and I think it's his blood," she said hoarsely.

"Did you check his pulse?"

Jess fought through another wave of panic. "I tried but

my fingers are numb, so I can't tell anything. You've got to call 911 right away before he—"

"They're on their way. Just stay on the line and keep talking to me."

Jess looked down, smoothing her coat over the motionless body. "How can you send someone if you don't know where I am?"

"You're going to give me directions right now," the male voice said calmly. "Keep him warm and be sure you don't move him, no matter what."

"Of course I won't move him. Do you think I'm a *complete* idiot? I know about trauma following an accident. There could be internal bleeding, spinal damage—"

*Or death.* All her fault.

Jess closed her eyes, shuddering. "Just send someone, okay? We're about three miles east of Port Angeles on Route 101."

Keys clicked at the other end of the line, and Jess realized he was typing at a computer. "Three miles east of Port Angeles. You're on the 101," he repeated. "North or south side?"

"South. There was a four-way stop just beyond the big hotel." She stared down at the man on the grass. "Hurry, please," she whispered. "It's so cold out here and he's still not moving." Her fingers tightened, shaking so hard the phone nearly fell. "Why isn't he *moving*?"

"Everything will be fine," the calm voice assured her. "What's your name?"

Jess squinted through the rain. "My name? I'm—"

Something stopped her from answering. She didn't know the man on the motorcycle; she didn't know the voice on the other end of the phone, and she had been attacked earlier.

No names, she decided.

"My name doesn't matter. Just hurry with that ambulance."

"They're five minutes away. Don't worry, it won't be long now. Is he breathing? Can you check that for me now?"

"It's hard to tell." Jess searched, trying to feel his breath. "I can't be sure. It's windy out here. Sweet heaven, just *hurry*."

"Stop shouting, will you?"

The voice was shaky, originating somewhere near her wrist, and Jess dropped the phone in shock when she realized it was the biker. His eyes were open, staring at her. "What the hell happened to me?"

"You're alive," she whispered, closing her eyes in relief.

The man on the ground rolled his shoulders and grunted in pain. "Yeah, I'm alive, even though you tried to flatten me with that damned Jeep of yours."

"Listen, I was trying to avoid you. First the van crossed into my lane, and then the truck was there, skidding toward me, and you—" Jess took a nervous breath. "I don't think you should be talking."

"Yeah, we'll argue the details later after my head stops feeling like razors drilling in from both sides." He dragged his backpack over his shoulder and struggled to his feet.

"Don't do that!" She lunged toward him as he pulled off his helmet. "You've been hit. You're not supposed to move at all after something like that."

"I'm okay," he growled, swaying.

Jess leaned into him, grabbing his waist when he started to stumble. "You're not fine. You can barely stand up."

Lights cut toward them. Both of them went still. A big blue van eased onto the shoulder and stopped.

"About time."

"Who's that?" Jess asked anxiously.

"Don't worry, they're friends of mine."

"How did they get here so fast?" Jess looked down at the cell phone she'd dropped on the ground. "Wow. Your friend must really be good."

A man in a nylon parka walked around the side of the van, carrying a medical bag. He looked at Jess, then frowned at the man she was struggling to hold upright.

"Mr. Randall, I take it?"

"That's right."

"You shouldn't be standing up. You shouldn't have moved at all."

Shaking his head, the man in the parka raised a small white penlight and flashed it briefly at Jess, then at the man beside her. In the sudden light Jess had her first good look at her victim's face.

*"You?"* She struggled out from beneath the man's arm and backed up fast. "You've been following me, haven't you? Listen, my sister's an FBI agent, and if you touch me again, I'm calling her." When she continued to back up, Jess banged into the fender of her car and grunted in pain.

"Hold on." The doctor frowned at her. "There's been a misunderstanding, but I'm certain we can straighten it out."

"Good luck trying. The woman's crazy." Her victim sat down abruptly on the opposite fender of her Jeep, swaying a little. "Tell Izzy she's the suspect I told him about."

*"Me?"* Jess glared back at him. "In that case, tell your Izzy, whoever she is, that *you* knocked me out and locked me in a hotel room."

"Because you were about to scream." The man on her fender shook his head, then winced. "What the hell were you doing in my shower?"

Jess preferred not to remember. It was a standard part of her hotel assessment to see if she could have other guests switched from their rooms, but it wasn't *her* fault that the clerk had agreed so easily. Nor did it explain how this man called Randall had bypassed hotel security and made his way into her room so easily. "Never mind me. How did you get inside? My door was locked, I'm certain of that."

The man on the fender of her Jeep simply shrugged.

"Who is he?" Jess snapped at the man with the medical bag.

"Someone who does . . . sensitive work," he said carefully. "For the government."

"For *which* government?"

The doctor laughed dryly. "For the U.S. government, trust me."

Of course he would say that, Jess thought. "Fine. But now that you're here, I'll be going. You obviously have matters in hand." She felt a little woozy, but managed to smile, one hand on the car as she lurched around to the driver's side. "Glad I could help."

The doctor followed her, shaking his head. "You can't leave."

"Afraid I can. Right now, no questions asked." She pulled out her cell phone and pretended to dial. "Remember my sister, the FBI agent? I forgot to mention that she's waiting for me down the road, and if I don't show up, she'll be coming after me with a few fellow agents." It was a complete lie, of course.

"No, you can't leave, because you're bleeding. You may have a head injury, ma'am." Frowning, the doctor leveled his penlight at Jess's face.

She blinked. "*I'm* bleeding? But it was his blood I felt."

"Take care of her first, damn it." The man on her fender turned up the collar of his jacket. "We need her conscious to answer questions."

Jess tried to protest, but something funny was happening in her chest. The Jeep seemed to sway sharply.

"Ma'am?"

Jess swallowed as the ground dipped. "Y-Yes?"

The doctor grabbed her arms and pushed her back against the driver's-side door. "You're sheet-white, and I think you're in shock."

"No, I'm fine." Jess watched fog trail across the road and wondered why the drifting strands made her dizzy.

"You can't drive anywhere until I've checked you out." The doctor had two fingers on her wrist, his eyes narrowed. "Take a deep breath."

Jess complied, which made her feel more light-headed than ever. "Okay, but I'm going as soon as you're done."

The doctor leaned down beside her, brushing some kind of swab over her forehead.

"You've got quite a bump, along with some bleeding. You must have hit something when you stopped the car. Your arm has a gash, too, I see."

Jess looked down, surprised to find blood on the sleeve of her sweater. Maybe she had hit the window or the dash. Funny, but she couldn't remember.

"I'll clean you up, but you need to come back to the hotel with us." The doctor continued to work on her forehead, unruffled and thoroughly professional.

"I can't go back to the hotel. I've already turned in my report, so it won't be safe." Jess focused on the doctor's head, which was slowly morphing into two separate images.

The man on the fender sat up, looking at her with sudden interest. "What report?"

"Never mind," Jess snapped.

"You two can sort this out later. For now you both need to rest."

"I'm not staying. No way." Jess staggered to her feet, shoving at the doctor's hands. "He's fine now. So am I." She knew something about legal procedure following a car crash. You couldn't leave the scene of an accident without rendering aid and complying fully with any requests from the police or investigating authorities.

But where *were* the police?

She frowned at the doctor. "Why aren't the authorities here yet? I need to give them a statement."

"No police." The man on her fender looked at the doctor and shook his head.

Warning lights flashed in Jess's head. Why was he so anxious to avoid the police? If he was a spy, maybe she shouldn't have tried so hard to save him.

The doctor cleared his throat. "We'll discuss police statements and determination of fault later. Right now both of you are getting in that van. Then we're heading to the hotel so I can do a complete workup. Are either of you experiencing shortness of breath, blurred vision, or headaches?"

Jess shook her head. The man on her fender grunted a *no*.

"What about chest pains or dizziness?"

"We'll both live," the man said grimly.

"He's right." Jess leaned around the hood of the car. She wanted a better look at the motorcycle rider in case he made later claims of severed limbs or cerebral hemorrhage. In the headlights of the doctor's van he looked pale, and the dark bruise at his forehead made her feel a moment's contrition. Going back to the hotel was exactly what he needed. If she trusted him, Jess would have gone along with him willingly.

But everything about the man felt wrong. In addition, she had her filed report to worry about.

"You better get moving, Doctor. He doesn't look so good."

A gust of wind struck her face. She shivered as more rain

began to fall. She decided to drive only a mile before she stopped to let her head clear.

Just far enough to escape her pursuer.

He was handsome in a rugged sort of way. Jess rubbed her neck, which had begun to ache. Actually he had the kind of hard jaw and rugged features that some women might find intriguing.

Not *her*.

She swayed a little, gulping in cold air.

"Are you going to faint?" He sounded disgusted.

"Me?" Jess laughed, hands on her hips. What kind of a lightweight did the man take her for? She *never* fainted.

She walked around the car, one hand on the fender, determined to tell him precisely what she thought of him and his nasty mouth and his bad driving, but her head throbbed and suddenly she couldn't shape her words into sentences.

Then she swayed, toppling straight forward, her face buried in his lap.

# chapter 5

**H**alf an hour later, Hawk's medical examination was finished.

He was in fair shape, all things considered, and the blood on his jacket wasn't his own. It belonged to the walking, talking ball of bad luck and ill will who was now asleep in the bedroom next door.

Just his rotten luck.

He was working under a tight deadline on a critical mission, and now he'd stumbled into the path of a crazy woman.

He frowned down at his chest as he wrapped a big elastic bandage across his ribs, then fastened it securely.

"No stunt diving or skateboarding, Lieutenant Mackenzie." The young doctor sent to take care of Hawk looked as if he'd seen everything. "Tomorrow you go for X rays."

"Sure," Hawk muttered. *Like hell he would.*

The doctor's mouth curved into a faint smile. "I've got to admit, the woman has style. She did a perfect swan dive right onto your crotch. Some men might enjoy that experience."

Hawk said one short phrase that made the doctor raise an eyebrow. Hawk had had enough problems for one lifetime involving Elena Grimaldi—or whatever her real name was.

"And don't get yourself mowed down by any more out-of-control vehicles."

"You get paid for medical advice like that, Doc?" Hawk shrugged on his shirt, wincing a little.

"Damn straight I do. And since you're determined to be a smart-ass, remember that you could have been killed tonight. That new prototype safety helmet you were using saved your hide. So did your skill handling that motorcycle of yours."

"It wasn't just me and the helmet," Hawk said tightly. "The woman had the right moves. That van was way out of its lane, and she had no other choice but to hit the shoulder. I tried to avoid her, but then I spun out on an oil slick. If she hadn't cleared out of my way when she did, I'd be steak tartare decorating her tires."

"Then I guess you owe her an apology. Meanwhile, I see no sign of any new damage to your ribs, but don't push it, Lieutenant. You're walking a thin line here. The new medication seems to be doing its job, but if you sustain further trauma . . . "

He didn't finish.

"Message received." Hawk checked his watch. "I wonder what's keeping Izzy. You could set the atomic clock by him."

The doctor shook his head at the sound of knocking. "The man is definitely spooky." Picking up his medical bag, he checked the peephole. "Denzel Washington, in the flesh," he muttered, opening the door.

The man in the doorway did bear a striking resemblance to Denzel Washington, except his eyes were older and harder. "Sorry I'm late." He studied Hawk intently. "You still alive, Mackenzie?"

"Barely." Hawk finished buttoning his shirt as the doctor quietly left. "You didn't have to come, Teague. The doctor said I'm good to go."

"I like to do my own site assessments." Ishmael Teague

surveyed the hotel room and then positioned a leather briefcase on the nearby desk. "Where's our mystery woman?"

"Fast asleep next door. She banged her head when she
hit me. The doctor said she could be in some pain when she
wakes up."

"If so, we'll deal with it." Izzy shot the locks on his briefcase
and pulled out a manila folder. "I've gone over your digitals
from the cliff. The print came from an expensive British-made
boot sold exclusively in Europe and via the Internet. I've gone
through channels to request a list of all purchases made in the
last two years, but that could take several weeks."

"So the print was a dead end," Hawk said irritably.

"Not exactly." Izzy pulled a sleek laptop out of the briefcase. "While we're waiting for their list, I figured I'd hack
into their server and have a look."

"Highly illegal, my friend."

"It would be if they ever found out. Their encryption
wouldn't have stopped my ten-year-old nephew," he said in
disgust. "I found out there were nineteen U.S. sales in the
last two years, and I'm running down the names now."

"You can add this to the mix." Hawk put his plastic evidence bag on the desk. "I picked up this piece of gum right
before the accident. It was on the ground near the last set
of tracks."

"So we may have a DNA sample. Nice work, Mackenzie.
I'll run it through some tests as soon as I'm done here."

As Izzy's fingers skimmed his keyboard, Hawk walked
over to the big window overlooking the coast. Lights bobbed
up and down on a fishing trawler steaming slowly north,
where clouds huddled on the horizon like listless sheep.

"I want to go back for one more look tomorrow. I still
can't shake this hunch that they're nearby, Izzy. After that I'm
mapping all residents in a five-mile radius of the cliff. Somebody out there may have noticed something that night."

"It's worth a shot." Izzy glanced at the file on the screen. "Here are all the people who purchased those boots. We're checking them against existing criminal and terrorist databases."

"Names are good, but how long until you get pictures?"

"Tomorrow. My people are paying a visit to everyone on the list, just to narrow things down."

"You mean, in case they're sick or dead."

Izzy nodded. "Never skip the one-on-one, because that's where you find the reliable intel." His eyes narrowed. "What happened out there tonight?"

"Bad weather, bad visibility and bad luck. The woman did all she could to avoid hitting me."

"Too bad she didn't succeed. How's the pain?"

"I'll survive." Hawk stabbed a hand through his hair. "Look, let's skip all the touchy-feely stuff."

"No can do, pal. If something happens to you, it's my ass in the sling."

"I'm holding it together, Teague. There won't be any unnecessary risks. You have my word on that."

Izzy frowned at the door to the neighboring room. "Any lawsuits or publicity right now would be devastating. So what the hell are we going to do with Cinderella?"

"We could get her shipped off to a reality TV show in Tahiti," Hawk said grimly. "She'll mow down her opponents before they guess what hit them."

"That bad? What about her sister, the FBI agent?"

Hawk shrugged. "Probably a lie. She was a little hysterical at that point."

"You sure she's still asleep?"

"Check for yourself."

Izzy walked quietly to the bedroom door and peered inside. Suddenly his body stiffened. "Shit."

"What's wrong?"

"*She's* what's wrong. I mean, what are the odds?" Izzy turned slowly. "She wasn't lying, Mackenzie. Her sister *is* an FBI agent, and a damned good one."

"How do you know—"

"Because I worked with her on my last assignment. And the woman lying on the bed in there is unmistakably her twin sister. Cinderella's real name is Jess Mulcahey."

"You trust her sister?"

"Yeah, I trust her. But she's not going to like finding out that Jess is anywhere near a government operation."

"I don't get it. If her real name's Jess Mulcahey, why the Elena Grimaldi business?"

"Beats me." Izzy paced the room slowly. "I found the name listed in the on-line hotel registry. It turns out that she's visited over twenty other hotels in this chain over the last six months. The whole thing's damned peculiar."

"If you think that's peculiar, you should have seen her worn-out sneakers next to the pink silk suit she had hanging in her closet. I'm no expert on women's clothes, but the combination seemed weird."

"I'll ask her sister for details when I call." Izzy sat down in a big leather chair and steepled his fingers. "Any problems from the accident?"

Hawk turned away, prowling restlessly. "I'm fine, just like I told the doctor."

"No new side effects from the medicine?"

"None."

"Blurred vision or dizziness?"

"There's nothing, Teague."

"I wish I could believe you, but I can't. I spoke to your medical team tonight, and they've got some bad news."

"Don't tell me. Blindness, convulsions, and death," Hawk said irritably. "I've got a week to live."

"Funny. But you *can* expect some major headaches."
Izzy frowned. "The headaches will get worse, too."

"Damn, can't you bring any good news?" Hawk kept his
tone light. Since his headaches had already become more
frequent, this latest information wasn't a total surprise.

"What else?"

Izzy rubbed his neck.

"Spill it, Teague."

"They're talking about pulling you."

*Damn the whole lot of them.* "I'm fit and able. Pulling
me would be a mistake."

"Exactly what I said in my last report." Izzy drummed
his fingers on the desk. "You've got twelve hours more,
then I'm to reassess your capacity." Izzy tossed Hawk a
bottle of pills. "Meanwhile, the geniuses at HQ said to give
you these."

"More experimental stuff?" Hawk shook his head.
"Thanks, but no thanks." He started to toss the bottle
back, but Izzy glared at him.

"Keep them, damn it. When you need them, take them.
Otherwise you're out of this mission."

Hawk shoved the pills into his pocket and turned back
to the window, his shoulders stiff.

"What about the other symptoms?" Izzy said quietly.

"Hell, Teague, can't a man have any privacy?"

"Not when you're on a mission, as you well know." Izzy
closed his laptop. "I was trained as a medic, remember? I'm
fully briefed on the action of the new medications they've put
you on. But I need to know if the problems are getting worse."

Hawk put his hands on the window, angry and knowing
he shouldn't be. "You want the gritty details? You want me
to tell you I feel juiced up like an out-of-control fifteen-
year-old with sweaty palms and a hammering pulse?"

"So your sex drive is affected because of the growth factors?"

"Hell, my sex drive is through the roof, Teague. The damned meds make me eat, breathe, and sleep with sex on the brain." Hawk laughed harshly. "Being in pain is about the only thing that keeps me balanced. And now if we're done with the medical interrogation—"

"Done. For now," Izzy said coolly. "If things progress beyond your control—"

"They won't." Hawk glared out at the rain. "I'm not fifteen, and nothing pushes me where I don't want to go."

"Glad to hear it. In that case, I'll get this gum back to the lab for analysis." Izzy closed his briefcase and studied Hawk. "I meant what I said about the headaches. If your symptoms turn severe, diminishing your field capacity, you are to report that fact immediately. Is that understood?"

Hawk rolled his shoulders and gave a noncommittal grunt.

"I'm waiting for a clear answer."

"*Yes,* damn it."

"Are you wearing the brace, Lieutenant?"

Hawk turned from the window and yanked up his shirt. "Right here." Irritated, he tugged at the heavy elastic bands. "Even if it does feel like sh—"

Fabric rustled at the bedroom door. Both men looked up as Jess appeared, her face pale and a purple streak at her forehead. "He called you *lieutenant.*"

"Ma'am, you should be—"

Her eyes were very dark as she studied the long bruises on Hawk's chest. "Lieutenant? In what branch of the service?

"It doesn't matter," Hawk snapped.

"Tell me."

"He's Navy." Izzy's eyes narrowed. "That's all you need to know.

# chapter 6

**H**awk shot to his feet. "You should be in bed."

"I've *been* in bed." Jess couldn't pull her eyes away from the deep bruises covering his chest. They left her queasy and guilty. "I need answers. Did I do that to you, Lieutenant?"

"The answer is *no*." Hawk turned away, pulling down his shirt with a grimace. "You didn't."

"Maybe I should introduce myself."

Jess paid no attention to the other man in the room. "Later. If not , then what did happen to you?"

Hawk shoved his shirt into his pants. "It has nothing to do with you. That's all you need to know."

"What did he mean about your headaches getting worse?"

"Never mind that, either," Hawk snapped. "Let's see your arm."

She fingered the new bandage carefully. "It doesn't hurt any worse than the last time I hurt it."

"What 'last time'?"

"Two years ago, when I fell off a banquet table in Seattle." Jess rolled her shoulders. "I get klutzy sometimes and—no, don't ask me for the gory details." She turned, studying Hawk's friend. "I take it you're not Denzel Washington."

"Afraid not."

"I recognize your voice." Jess thought for a moment. "You're the man on the phone."

"The name's Izzy Teague. And I knew you and your sister were twins, but seeing you up close still packs a wallop, Ms. Mulcahey."

"You know my sister?"

Izzy nodded, his eyes unreadable.

He looked the type for government work, Jess realized. A professional who was silent, efficient and deadly. Both men looked like poster boys for commando work.

While she was working, her sister had that same total focus.

Hawk pulled his helmet off the chair near the window. "You should sit down."

Jess shook her head. "What happened out there?"

"You fainted, among other things."

"I never faint." Jess took a deep breath. "Okay, I guess I did faint. Things are pretty much a blur in my mind. I didn't eat because I was trying to finish my inspection, so I could leave. Then I came out of the shower and . . . found you there."

"You haven't eaten?" Hawk glanced at Izzy, who vanished into the bedroom. "About what happened earlier —"

"I want you to know that I was just doing my job." Jess sounded defensive, and the knowledge left her irritated. "I've done hundreds of room switches, and no one ever *attacked* me before."

"I don't understand."

"I'm a hotel inspector, Lieutenant. I'm called in when a facility receives too many complaints. I waved around a fifty dollar bill until I managed to have a hotel guest bumped to a different room."

"Why?"

"A test. To see if it's possible, of course."

"I still don't follow you."

"My job is to check out possible areas of irregularity or noncompliance with national chain standards." Even as she spoke, Jess catalogued further problems with the room. Dusting was below par, as was rug and upholstery cleanliness, and the desk needed to be replaced because of surface damages. She made a mental note to add these details when she e-mailed a follow-up to her report. "Now do you see?"

"Not a clue."

"Since this particular hotel has a reputation for problems, I was sent in incognito. I'm afraid that you were the guest that got bumped after I waved around the big tip."

"So that's what you were doing in my room." Hawk winced as he sat down across from her. "Entrapment?"

"It was nothing like entrapment," Jess said curtly. "And you don't need to hide the fact that you're in pain on my account."

"What makes you think—"

"Don't worry, your little secret is safe." Jess noticed his leather jacket hanging from the chair at the desk. Frowning, she fingered the long gash on one sleeve. The man could have died out in the rain.

Partly to distract herself from that grim thought, Jess grabbed her purse from the floor and fumbled inside.

"What are you doing?"

"Stitching up your jacket."

"You can't fix a cut like that one."

"All it takes is a very sharp needle, and I carry a whole set of them when I travel." Because she didn't have time or money for complicated repairs, Jess thought wryly.

But she definitely wasn't veering off into that subject.

"Look, don't bother. I'll manage something."

"Like what, duct tape? Glue and staples?" She was already at work, her needle slipping in and out of the soft leather. "I'll be done in a few minutes, Lieutenant, so relax. Stop giving me orders, while you're at it."

Hawk shook his head and muttered something that she couldn't quite make out.

"By the way, what were you doing out on that road?"

"Relaxing." He drummed his fingers on the table. "Taking a drive down to the beach."

Jess's head swung up. "In the middle of a storm?"

Izzy reappeared, holding a basket full of fruit. "I've got some food here. What's she doing to your jacket, Mackenzie?"

"Stitching it."

"Can you do that to leather?"

"Apparently you can."

Izzy sat down next to Jess and put two oranges on a plate. "Room service should be here shortly."

"Not for me." Hawk stood abruptly. "I need to be pushing off."

"Actually, you're staying right here so you can eat." Izzy handed him an orange and a protein bar that looked squished.

"You call that food, Teague?"

"It will hold you until the caviar and baked Alaska arrive," Izzy said dryly.

Jess watched the byplay with interest. "You're in the military. So who's got the highest rank?"

Izzy took an apple and tossed it up in the air, catching it behind his back. "That depends on who you ask, Ms. Mulcahey."

"Very funny, Teague." Hawk glanced at the door. "How long until that food arrives?"

"Less than ten."

Something came and went on Izzy's face as he looked at Jess.

"What's so funny?" she asked.

"You. You're very different from your sister."

"Everybody says that. Summer's wonderful, a hundred times more capable than I am. Even if she does tend to get a little . . . "

"Married to the job?" Izzy murmured.

"No doubt about it." Jess's needle moved swiftly as she closed the tear. "I appreciate your ordering food."

"Least I can do. So why did you register as Elena Grimaldi?" Izzy asked.

"It's safer that way. Hotel managers develop a second sense about investigators, and sometimes they retaliate after a bad rating. I know one hotel examiner who was stuffed in a trash compactor, and it wasn't pretty. Another inspector went back for her suitcase after her report was filed." Jess frowned at Hawk's torn sleeve. "In her case, the trash compactor looks good by comparison."

"Why do these people care so much about a single report?" Hawk cut in.

"Because management bonuses are based on compliance rates. Even a drop of one star in an investigator's report can mean thousands of dollars lost. Staff bonuses are cut too, which means big bucks." She finished the seam and studied the effect. "What are you people doing here? Is this some kind of secret mission?"

Jess didn't want to talk about towel allotments and personnel evaluations. She was far more interested in her mysterious new friends.

"Forget about us. I want to hear more about this retaliation stuff." Hawk's face was grim. "Has that happened to you?"

Izzy left the room again, talking on his cell phone, and

they were alone. "First tell me what you were looking for this morning."

"What do you mean?" Hawk said tightly.

"You wanted to know where I'd put something—and you seemed pretty damned concerned."

"You must have misunderstood."

"I know what I heard," Jess said quietly, holding out his finished jacket. "You were looking for something important you thought I had. It had to do with my laundry carrier."

He ran his fingers along the neat seam. "Drop it, Jess."

"More orders, Lieutenant?"

"Call me Hawk, damn it."

Dishes rattled outside in the hall and Izzy reappeared, pushing a cart covered with dishes. "Quesadillas, steak, and fries. Stop arguing and start eating."

Jess took a deep breath. Both men were hiding something. Her sister would know how to handle something like this, but Jess wasn't Summer.

So she'd eat and then hit the road. She was smart enough to know when she was in over her head.


"Explain to me again how this thing of yours works?" Hawk was demolishing the last of an exceptionally good quesadilla as he studied Jess. "You're supposed to be related to the king of Monaco?"

"Monaco has a prince, not a king. And I'm not necessarily from Monaco. It's important to keep changing the details, so sometimes it's Hungary, sometimes it's Luxembourg, or maybe Spain. Not many people stay current on lesser branches of European royalty."

Hawk shook his head. "So people believe you're some kind of minor princess when you offer them a bribe?"

"The pink heels and pink silk suit help." Jess raised an

eyebrow. "I'm very good at my job, Lieutenant Mackenzie," she said in accented English.

"I have no doubt, and call me Hawk." He eyed the food untouched on Jess's plate. "Aren't you going to eat?"

"I'm working on it." Jess was feeling edgy, though she couldn't figure why. The weird stuff happening to her? Or was it this uncomfortable awareness of the commando type sitting across from her?

"If you're not going to have those fries, maybe—"

"Be my guest." Jess slid a mound of french fries onto his plate. She couldn't eat, mostly from stress. Since she currently had six dollars and twenty-three cents in her pocket and not a whole lot more in her bank account, she was looking at a lot more peanut butter sandwiches and free snacks from the hotels she visited.

None of which was anyone else's business.

"By the way, I meant to thank you for your excellent driving today."

"I still hit you. I should have been faster," she said tightly.

"It was my fault, not yours."

"Okay, you can take all the guilt for the accident." Jess took a deep breath. "That's one sweet piece of metal you were riding. A Husky, isn't it? Four-stroke cylinder and electric starter?"

Hawk snagged another one of her fries. "You follow motorcycles?" he said in disbelief.

"Only Ducatis and Huskies. Nothing else comes close."

"You won't get an argument there. I made some modifications on the motor, and the throttle tends to run a little high, but that makes for a nice edge off-road."

Jess swallowed, reining in her excitement. "You retooled the system yourself? *Now* I'm impressed."

Hawk shook his head, laughing dryly.

"Probably you should tell me why that's so funny."

"Because I can almost see you flying along in a beefed-up off-road bike, edging every turn hell-for-leather, and loving every damn second."

Jess smiled slightly. "I certainly try." But lately there hadn't been many chances to ride. She had been too busy doubling and tripling her assignments in an effort to pay off her debts.

Hawk rocked back in his chair. "I've got a Ducati SS1000 that's as sweet as they come."

Jess let out a little breath as one of her biggest fantasies came roaring to life. "I'd love to take it through a few turns and then open it up on the straightaway." She gave up trying to be casual. "OK, I admit it. Give me a Ducati and an open road. Life doesn't get much better."

Hawk's head tilted. "Who got you interested in motorcycles? Was it your father, brother?" His eyes narrowed. "Lover?"

"None of the above. One summer in high school I worked in an auto shop, and the mechanic—"

"Wait, let me get this straight. You worked in an auto-repair shop?"

"Why not? It paid twice as much as the local fast-food joint. In the town where my sister and I were living, that was the full range of choices." She toyed with a slice of lettuce. "The mechanic had to have cataract surgery, so he gave me a manual and told me to memorize it. The next day I was under the hood, helping him keep his wires and valves straight. I learned a lot about engines that summer."

And she had relished the freedom. Jess still remembered every detail of her first ride.

Wind like a cool caress, the growl of a powerful motor, and the effortless sense of speed that spelled complete freedom.

"What about your current job? People don't like to be spied on, generally."

"No, they don't." Jess sat stiffly, holding her plate. "Sometimes they get nasty."

Hawk bent forward. "Nasty how?"

Jess was surprised at how angry he looked. "One time they shredded my clothes." She looked away, trying not to remember the sense of violation and helplessness. "Another time they went after my Jeep. They pulled some wires, slit the seats, cut the brake line." Her car had never worked as well after that and Jess had hoped to trade up to a newer model, but she'd lost her savings overnight and then spent the next two years trying to dig her way out again.

She was still trying. One more year would do it, as long as she watched every penny.

"No brakes?" Scowling, Hawk sat forward. His eyes could have scored metal. "You could have been hurt, maybe killed."

"I always check my car after I turn in a report, Lieu— Hawk. Don't worry, I caught the problem in time."

Jess realized she was leaning forward, their faces barely a foot apart. With the rain hammering on the window, the mood in the room had suddenly turned personal—and slightly intimate.

She stood up tensely. "Look, storm or not, I need to get moving."

"It's too late to go anywhere given these road conditions." Hawk moved in front of her. "Izzy's reserved the room next door for you."

Rain sluiced down the windows, blurring the darkness. All Jess's tension returned. "I can't stay. I need to get to Portland. I especially need to leave this hotel."

"Just keep your door locked if you're worried."

Her eyes narrowed. "As I recall, a lock didn't keep *you* out this morning."

"That was different." Hawk stabbed a hand angrily through his hair. "Look, only a fool would leave in this weather. Somehow you don't strike me as being a fool."

Jess looked out at the darkness. The wind moaned shrilly, whipping rain and twigs against the windows.

Her common sense was fighting a hard battle with her anxiety.

"You can trust me, Jess. I'm a light sleeper. All you have to do is bang on the wall if anything worries you."

"That won't work. I won't be next door or down the hall." Jess turned, meeting his eyes squarely. "If I have to stay, I'll be sleeping right here."

# chapter 7

*ere?* In my room?"

"Don't worry, this isn't a proposition. Cool your jets, because I'll be the one on the couch."

Hawk shook his head grimly. "No."

"Well, it's here or I'm out of here, Lieutenant." Jess stared out the window. "I don't intend to be a name on someone's accident report tomorrow." She took a deep breath and then began pulling cushions off the sofa, stacking them neatly on the floor. "Maybe you should take first turn at the bathroom."

Hawk turned her around to face him. "Stop calling me *lieutenant,*" he growled. "And believe me, staying in my room isn't a great idea."

"Because you think I'll jump you?" She smiled crookedly. "Don't worry, I'll be asleep in five minutes. I won't hear any state secrets you blurt out in the night."

Hawk bit back a curse. Why didn't she act like any other woman he knew? "I don't talk in my sleep," he snapped.

"Glad to hear it. In that case we should both get some decent rest."

"Look, Jess, I don't sleep very well. I'll probably be up and down prowling all night."

"No problem." Jess unfolded a blanket and tossed it across the couch. "My sister tells me I can sleep through anything."

Was there *any* way to get through to her, short of a tank or a SWAT team?

A cell phone chimed shrilly and she grabbed her purse. "That's probably my sister now. If I don't answer, she'll send half a dozen field agents to surround the hotel." She pulled out her phone, waving her hand. "Stop staring at me. Everything's going to be fine here. You really need to learn how to chill, Lieutenant."

She turned away, talking on her phone, oblivious to his anger.

*State secrets?* And when had *he* morphed into the protectee? The scenario was so unsettling that Hawk grabbed his knapsack and headed for the bathroom, scowling.

"Slow down, Jess. Why are you still at the hotel? You're supposed to be on the road to Portland by now." Summer Mulcahey sounded harassed, trying to make sense of what Jess had just told her. "You always leave after you file a report."

Jess struggled to open the big queen-size sleeper sofa. "Something came up. A storm and . . . other things."

"They had to be something big for you to break a cardinal rule. Hold on a moment." Jess heard her sister turn away from the phone, asking for an update on a forensic report.

Jess didn't understand the rest of the conversation, which was carried on largely in some kind of jargon known only to the FBI. When her sister returned, she sounded more harassed than ever. "Sorry, Jess. Tell me what went wrong tonight."

"Okay, but don't go ballistic on me."

"What *happened*?"

"I had an accident." Jess blew out a breath. "A very minor accident."

"What do you mean, a *minor* accident? Are you hurt?"

"I'm fine." Jess winced a little as she spread a blanket over the lumpy mattress. Her head and back were bothering her, but she didn't mention that. "A bump on the head. A few stitches, but nothing major. I thought I killed a man on a motorcycle, but he turned out to be fine."

Her sister's voice turned shrill. "You had stitches? Tell me exactly what happened."

"It wasn't like that, Sum." Jess frowned as the shower began to run. "Look, the man is fine, and so am I. By the time we got things sorted out after the accident, it was too late to drive anywhere."

"I suppose that car of yours bit the dust. I keep telling you, if you need money for repairs, I'll send some and—"

Jess's face tightened. Summer was older by only a few minutes, but she had always been overprotective. Even though Jess knew her sister's motives were good, they had a way of pushing all her sibling irritation buttons. "My Jeep is old but in excellent shape. You know I do all the work myself. No mechanic is going to rob me blind."

"Don't I know it. I keep wishing you'd have a look at my Explorer." Summer took a deep breath. "I just . . . worry, Jess. All day I've felt off, and I couldn't stop thinking about you. It's that spooky twin thing again, isn't it?"

"I can always tell when you're in trouble, Sum. Like when you were down in Mexico with Gabe on that assignment."

"Not over a cell-phone line," her sister said quickly. "So now that I know you're safe, tell me about this man on the motorcycle."

"He's taking a shower right now, but he's fine. A little

bruised, actually. Funny, he told me the trauma came from an old accident."

"You're sharing a hotel room with him?" The shrill edge was back in Summer's voice.

"Don't worry, he knows your friend Izzy, so everything will be fine."

"Izzy Teague is there? You saw him with this man?"

Jess heard someone ask Summer a question. She barked at them to wait, which wasn't like her. "He just appeared after the accident, Summer. The man is completely gorgeous, by the way."

"Put Izzy on the phone," Jess's sister ordered.

"No can do, Sum. He left." Jess bit back a yawn. "I'm going to sleep now. It's been one heck of a day and I'm dead on my feet." Jess looked up as the bathroom door opened, and her heart did a double back somersault.

Hawk was shirtless and barefoot, water glistening across his muscled chest. "Oh, my," she murmured.

"Oh, my *what*? Jess, I need to know exactly what—"

"Talk to you later, Summer." Without a hint of regret Jess broke the connection. Her exhaustion had vanished the moment she set eyes on Hawk, damp, disheveled and dangerous.

Before she could say a word, he tossed his shirt and towel down on the open sofa bed. "Get moving," he ordered. "I'm sleeping here."

"That's not necessary. You'll be more comfortable on the bed."

He nudged her out of the way like a tank plowing over soft sand. "I'll keep an eye on things out here. This way I can hear the door."

There it was again, the cool way he simply moved in and took over.

But Jess didn't need anyone to take over for her.

Okay, so she was currently in financial freefall thanks to her lousy investment strategy, and her car was maybe held together with duct tape and chewing gum. Probably her job choice was lousy, too, but she had her independence, and this tough-eyed stranger had no business muscling his way into her plans.

It was time to draw a line in the sand.

"I'll sleep here." Jess crossed her arms and didn't move.

"You want to go one-on-one, Jess?" Her name was a harsh whisper. She was mesmerized by the challenge in his eyes as he tossed a pillow onto the bed.

His hands went to the waistband of his jeans, and the button popped open. His zipper hissed down.

Though it took incredible willpower, Jess didn't allow her eyes to follow his zipper, because there was absolutely *no* reason she should be curious about what lay beneath.

"If this is some kind of perverted test of wills, I remain unimpressed."

*Ugh. Too prim,* Jess thought. Why did this man bring out the worst in her?

"It's no test. I'm dead on my feet." His fingers hooked in the waistband of his jeans. "In three seconds, the jeans and anything else I'm wearing will be gone. If you're still here, that's your problem."

Despite all her willpower, Jess's eyes flickered downward. Dark hair arrowed across his chest. Taut muscles lined his open jeans.

Jess swallowed, her face filled with heat. She had to explain things clearly. "I need to leave my bedroom door open. It's . . . a thing I have. I don't like small spaces."

"No problem. I'll make a note not to lock you up in the trunk of a car anytime soon."

Jess heard fabric rustle. His jeans shifted and began to fall.

She spun around quickly. "Fine, be a jerk." Grabbing her purse, she headed toward the bedroom, trying not to hear his soft laugh or the sound of his jeans hitting the floor. The sound left an unforgettable vision of a naked male body imprinted on her brain.

The sofa bed squeaked, protesting beneath Hawk's weight. "Any other grave secrets I need to know before I go to sleep?" he called.

So he assumed it was some kind of joke. Maybe that was just as well. "No more secrets," she answered shortly.

"Good." His voice wasn't quite as cool as it had been. " 'Night, Ms. Mulcahey." The light switched off in the room behind her.

Jess stared at the partially open door. He didn't understand at all.

With luck he never would.

Summer Mulcahey paced anxiously outside a dilapidated warehouse, imagining her sister trapped in a hotel room with a psycho. Given her FBI experiences, her imagination was far too concrete and detailed.

She probably worried too much, but the thought didn't make her stop sweating. When her cell phone chimed, she answered immediately.

The number was blocked, she noted. "Jess, is that you?"

"It's Izzy Teague, Summer. I just got your message."

Reining in her nerves, Summer walked away from the team of forensic experts finishing a crime-scene assessment nearby. "Izzy, what's going on? My sister said she saw you tonight. She also said she was in a car accident. If Jess is in some sort of trouble—"

"Jess is fine, Summer. Her Jeep spun out in a storm, and I smoothed things out."

Summer Mulcahey glared at the phone. She didn't for

one second believe the story was that simple. Izzy Teague was a security operative with class-A clearances, and he didn't wander onto lonely country roads to handle random motor accidents. "Try again," she said flatly.

"Okay, it wasn't just a simple accident." Izzy blew out an irritated breath. "You really need to hear this now?"

"I really, *really* need to hear this now."

"I'm involved in a project here, Summer. My friend was finishing his surveillance when your sister took a detour onto the shoulder. He couldn't see her until it was too late, but he's fine now. So is your sister."

Summer hunched over the phone, speaking quietly. "She's my sister, Izzy. Since I know *exactly* what kind of work you do and the kind of men you do it with—"

Izzy laughed dryly. "Of course you know. You're married to one of those men."

"That fact is irrelevant. I don't want Jess involved in my world or in yours. I mean that, Izzy. There are . . . reasons."

"Care to name them?"

"No, and don't cross me on this. If Jess has wandered into the middle of a mission, get her out." Summer's voice hardened. "Otherwise, I'll come out there and see to it myself."

Jess was floating on a small boat in the Aegean. Waves rocked her gently, slapping against the hull while she slept beneath a hot, glorious sunset. Yawning, she decided to take off the top of her swimsuit and slather on more oil. . . . She shrugged off the straps, feeling the heat of the sun on her shoulders—

She woke up with a start, on a strange bed in a cold room. As rain pounded against the window, driven by a hammering wind, she remembered where she was and why she was still there.

For long tense moments, she didn't move, letting the blurred edges of sleep slip away.

2:21 A.M.

So much for her vaguely sexual dreams.

Abruptly her stomach growled. She had been too keyed up to eat very much after the accident, and now hunger pangs hit her in earnest.

She glanced at the clock again.

2:22 A.M.

After a mental review of her possessions, she realized her options were limited to a raisin granola bar and a few other snacks, but all were stashed in her suitcase, which happened to be next door in the living room.

Of course she wasn't going near Hawk or the bed where he slept, probably wearing nothing.

With a mental curse, she pulled the pillow across her head, ignoring her growling stomach. She was successful— for about twelve minutes.

Finally convinced that further sleep was impossible, Jess sat up, staring into the darkness.

She would simply pull on her robe, creep next door, and carry her suitcase back down the hall. Hawk would probably sleep right through, so there was no reason for her to be so jumpy.

Even if he did sleep naked, probably with no covers over that phenomenal body.

She pulled on her robe and crossed the bedroom. She never closed her door completely when she slept, so turning the knob didn't pose a problem, and when there was no sign of movement next door, she moved down the hall toward the living room.

Silently she inched through the darkness around a fake

potted orange tree. The rain was hammering hard, and she was certain Hawk wouldn't hear her.

She took another step and stopped, her heart pounding as something struck the window.

She jumped nervously when a second pebble struck the glass, tossed by the wind. Some instinct of danger made the little hairs stand up at the back of her neck.

Which was ridiculous. Hawk had promised she would be safe here.

Not that she believed him completely. She was pretty sure he wouldn't jump her, at least.

With the shadows stretching around her and the storm raging in the night, she began to play back everything he had said earlier. What if he and his friend were criminals, not government agents? What if she'd stumbled into the middle of something they wanted to keep quiet; something her sister didn't know anything about?

Jess realized she was shivering. Bending carefully to pick up her suitcase, she heard her stomach growl loudly. Wind rushed across her face, and then she was spun around, pinned immobile against the wall. Callused fingers gripped her throat.

Choking her.

# chapter 8

The movement came so fast that Jess had no time to fight back. She was falling before she knew it, her heart slamming in her chest as panic set in.

Even then he didn't speak or offer threats. He simply gripped her, silent and ruthless, until the room began to blur around her.

Jess gasped for air.

Suddenly his hands loosened and his arm shot around her shoulders, to keep her from falling. "What the hell are you *doing*?"

She tried to talk, but could only manage a dry cough.

"Tell me, damn it."

"Not—" Jess bit off another cough. "Not meeting spies from a hostile government."

His voice was flat and emotionless. "Then why were you out here?"

Jess drew in a gulp of air. "To find the last granola bar and the other food I usually carry in my suitcase." She shoved impatiently at his arms, more irritated than frightened now. "Because I was hungry, okay?"

He muttered a curse. Only then did she realize that in her irritation she had elbowed him in the ribs. "Sorry." She leaned closer, trying to see his face in the darkness. "How bad is it?"

His body was wedged against hers, trapping her against the wall. His hand seemed to burn through the thin cotton of her nightshirt.

The old, awful fear kicked in. *Small places. Locked doors. Darkness.*

*Trapped.*

A moan broke free, and she twisted, frantic.

A second later Jess was free.

"You should have listened, damn it. I told you I was a light sleeper. Your suitcase is on the desk, so grab your granola bar and whatever else you need, then go back to bed. And this time, *stay* there," he said tightly.

Jess rubbed her wrists, which still stung from the force of his grip. What kind of dark world did this man inhabit, where threats lurked around every corner?

She decided she didn't want to know. Her sister inhabited that same world, and Jess had seen her sister's face all too often after a tough assignment, ruthlessly stripped of any emotion. Sometimes it was days before Jess heard her sister laugh again.

Summer loved her work, but Jess knew that she paid a high price for dealing with the darker side of human nature.

Jess realized that this man had learned to pay that same price. But his choices were none of *her* business.

In a blur she turned, carrying her suitcase down the hall, but by then she'd lost all hint of an appetite.

Hawk didn't move.

If he was getting well, his fractured ribs had an odd way of showing it. Jess's jab with her elbow hadn't helped the pain, but Hawk didn't hold that against her. Most women would fight if they were suddenly slammed up against a wall and attacked in the middle of the night.

Scowling, he sat on the sofa bed, listening to rain hammer at the window. He had simply acted by training. First a noise, then a shadow—and he had shot awake into full attack mode, cutting her off before she could move.

It was simple ingrained habit now. Recognize a threat and then immobilize it.

Except that tonight, Hawk wasn't dealing with a sociopathic assassin or ruthless bioterrorist. Tonight his hands had closed around the neck of a guileless woman without a clue to the dangerous currents sweeping around her.

He closed his eyes, remembering her moan of panic when he had pinned her against the wall, hands to her throat.

She'd been terrified beyond what he'd expected.

Why?

Not that it was his problem. The woman was trouble, and the sooner he was gone, the better, because he didn't have even one damned inch of room for *more* trouble in his life.

Three hours later, the rain was still hammering at the windows.

As Hawk finished shaving, he looked at the pills Izzy had given him earlier. The headaches were more frequent, almost once a day now, and the other side effects were just as noticeable.

Having the hormones of a reckless fifteen-year-old boy wasn't all it was cracked up to be. He was a man who enjoyed being in control—always—and the distraction from the damned meds the Navy had seen fit to give him was a serious annoyance.

Not to mention the rest of the side effects.

Thanks to his enhanced libido and markedly extended arousal time, his mood was becoming downright surly. He was dedicated to serving his country, but being a medical guinea pig was taking things a step too far.

Frowning, Hawk rolled the cool plastic bottle between his fingers. Then he dropped the meds into his backpack.

After he finished dressing, he checked on Jess. She was sound asleep, one arm wrapped around a pillow, her body curled in a tight ball. With her bare legs dangling over the edge of the bed and the covers askew, Hawk could see the curve of her hip beneath her simple pink nightshirt.

His body responded with instant, savage force.

Biting off a curse, he scanned the room, gray in the predawn light. Her clothes were folded neatly on a chair, her notebooks lined up on the desk. She was all packed, ready to leave as soon as she woke. Recalling her anxiety about retaliation for her negative report, Hawk had already taken precautions with Izzy.

But neither man believed that she was in any real danger. Izzy had checked, and there was no record of her real name anywhere in the hotel database, and there were no internal memos about her inspection.

Wandering to the closet, Hawk picked up a pair of boots on top of her suitcase. He noticed a hole the size of a quarter in the bottom of one sole. She had wedged a piece of cardboard in place to cover it.

If she was out of money, why didn't her sister help out? Or why hadn't Jess asked?

Nothing about the woman made any sense.

*Not your problem,* he thought coldly. *And you couldn't help her even if it were.*

*Coffee?*

*Yes.* Jess opened her eyes and inhaled deeply, praying

that the intoxicating scent filling her lungs wasn't a by-product of her strange dreams.

"Are you decent in there?"

She pulled the covers up hastily at the sound of Hawk's voice beyond the half-open door. "Decent enough."

He opened the door, fully dressed, carrying a tray. There were lines on his face that she hadn't noticed the day before. "I thought you'd want some breakfast." He put the tray on the corner of her bed. "Considering all you got from me a few hours ago was a lecture and a granola bar."

It wasn't an apology, but Jess decided it was close enough. "If you've got coffee on that tray, I might have to kiss you." She sat up and propped her elbows on her knees. "What time is it?"

"Almost six. Your sister called a few minutes ago. When I told her you'd call back shortly, she wasn't exactly thrilled."

"Summer is convinced all men are out to dupe me and I'll be too naïve to notice it." Heat filled her cheeks as she realized how that sounded. "I don't mean that my sister's not wonderful," she added quickly. "Or that I've never—that I haven't—" She cleared her throat. "Because I have, you know. Summer's just protective. Maybe overprotective." Jess was still trying to figure that out, working through the whole twin dynamic thing, and she knew by now that it wasn't an easy relationship to explain. Sisters were close, but twins were part of each other, sometimes linked mind to mind in a way that bordered on freaky.

Not that he'd be the least bit interested in her family background or sibling issues.

She waved a hand. "Never mind. It's just one of those family things."

"You're identical twins?"

Jess nodded.

"When I was a kid I always thought it would be cool to have a twin." Hawk stared out the window at the rain. He turned, his eyes following her as she stood up and slipped on a pink fleece robe. "I left the newspaper here for you." He took a step back. "Now I'd better get moving."

"You don't even want coffee?" Jess bent over the tray, lifting lids and checking pots. "Especially coffee that smells as wonderful as this? Come on, tell me how you like yours."

Hawk hesitated.

"A few minutes won't kill you, Lieutenant. That storm outside is going nowhere."

"No sugar. A microsplash of milk."

Amused, Jess filled a cup, added a single splash of milk, then held the coffee out politely.

She tried to act calm and polite, not at all flustered, as if she wasn't wearing a nightshirt and they hadn't shared hotel accommodations the night before.

As if he hadn't taken her for a spy and tried to strangle her.

Hawk accepted the cup, his jaw hardening.

"Are you okay?"

"You don't have to serve me," he said coolly.

"It's no bother. How about half of a grapefruit? Or maybe a croissant with butter and jelly?"

He stabbed a hand through his hair. "I really need to get out of here now." He sounded tired and tense.

"Don't be an idiot." Jess shook her head. "I know how much energy it takes to ride a motorcycle off-road in the mud, so stop arguing and eat."

Hawk stared at her. How long had it been since a woman fussed over him, worried about him, bothered to ask his coffee preferences? He couldn't begin to remember.

"Get the lead out, Lieutenant."

When Hawk looked up, she was chewing a wedge of

grapefruit enthusiastically, while a bead of juice trickled down the corner of her mouth.

It seemed as if a switch were thrown somewhere, pumping up every nerve and muscle group in his misbegotten, unpredictable body. Not that Jess was remotely his type. She was clearly a one-man woman, the kind who believed in three kids, chasing fireflies and staying in love until you died of old age. The sight of her eating shouldn't have been remotely sexy, but somehow Hawk kept thinking about licking away that trail of juice, exploring her tongue, enjoying all the warm corners of her full mouth.

*Back off, Mackenzie.*

He knew the distraction had to be from the meds they were giving him. Something about freeing the bioavailability of testosterone and activating his growth hormone production to aid healing, they had explained.

So far the symptoms had come exactly the way Izzy had described them.

Frowning, Hawk finished his croissant and took another one.

Outside, the storm hammered on.

"Do you have far to go?"

He shrugged.

"Sorry. I ask too many questions." Jess frowned at him. "I'm probably not supposed to ask. What you do is some kind of military secret, right?"

Hawk stood up and reached for his backpack. "I'd better shove off."

"Take some coffee with you." She filled a big insulated travel mug and added milk.

Just a splash. No sugar. Exactly the way he liked it.

Suddenly the room felt too small and far too intimate. Hawk took a step back. "The road is out down the coast."

He handed her a map with the problem area circled in red. "You'll have to detour west a few miles. I marked the turns for you."

She frowned at the map for a few moments, then pulled a pair of reading glasses out of her purse. "Say one word, and you're a dead man," she muttered.

The glasses were pink with blue stripes, and for some reason Hawk found them sexy as hell. "Aren't you a little young for—"

"Not a word."

Hawk watched her study the map. "Okay, I'll shut up about—about the things you're wearing. By the way, Izzy had your Jeep checked out last night. Nothing major was broken, but he had a few things replaced, including your bumper. Your treads were worn on the right front tire, so he took care of that, too."

"Thank you," she said gravely. "Things have been a little tight financially . . . but never mind about that. I fixed this for you."

Hawk realized that she was holding out a plastic bag. "What's this?"

"You're going to need energy today, so I put in two apples and a jelly donut."

As he took the plastic bag, her wide, generous smile warmed the room.

To his shock Hawk felt a tiny moment of regret at leaving.

But he didn't have time for anything soft and pleasant. The wind was growling and the headache ratcheted up a notch as he zipped his jacket and stashed her plastic bag of food. There was no reason for him to delay any longer.

"Watch those turns in the rain," he said. "That Jeep of yours is tough, but it's no Ducati." Then he shouldered his backpack and headed outside without saying goodbye.

Packed and dressed, Jess stood in the elevator and watched the big metal doors close.

For some reason she couldn't get the tall, unsmiling lieutenant out of her mind.

Stupid. Worse than stupid.

She was smart enough to know that the man had *danger* written all over him. Any doubts had vanished with painful clarity when he loomed out of the darkness and pinned her against the wall in a chokehold. All because she'd gone for a smashed granola bar in the bottom of her suitcase.

Of course, he'd warned her that he was a light sleeper.

"Fine," she muttered. *And stop apologizing for the man.*

Jess tapped her foot nervously as the elevator stopped at floor after empty floor on a slow descent. Someone appeared to be playing a joke with the buttons.

She closed her eyes, taking a deep breath. She hated elevators. Every stop jangled her nerves a little more.

The doors closed again. With a little lurch, the elevator started down once more while Jess stared at the floor indicator.

Just before leaving, she'd found out that the hotel manager had filed an angry protest about her report, which meant her records would be checked and rechecked, every name and detail verified.

And Jess was suddenly tired of the pretenses, tired of traveling three hundred and forty-five days a year under an assumed name.

But three years at a small liberal arts college didn't provide the background for technical or professional work, and the thought of working in sales left her cold.

One floor down, the elevator doors opened again. A man in a leather coat and small, expensive designer glasses

got on, studying her avidly. "You here with the orthodontists' convention?"

"Afraid not."

He looked her up and down, then shrugged and stepped
off at the next floor.

As the doors slid shut, Jess felt a stab of anxiety. She
gripped her suitcase, frowning when the lights flickered
several times. Probably from the storm, she thought nervously. Maybe she should get off at the next floor and walk
down.

But when the doors opened again, she was stunned to
see Hawk walking toward her. "I can't get away from this
place. Damned orthodontists' convention has the stairs
blocked six flights up and six flights down. They're gathered in every corner discussing implants and root canals."

Jess barely heard. She was too busy watching the floor
button and wishing she had taken the stairs.

"Something wrong?"

"Not a thing." *Absolutely, definitely,* her mind snapped
at him. She wanted out, and it was getting harder to hide
her anxiety. "The lights—they went off a few times," she
said tensely.

"Probably from the lightning." Hawk hit a button and
the elevator doors closed. "The wind's picking up, too."
He leaned against the wall, crossing his arms. "Not that it
matters. These hotels always have backup power sources."

Jess nodded calmly, but her nails were digging into her
palms. Taking deep breaths the way she'd learned in a
dozen relaxation classes, she watched the floor indicator
click downward. Suddenly the piped-in elevator music
broke up into static.

Another fragment of Jess's reason fled, victim of the old
terror. The man behind her was irrelevant, a mere sliver of
her memory as she capsized beneath a wave of panic.

It wasn't fair, she thought wildly. After months of therapy, she had finally managed to condition herself to face small spaces and crowded rooms. She had closed herself inside closets, even taken short elevator rides so she could resurrect her blurred memories.

By now those memories should have been healed and forgotten.

*Have to learn how to behave, little girl. Strict rules and strict procedures make good behavior for everyone.*

Jess shook at the memory, feeling the darkness and four walls close in on her, just the way they had in the clinic where she'd been sent, years before, rebellious and stupid as only someone of sixteen can be.

*Just memories.*

She closed her eyes. She wasn't crazy or stupid. She damned well knew the difference between *then* and *now,* and the clinic was just a memory.

But knowing didn't help. The walls were closing in on her again, and she was fighting to breathe.

Jess's palms began to sweat, and her throat felt dry.

With a lurch, the elevator came to an abrupt halt. The lights flickered and then went out.

# chapter 9

Hawk hit the DOWN button. When the elevator didn't move, he tried the red EMERGENCY button. Nothing happened either way.

Air hissed down the elevator shaft. A set of dim interior lights flickered on. Judging by the interim lights, there appeared to be a backup generator at work, but Hawk didn't plan to wait around for a repair crew. He opened the instrument panel and checked the wiring.

When the control panel provided no help, he banged loudly on the wall, but there was no answer. The three cell calls he placed to Izzy were equally unsuccessful.

Damned storm.

As wind roared down the overhead shaft, the elevator rocked slightly. "Hang on, because we may be here for a few minutes." Flipping out his cell phone, Hawk tried Izzy one more time, cursing when the signal dropped again. He checked the opposite wall panel for an emergency phone, but the line was dead. "Hell."

When Hawk turned around, Jess was wedged into the corner, her purse clutched to her chest.

"We're safe here. This is not a big deal, Jess."

She just stared at him, her face sheet-white.

Hawk remembered then what she'd said earlier about keeping her doors open. If she had space issues, being caught in an elevator like this had to be gut-wrenching. "Look at me," he said roughly. "We've got plenty of air, plus auxiliary power for the lights, and we shouldn't be here long. No doubt Izzy has already checked and located the problem." At least, Hawk *hoped* he had.

Jess's fingers shook and her handbag dropped to the floor. "Small spaces—no air." She closed her eyes. "I have to get out. *Now.*"

"Try taking a deep breath." He put his hands on her shoulders. "Look at me." When her eyes opened, her gaze kept slipping to the closed doors. Hawk put one finger under her chin, lifting her face. "No, here. Look at *me.*" He felt the tension gripping her body. "Breathe. Stay calm."

There was panic in her eyes. She looked desperate, like a swimmer losing strength right before going under. "I—I can't breathe. It's too small, too tight." She twisted away, her trembling hands moving frantically over the walls.

"Jess." He pried her fingers away from the wall. "Listen to me. I wouldn't lie to you." Her teeth chattered, and he pulled off his jacket, smoothing it around her shoulders.

With great effort she seemed to refocus on his face. Her fingers gripped his shirt. "They're going to come soon. We won't be locked in here, will we?"

He chose his answer carefully. "I'm sure they're already working on a repair. We'll be out of here soon, honey."

Something tore loose and rattled down the elevator shaft, clanging against the metal roof. The elevator cables creaked loudly.

White-faced, Jess lurched back and dug at the doors, trying to pry them open. Blood streaked the ends of her fingers and tears mottled her face.

When Hawk tried to pull her back against his chest, she fought him blindly.

"Jess, stop. You're hurting yourself."

She was oblivious, her fingers tearing wildly at the door, leaving dark smudges of blood on the metal.

"Jess, *stop,*" he said in a low, viciously controlled voice.

"Open the door," she rasped. "Even a crack. Then they'll hear us."

"I can't force the doors, Jess." Hawk gripped her hands against his chest. "Listen to me. Trust me."

"I can't. You don't understand."

The wind was howling overhead as he cradled her cheeks between his callused palms. "I do understand. You're claustrophobic, right?"

"You have to do something. Please," she whispered.

"I'm trying, honey." Even when she twisted, slamming one elbow against his ribs, he didn't release her. "Tell me what happened, Jess. Tell me what did this to you."

"Why do you care?" Jess stared at him gravely.

"Because I think you need to tell someone what happened."

"Psychological unburdening?" She gave a broken laugh. "If you only knew how many things I've tried." She turned away, her body rigid. "It won't help, believe me."

"Try." His voice didn't rise. "First you have to remember—and then you can start letting it go."

Jess sighed. "If only remembering didn't hurt so much. . . ." She squinted up at the ceiling. "My father was in the Navy, gone most of the time." Her mouth flattened. "Secret work, I guess, to places he could never mention. My mother couldn't cope after he died. My sister was the strong one, while I . . . I had behavior problems. An eating disorder." Her shoulders lifted, then fell. "Alcohol on occasion. Maybe on lots of occasions." She looked away again, but Hawk turned her face gently back to his. "I just couldn't believe how fast it happened. One day they were both there, and then it was only Summer and me left."

"Go on."

"You don't give an inch, do you?"

"Generally, no." His thumb traced the little hollow beneath her cheek. "I'm waiting, Jess."

She took a hard breath. "Eventually the people from foster services sent me away for treatment, out to a clinic in the middle of nowhere. Their specialty was something called 'reality-based behavior modification.'" Hawk saw emotions churn up, chasing across her face like angry clouds. "There were ten rules in that place. Ten things that could never be done. I broke four rules my first week."

As she spoke, her hands twisted restlessly. Hawk slipped his arm around her shoulders. "What did they do to you?"

"The director said that it would save everyone time and trouble if I learned the house rules right from the start. I laughed when she told me that, because I thought it was going to be detention or garbage duty, humiliating things like they do to you in school."

Hawk waited, trying not to show his tension. "But it wasn't."

Jess laughed bitterly. "The director marched me outside and locked me in the storage shed. I was crammed in between two lawn mowers and a wall of gardening supplies. I'll never forget the smell of gasoline and peat moss." Her shoulders slumped. "I yelled until my throat hurt, and I pounded on the door for an hour, but no one came. It was only a matter of time until I stopped yelling, like all the others."

Hawk didn't know when he moved, drawing her grimly against his chest. "How long?" he asked gently.

"Three days." Her hands clenched. "Three days, eleven hours, and twenty-six minutes." She trembled, her hands closing on the front of his shirt. "All those years," she whispered. "And it still feels like yesterday."

Hawk didn't answer. He was too busy fighting an urge for cold, premeditated murder. "Maybe you and a few friends should pay that clinic a visit," he said harshly.

"There's nothing left to visit. The director died two years ago, and the clinic is closed, all the staff gone. They've rented out the grounds to a training school for guide dogs." She managed a small smile. "The dogs were beautiful. You know what they say, *Not with a bang but a whimper.*"

Hawk cursed so inventively that her eyes widened.

At least the cursing made him feel better as he ran a hand over her hair, wishing he could erase her bleak memories. "Didn't you tell anyone? What about your sister or the people at foster care?"

Jess winced as he brushed her bloody fingers with the corner of his shirt. "I told them afterwards. My sister was furious, and the foster care people were ... upset, but they sided with the clinic. After all," Jess said bitterly, "they were the professionals, right? They had a clinic and they had all the training and the degrees." Her head sank back against the wall. "What's that thing they say? Something about what doesn't kill you makes you stronger. My time in that shed did make me stronger, even if I left a piece of my childhood behind there. Summer's one of the few people who know what really happened. Now you know, too."

"The whole damned place should have been put out of business," he said harshly. "Then the director should have been horsewhipped and locked in the shed herself for a few days."

She looked startled by his fury, and he concentrated on

relaxing, blanking out the violence of his emotions. At least *she* seemed to be calmer now.

Too bad he wasn't.

"Jess, do you have any more food in that bag of yours?" It had occurred to him earlier that she made it her duty in life to feed people, even when she couldn't buy a decent pair of shoes.

"Food?" She frowned at him. "You're hungry? Now?"

"I am," he said gravely, relieved to see her lower her head to look at her bag.

"Food . . . yeah. Great idea." She took a deep breath and seemed to focus inward as she abruptly sat down on the elevator floor, unzipped her purse and dumped all the contents onto the floor. Sitting probably made the space seem larger, higher, Hawk realized. "There must be something here that will help." She sorted through bagged pretzels, toothpaste, and a pile of receipts neatly organized with colored paperclips. Now her hands were barely shaking at all.

Leaning past her, Hawk pulled a deck of cards out of the pile and sat down. "While we eat, we can make use of these." He opened the box and shuffled the deck expertly.

Jess watched his hands move. "Cards?"

"Not just any cards, honey. We're talking poker here—the most perfect test of intellect and guts devised by man. Texas Hold 'Em, aces high. Get ready to lose your shirt—and any other articles of clothing that happen by."

He was relieved to see her eyes widen in something besides panic, and her mouth slid up in the glimmer of a smile.

She glanced up at him, her eyes smoky, considering . . . then just a little reckless. She took another deep breath, then focused on the floor in her immediate range of vision.

"Okay. Ten minutes. I'll take it ten minutes at a time. Go ahead and deal the cards, partner."

Fifteen minutes later Hawk had lost four dollars and eighty-six cents at poker. Jess had surprised him with her flair for the game, occasionally losing a hand, then catching him with a burst of sheer bravado.

The woman definitely knew how to bluff.

Making herself comfortable, she removed her fashionable pink stiletto heels and shifted to sit cross-legged on the floor, studying her cards, while Hawk concentrated on trying not to notice her long, slender legs.

She toyed with her hand, frowned, shifted. Every few seconds she glanced up, trying to read Hawk's face.

Not that she'd succeed. No one read his face, whether playing at cards or anything else.

He leaned back against the wall, enjoying the snappy play almost as much as her artless questions about poker rules.

"Hit me," she said breathlessly.

He did.

"Flush." She shot to her feet and danced in a little circle.

Hawk tried hard not to stare up her skirt.

Damn if she hadn't beat him again.

It seemed that learning the finer points of poker kept her mind off the stalled elevator, and for that, Hawk was willing to lose all his cash. Especially when her victory left her eyes shining and her cheeks flushed.

Sitting down again, she stacked her cards and set them neatly in front of her. "We forgot about our snack break." She searched through the bagged items on the floor. "We have an array of choices for your dining pleasure today, including one smashed cinnamon croissant, half a strawberry granola bar, and a slightly bruised apple."

Hawk leaned back and crossed his arms. Her face was still white, but she definitely got the prize for spunk. "I'll split the croissant with you."

It was getting colder in the elevator, he noticed. "You're shivering."

"Not from the cold."

Frowning, Hawk pulled a wool scarf out of his leather pack and slipped it around her neck, his hands lingering on her shoulders as she held out half of her croissant. He angled his head, taking a bite from her fingers.

Big mistake. There was something entirely too intimate about taking food from her hand. At the first brush of his mouth against her fingers, he forgot about the rich pastry and fought the urge to grasp those fingers, guiding them down. . . .

Color swirled into her cheeks. "Don't you want more than a bite?"

He wanted more, all right. But not of food, of *her.*

Fighting a sharp awareness of her hip cradling his thigh, he shook his head. Despite his effort at control, his hands tightened on her shoulders.

She made a soft sound, her hands flat against his chest. Her head tilted. "Why are you looking at me like that?"

He could have shrugged or explained. He could have pulled away. He could have let the whole damn subject drop. Instead he brought his mouth down against hers, exploring her slowly, feeling every nerve in his body ratchet up to full, screaming awareness. When she didn't protest, he pulled her closer and drank in the lush taste of her mouth. Hawk had never tasted anything so heady, sweet with cinnamon and a hint of strawberries. He forgot everything but Jess as he slipped his hands into her hair and drew her forward until she straddled his thighs. Already aroused, his body tightened, clamoring for release.

He cursed, aware that the meds were pushing him way out of his comfort zone. His hands shook faintly with his effort at control. "I can't be doing this. And you shouldn't be letting me."

"The operative word is 'letting.' My choice, my decision," she said, a breathless hitch in her voice. "Clearly, you want this as much as I think I do."

If his body made the rules, the answer would have been a flat-out yes. At that moment he would have liked nothing more than to pin her against the wall and take her, fast and rough. "Let's forget this. Chalk any reactions up to too much closeness and not enough options."

"Why don't you just shut up and distract me, Lieutenant?"

When her hand slid down his chest, Hawk stopped her. His sense of touch was excruciatingly sensitive, every nerve stretched like wire. Her warmth was seductive, and even the scent of her shampoo was torture. Just his damned luck to be locked in an elevator with the kind of woman who was completely out of bounds.

He cleared his throat, pushing her away. "Nothing more to say. This is a really bad idea, Jess. We can't just strip naked and—"

Their bodies were thigh to thigh, and she made a husky little sound as he reached out, tracing the edge of her lower lip. Touching her this way was dead wrong, he thought. Dead stupid, too.

He shook his head, trying to remember all the reasons touching her was forbidden.

When that didn't work, he resorted to the cold habit of control, driving his body to stillness.

"Tell me why you always do that, watching the people around you, cold and calm, absolutely quiet."

"Does it frighten you?" Hell, it seemed to frighten most people, Hawk thought. Why not her?

She tilted her head, frowning. "You told me to trust you. I think I do."

His thumb touched the pulse racing wildly at her throat. "Good thing that we both know you're not the kind of woman for casual sex in an elevator."

"You don't know anything about what I am. I've waited years for the violins and the roses, but they never happened, so right now I'm open to alternate suggestions."

"Like casual sex?" Hawk's voice was hard. He smelled the scent of her hair, felt her body tremble.

"Forget it, Jess."

"If you're saying no because I asked first—"

"I'm saying no because it's a stupid idea." Hell, he didn't even have protection with him, Hawk thought grimly. That was a rule he'd never been stupid enough to break. "The whole idea is—"

Before he could finish, his cell phone rang. "What took you so long?" he snapped.

It couldn't be anyone but Izzy on his secure line.

"It's the night of the living dead out here." Izzy's voice crackled in sudden static. "Where the hell are you?"

"In a stalled elevator at the hotel. I've been trying to reach you without any luck."

"This storm has knocked all our communications off-line. What's your situation?"

"We've got auxiliary lights, but no service." Hawk spoke quietly, aware that Jess was following every word. "How soon can you get a team over here?"

"Not anytime soon. Several towns have flooded and there are downed power lines all over the county. Most of the roads have been closed, too." The phone signal faded. Then Izzy's voice came back, echoing hollowly. "I doubt if

I'll be able to get anyone there in less than an hour, but I'm doing all I can. Meanwhile—"

Abruptly the words broke up on a burst of static.

Hawk powered down the phone, praying that Jess hadn't heard.

"He said it would be an hour before someone came," Jess said hoarsely. As she spoke they heard a noise on the other side of the elevator door.

"Hello? Is somebody in there?" a male voice called.

"Damned straight somebody is," Hawk called loudly. "Get the manager over here."

"I *am* the manager. The hotel is currently limited to an auxiliary generator until the electricity is restored, but we're having some problems with the wiring in this building."

"Then fix them," Hawk snapped.

"We're trying. We've phoned all over the state, but no one has repair crews mobile yet."

Hawk slid an arm around Jess's shoulders, pulling her against the warmth of his body. "Isn't there some way to open the doors manually from the outside?"

"Afraid not. Our manual access was removed a few years ago after a man tried to crawl out of a stalled elevator here. He dropped seven floors, broke his neck, and his family sued the hotel for millions. After that the manual override was removed. But don't worry, we'll have you out soon."

Soon wasn't good enough, Hawk thought grimly, feeling Jess's nails digging into his back.

"Do you need food or water? I could try lowering something through the roof. That center panel above your head can be removed."

Hawk looked down at the snacks on the floor near Jess's purse. "We're fine for the moment. Keep me updated on the situation with your power."

As footsteps tapped away from the doors, Jess took a ragged breath. "You heard him. He said the whole state's been affected. Your friend said it would be an hour before he got here."

Hawk caught her fingers gently in his hands. "We'll get by, Jess. You're going to have to trust me."

"Trust won't help me." Her eyes fell, focused on his hard mouth.

Hawk bit back a curse. She couldn't be serious about having sex.

"We could be locked in here for hours." Her hands tightened, fingers linked tensely. "I need you to help me, Hawk."

"Jess, this is nuts. I won't—"

The elevator swayed gently beneath them. "I want you." Her eyes were dark. "Don't tell me I don't know what I'm asking."

"You *don't* know what you're asking," Hawk said savagely. "I'm a stranger, for God's sake."

"You're not a stranger anymore." Her fingers traced an old scar on his neck. "Besides, only an honorable man would try to talk me out of it. That proves I'm right."

"Forget it, Jess. It's not happening."

Her hand slid down his chest, stopping at his belt. "Especially when that man is as aroused as you appear to be."

Hawk gripped her hand and held it locked against his chest. "You don't know what you're getting into."

"Then tell me." She studied his face. "Everything seems to be present and in working order." Her fingers wriggled open, exploring the heat of his chest.

Hawk knew his erection was unmistakable as their bodies brushed intimately. "Damn it, Jess—"

"Is there some physical problem?"

"There's *no* physical problem."

"Then what are you waiting for?"

"Because one of us has to be sane."

"Why?"

"Because men are worthless shits and you'd better remember that."

"Okay, I've got that clear. What other advice do you have for me?"

"I'm serious, Jess. There are reasons," he said harshly.

Her hips moved as she brought their bodies closer. "You're a very scary man, Lieutenant. You talk cold and you look cold. But for some reason, I don't think you're as buttoned-down as you look. In fact, you don't scare me at all," she whispered.

"Then you're a fool." His hands tightened on her shoulders. Hawk wanted to feel her body rise against his. He wanted his hands buried in her hair while she lost all her reserve and moaned his name. "I could take you whether you liked it or not, Jess. I could say when and how much and you wouldn't have any choice." The damned woman needed to see just how dangerous the situation was, he thought grimly.

And then, before he could finish trying to frighten her, she kissed him.

Her first attempt was tentative, even a little awkward. When Hawk didn't move or respond in any way, she kissed him again, this time with teeth and a whole lot of tongue.

Hawk cursed. "You just opened the wrong door, honey."

"Good." Her fingers moved, tugging at his belt. "I've always loved surprises."

"In that case, there have to be a few damned rules." Was he insane? Hawk wondered. Even if he was, it didn't seem to matter now.

He stood up slowly, pulling her along with him. "Rule number one. No questions. No matter what."

"But why—?"

"Yes or no, Jess?"

"Okay," she muttered, then traced his mouth with such gentle concentration that Hawk cursed silently.

"Rule number two. Your hands stay where I put them, no matter what."

"But—" Jess stopped, studying his face.

"Yes or no?" Hawk realized his hands were rigid, his need building fiercely.

"Yes."

He sighed, almost angry that she wasn't giving him any reasons to say no. "What if you regret this tomorrow?"

"I won't." She sounded absolutely certain.

Fighting back a curse, Hawk leaned down, letting her see the hunger he'd managed to push beneath the surface. If she planned to turn back, he needed to know now. "You realize exactly what you're offering me, Jess. *Everything*." His hand cupped her breast, stroking her slowly through the thin silk of her blouse. "Are you still in?"

She blinked at him. Her eyes darkened as his fingers tugged at the tight crest thrusting against her blouse. "I'm not sure I can think when you do that."

Hawk laughed grimly. "I'll be doing a lot more than this in a minute, honey. So give me an answer."

Jess gnawed at her lip, making a soft sound of surprise when Hawk's hands slid beneath her blouse, shoved aside her bra, and closed over her nipples.

Her skin felt hot and tight against Hawk's callused fingers.

His breath was rough. He couldn't manage to act casual much longer. She was too exciting and he wanted her too badly.

If she didn't scare off soon, he wouldn't be able to stop.

He leaned down, one arm at her back as he kissed her neck, her shoulder, the perfect curve of her breasts.

His tongue circled her slowly, like a cat savoring warm cream, working the dark pink nipple between his teeth until her breath hissed and her nails dug into his back.

"*Good*," she whispered. "I mean, yes. I'm *definitely* in. Don't even think about stopping now."

Emilio Chavez moved restlessly through the quiet room. His stocky body was tense, his energy barely contained.

Finally he came to a halt. "Have you found the animal yet?" He used the hard, colloquial Spanish of the mountain village where he'd been born in Colombia.

The two other men in the room avoided his eyes. Both men knew that the news they brought was *not* the news that their employer wanted to hear.

As the silence stretched out, the stocky Colombian ex-general moved to the window and stared out at the rain-swept harbor.

"I gave you twelve hours, and you gave me only promises." Chavez drummed his fingers on the chipped windowsill. "Then I gave you another twenty-four hours. And still you mutter and delay, with nothing of any value to show me." The two men behind him were sweating now, although the room was cool.

"But, sir, we followed the roads. We checked the map and the towns nearby." The man was interrupted by footsteps outside.

There was a single quick tap at the door. "What is it?" Chavez called angrily.

The door opened. "The satellite weather maps you asked for are here, sir."

Chavez glared at the nervous man in a black rain poncho. "Put them on the desk, then have my boat fueled."

"Yes, sir. Immediately, sir." The door closed quietly, and the three men were once more alone.

Chavez watched lightning break out at sea and sighed. He pulled a bottle of whiskey from a hidden shelf and carried it across to his desk, where he filled three glasses, then motioned the other two men forward. "You have ten hours from this moment. Before you go out, we will share a drink for good luck. This whiskey is excellent, as only the mad Scotsmen can make it. But remember that I am not a patient man." He raised his glass in a toast to the others. "To the first one who finds the animal. He will sleep in silk sheets, with more money than he can spend in one lifetime."

Glasses clinked and greed lay heavy in the air. As Chavez savored the expensive aged whiskey, he noticed with distaste that the others tossed their drinks back with no respect.

Crude killers, he thought. Men with no hearts.

But he paid them to be nothing else. Smiling gently, he watched them over the rim of his glass while rain beat at the window.

The man nearer to him swallowed hard and sank down onto the chair beside the desk.

"Is something wrong, Diego?"

When the man didn't answer, Chavez waited calmly, steepling his fingers.

Five seconds later, a glass shattered on the unpainted wood floor. With a sharp gagging sound, the man named Diego collapsed, his feet bumping loudly in his convulsions.

Chavez moved casually to the body that was still twitching. "Never question my orders. Never make excuses," he said coldly, driving the ornate metal toe of his expensive boot into the back of the man's head. He looked up slowly at the frightened man who remained. "And now you have only nine hours and fifty-seven minutes to find the animal. Otherwise, you will die worse than this one did."

Emilio Chavez didn't look back when the door was

yanked open, footsteps flashing up the metal steps. His eyes were narrow and intent as he tossed the used glasses into the garbage. With no change in expression, he bent to wipe the blood and brain tissue off the toe of his boot.

"Nine hours and fifty-five minutes," he said to the empty room.

# chapter 10

**H**awk straightened his leather jacket around Jess's shoulders.

She realized his game plan was set and there would be no deviations.

But now that she'd watched his eyes darken as he touched her skin, Jess decided the rules weren't so important.

She closed her eyes as the elevator swayed slightly. Sweat beaded up over her forehead.

She hated being weak like this, hated for anyone to look deep and glimpse her fears.

But Hawk hadn't laughed at her. He didn't move away as if she had some kind of disease.

Jess closed her eyes. She wanted to blurt out that she didn't usually accost semi-strange men or propose sex in public places, but she caught back the words.

*No explanations.* Just Hawk. Just this need to be close, to be held and feel his skin warm against hers.

With her head bent, she shoved away the fear and focused on the scent of his jacket. Wearing it felt sharply intimate.

Old leather.

Sea wind.

Apples, probably stuck in an inside pocket. The mix of smells mesmerized her, even as the old fears returned.

*Three days. Eleven hours. Twenty-six minutes.*

*Dear God, no more memories.*

Jess squeezed her eyes shut.

She wanted to be in the present. She wanted to move against Hawk's body. By concentrating intently on the scent of his jacket, she managed to block the vision of cold walls closing in.

"No questions," she said, studying the walls fixedly. "But I need to know the time, how long until someone will come."

Hawk pulled off a watch with a luminous dial and multiple time zones. "Take mine."

"Only until . . . this is over." Frowning, she pulled on the big watch, feeling the heat of his body in the metal.

Hawk pulled off his sweater and hung it from the rim of the molding at the top of the elevator.

"Why—"

"Because there's a camera up there and I'd rather not have an audience," he said dryly. He shifted the sweater to one side, then turned back to her.

"Don't talk," Jess said quickly, afraid if she talked she'd lose her nerve. She didn't want to be afraid.

She rose on tiptoes, skimming her hands across his chest, his ribs, just above his waistband. "Hawk, I need—"

"I know what you need," he said roughly. "I was thinking about it in high-resolution detail most of the night."

Jess wondered that she wasn't embarrassed by the brush of his hands tugging her blouse free of her skirt.

Hawk leaned down, his face tense. She caught the scent of apples and sea wind again.

Her blouse opened.

"There's still time to change your mind." His voice was slow, like cold water dropping over deep gravel.

"My mind's made up."

"You're making a mistake." He gripped her waist, turning her slowly.

"If so, it's *my* mistake." As Jess spoke, her gaze drifted to the walls.

His eyes narrowed, dark points that seemed to pull her soul into their depths. "You don't go easy on yourself, do you?" He tilted her face up carefully. "You're soft outside, easy with words, but tough where it counts."

Jess didn't answer.

The emotion in her eyes kicked hard at Hawk's chest.

She was the bravest woman he'd ever met, wrestling demons that would have toppled many a strong man.

The thought of her locked in a shed left his hands clenched into fists. He wanted to right the old wrongs, repay the idiots who had hurt her years ago.

But she didn't want his pity or his anger.

He'd listened to her story with all expression locked down tight, aware that Jess didn't need complicating emotions. All she wanted was to forget, facing the past dead-on rather than denying it. Even when the situation grew worse, she'd held tight to her sense of humor as she disgorged the contents of her purse in search of possible distractions.

And then she'd faced him without a qualm and asked for the solace of his body, for sex in any way he chose to have it.

The memory still left him unsteady. Hawk was a generous lover who knew how to stir a woman's body. He knew he could touch Jess with fire and make her moan his name as she raced along the razor's edge of passion into oblivion.

But Jess wasn't like the other women he'd known. She

was smart and stubborn, yet beneath that prickly exterior he glimpsed a dreamer who woke every day with a resolve that better things were just around the corner.

Hawk didn't want to be the man who ruined those dreams. She swore she would have no regrets, but she was wrong. Because she wasn't a woman who gave her body lightly, she'd leave a part of herself behind, too generous and too innocent to wall off her feelings the way Hawk had long ago learned to do.

The women he chose as partners knew how to create that distance. They laughed easily and drank with calm deliberation, asking no questions so that nobody got hurt and nobody expected more than either one could give.

Until Jess, that kind of sex had been easy.

Until her cocky smile, endless questions, and trembling hands twisted something in his chest and made him want more, though he couldn't find a name for it.

God knows, it wasn't love. Hawk hadn't believed in love since he was twelve and he watched his father push his mother down a flight of stairs.

His fingers tightened, then he released them quickly, all too aware of how easy it would be to mark her, to hurt her.

Because with every gentle touch, she left him aflame, reckless to give her the oblivion she craved. But there was always a cost, he thought grimly. And now the medication he was taking pushed him to the very edge of his control.

His muscles clenched as she traced old scars on his neck.

A knife fight in Mexico City.

A river ambush in Thailand.

Burns from fast-roping off a chopper in the South China Sea.

She cared about those scars, Hawk realized. She touched them slowly, her breath tense. And he sensed that she wanted to touch the man beneath the scars, the one that Hawk never let anyone see.

But who would touch her back—the lethal warrior or the stranger he glimpsed occasionally in mirrors and windows? A man he'd all but forgotten since anonymity and transience had become the mainstays of his life.

If his life had taken a different, less violent path, he might have met a woman like this, might have fallen in love and married her without thinking twice. Right now he could have been a high school teacher in Portland, with a fence and a mortgage and three noisy kids.

Instead of a man with too many scars and too few dreams.

*Hell.*

She was looking up at him, a mix of hope and desire on her face, and he wanted to tell her there was nothing here, that he couldn't help her. That in the end he was bound to hurt her.

But he didn't say any of that, mesmerized by the depths of her smoky green eyes. Paralyzed when her hands slid beneath his shirt, curving smoothly over his chest while her perfume tangled up all his too-acute senses.

And then he was lost, tracing her neck, the line of her shoulder, shoving off her blouse to explore the silk of her skin.

She sighed when he released the catch of her bra with its simple white straps. The feel of his mouth seemed to stun her, and she said something Hawk couldn't hear.

He'd been certain that she'd push him away, but her hands slid to his face, tightened, then moved down, shoving hard at his T-shirt.

The touch of her fingers on his skin nearly undid him, nearly made him forget his plan.

To give without taking. Because that's what she needed most from him.

"Hawk—"

His lips opened, cutting her off. Whether it was a question or an explanation, he would never know. With need like thunder in his head, he slid away her skirt and one final scrap of lace until all she wore was his big leather jacket, askew around her shoulders.

And damned if his battered jacket didn't suit her just as much as the nakedness did.

His rough hands scraped slowly up her thighs and curved around her hips while he tasted his way recklessly across her chest, nudging aside the leather so he could mouth her taut nipple.

Her body trembled, her fingers digging into his shoulders, but Hawk refused to give either of them time for questions.

*I love the weight of your breasts,* he wanted to say. *I love the way your breath catches when I find the hot, wet place between your legs.*

But he showed her instead, pulling her to the floor with locked arms until she lay beneath him, pale and restless against the dark leather of his jacket.

And then he loved her, his mouth slow and relentless on her thighs, and then higher, exploring her wet folds, driving her up while she gripped his back and raked her nails across his skin.

He wanted her taste on his mouth. He nuzzled, then scraped her gently with his teeth.

When she shuddered, he eased her legs apart, tracing her with his thumbs, giving her time to accept his mouth.

As she moaned brokenly, Hawk eased one finger inside her.

Seconds passed. She moved against him in aching intimacy, her breath rising in inchoate words.

With a dark smile, he drew her against his mouth, searching for the tiny ridge hidden in slick folds.

When he found it, she was wet and ready, trembling on the edge, all fears forgotten.

His own needs seemed distant, and Hawk realized he wanted her nails driving into his back while pleasure rained over her and the wind hissed down the elevator shaft around them.

"Hawk—"

"Shh."

*No words,* he swore. No questions. Only hot, silent pleasure while her body rose against him, arched in need. He slid another finger inside her while he took her with mouth and tongue until she cried out his name and her heart banged in her chest and she collapsed in exhaustion, slick with sweat.

Mustering his control, Hawk curved his body against her, one arm wrapped protectively around her waist. With every breath, her soft hips rose and fell, cradling his erection, stretching every nerve to the breaking point.

Then, with a sigh, she burrowed against his chest, one hand at his neck, the other inches from the taut line of his zipper. Completely oblivious, she draped her warm body across him and fell asleep.

# chapter 11

**S**ummer Mulcahey hated computers and the feeling happened to be mutual.

Scowling, she stared down at the screen of her frozen laptop. Why did the wretched thing work without a hiccup around her husband, but freeze completely around her?

Abruptly the screen unlocked, flickered twice, and then Microsoft Windows crashed.

Muttering, she rebooted the computer and went through the laborious steps to track down the digital culprit, managing a successful reboot. Ten minutes later she had forgotten the cucumber mask slathered over her cheeks and was peering at weather forecasts for Washington State.

The reports were ominous. Forty mile-an-hour winds were already pounding the Olympic Peninsula and more rain was predicted over the next forty-eight hours.

She looked outside at the snow falling in dark Philadelphia streets. Summer had a strong suspicion that more than a storm was at stake in Washington. In the last week, four senior field agents from her office had been quietly reassigned to the Northwest, with no explanations offered. Questions were met with silence.

Which meant that a highly classified operation had been initiated.

And if Jess had stumbled into the middle of that operation . . .

Summer closed her eyes. Her twin sister was smart, responsible, and able to take care of herself, but worrying about Jess had become one of Summer's oldest habits.

Sighing, she turned back to the weather maps, trying to gauge the storm's progress. What was the name of her sister's latest hotel assignment? Was it the Meridian or was it the Marathon—

The doorknob turned behind her.

Summer's frown burst into a radiant smile as a tall man in a Navy uniform filled the doorway. She jumped up, knocking her chair down in the process, and the force of her hug drove him back against the wall. "You're home!"

"Sorry I'm a day late. Something came up." Her husband didn't say more, and after a glance at his face, Summer didn't ask. Work generally meant secrets neither could reveal.

Gabe caught her with one arm, grinning. "Got off the plane twenty-five minutes ago. One of the men offered to give me a ride, and we drove straight through from Virginia."

Summer shoved at the buttons on his jacket. "The last four weeks have felt like a few decades. In fact, I'm probably an old hag with gray hair already."

The SEAL held her a little away from him and studied her face. "Not a gray hair in sight, but it looks like the aliens have landed."

Summer shoved at his chest, laughing. "I forgot I had this gunk on my face. Jess sent it a few weeks ago and insisted I try it out. I'll go clean up, but I don't want you to move an inch." As she raced to the bathroom, she called over her shoulder. "Have you eaten anything today?"

"Nothing that I want to remember." Gabe stripped off his uniform jacket and laid it on the leather chair near the door. "By the way, Izzy said to tell you hi."

Down the hall water ran, then was abruptly shut off. "Izzy? You saw Izzy?"

"I passed him in the hall a few days back. Nothing formal." Gabe chuckled. "He said to tell you that married life agrees with me."

Summer appeared, minus the green gunk, her hair pulled free of its rubber band and curling softly around her shoulders. "I'm delighted to hear it, Lieutenant Morgan."

"You should be, Mrs. Morgan, since you're largely to blame."

In one stride, Gabe had his arms around her, his mouth hot and impatient.

When Summer could break away to speak, she looked down, enjoying the sight of Gabe stripping in record time. "Just so you know, I fell asleep in the tub working on my current case. But I used that pineapple bubble stuff you like, and then the coconut oil lotion Jess sent me for Christmas." She toyed with the belt of her robe. "Not wearing anything else. Just in case you're interested."

Gabe's eyes darkened and he said something under his breath. His hands loosened her belt and slid inside her robe. "In that case, we ought to do something about it."

"Anything particular in mind?" One side of her robe gaped free.

"You're damned right I've got something in mind." Gabe planted slow kisses down her neck and shoulder. "I haven't thought about anything else for the last four weeks."

Summer yanked at his belt. "The bedroom's probably cold. I opened the window earlier and then—"

"Forget about the bedroom, honey. We're not going to make it." Gabe opened her robe and filled his hands with her. His breath was harsh and strained. "Right here, Summer. Right against this wall."

Snow brushed the window, leaving little white tracks as he shoved off her robe and brought their bodies together.

Summer stretched slowly, every muscle in her body unkinked and luxuriously relaxed. "Wow," she said.

"Well said, honey." The snow was still whispering against the windows.

Now Summer watched it from bed, burrowed beneath a thick quilt.

Gabe's job as a Navy SEAL meant all of his work was classified, and much of the same held true for her assignments as an FBI field agent. Both of them were keenly aware of the heavy security issues imposed by their jobs, and both were scrupulous about observing those rules.

At the same time, they were both struggling with the whole concept of marriage, still waking up amazed to be together. When the distance was factored in, with Gabe based on the West Coast and Summer here in Philadelphia—

She closed her eyes. At least their distance problem would soon be resolved. In a month Gabe was set to be transferred to Little Creek, Virginia, while she was being assigned to a field office in Maryland.

Meanwhile they met when they could, talked often, and managed to stir the embers through long-distance phone calls that had grown increasingly heated.

In fact, Summer had discovered a definite talent for phone sex.

But she had never had much experience with normal relationships as an adult, and as a female agent training for the FBI, her world became even more proscribed. Because she wanted her marriage to Gabe to succeed, she was determined to master *normal*.

Of course, she still hadn't figured out what *normal* meant. She stopped tracing Gabe's muscular chest and rolled onto one elbow. "Are you hungry? I made some spaghetti sauce yesterday and—"

The SEAL cracked open one eye. "You *cooked*? With pans and cutlery and real garlic?"

Summer flushed. She refused to tell him that she'd spent three hours hunched over a cookbook, trying to make sense of unknown spices and the proper method of timing al dente pasta. After all, other women made spaghetti in their sleep. Other women actually made pasta from scratch, mixing the dough and rolling it out in expensive little machines.

It infuriated Summer that it took her three hours to come up with a reasonably palatable approximation of a simple, home-cooked meal.

But she refused to admit that to him.

If he wanted normal, he was going to get normal.

"No big deal. I can handle cutlery. As a matter of fact, Jess sent me a new cookbook, and I decided to try it out while you were gone."

Gabe cupped her chin and turned her face up to his. There was something unreadable in his eyes as he slowly traced her cheek. Summer had forgotten the small bruise on her neck, but Gabe kissed it carefully. "New case?"

"Yeah."

"Rifle recoil?"

Summer shrugged.

For a moment something came and went in Gabe's eyes. "I can't tell you to be careful, can I?"

"It's my job, Gabe. If I'm thinking how to protect me, I can't think about protecting everyone else."

He said something under his breath, then kissed her fiercely, his hands locked in her hair while he captured her beneath him.

Summer finally pulled away and took a deep breath. "What was that for?"

"Thank you."

"For a few cups of spaghetti sauce?"

"For being the best at what you do. For making me food when we both know you hate the thought of cooking." Looking down, he traced the slender gold band on her finger. "For being everything I've ever wanted in a woman."

Summer blinked hard, struck with a wave of emotion. Just when she thought she had this man figured, he said something that turned her inside out.

Maybe being normal wasn't so important after all.

"Okay, it did take me three hours and the kitchen looked like the evacuation of Dunkirk by the time I was done, with olive oil over most of one wall. But when you get the garlic just right, the smell is amazing." Summer's eyes narrowed as she saw Gabe's crooked grin. "Well, it is," she said defensively. "And the thing about olive oils—who knew they could all be so different? Like handguns, you know what I mean? They all do the same job, but they're worlds apart."

"Honey, only you could compare extra virgin olive oil to handguns." Gabe nuzzled her breast, tugging the sensitized skin with his teeth until Summer made a breathless sound.

Suddenly she froze. "Wait a minute. You said you saw Izzy?"

Gabe nodded.

Alarm bells rang in Summer's head as she realized that Gabe hadn't volunteered any details.

So this was work, probably classified.

But classified or not, her sister's safety was in question and Izzy had the answers. "Jess told me she'd run into Izzy out in Washington. I'm worried that she's landed in the middle of something dangerous."

Something closed down in Gabe's face.

"You can't talk about it, can you? I understand that, Gabe. I've never asked before, and I won't ask now. But if Jess is in danger, I can't stand by and keep quiet. You know how impulsive she can be."

"It's part of her charm."

Summer's hands tightened on the quilt. "If—if something ever happened to her—"

"Nothing's going to happen to her," Gabe said quietly. "I'll ask a few questions and tell you everything I can."

Which might be very little, Summer knew. She was bound by the same rules in her work. But something was better than nothing.

"If Jess is tangled up with Izzy, it's a bad sign," she said slowly. "I know the game plan, and I won't pry. But I'm calling her." There was a catch in her voice. "I need to know that she's okay."

"You worry too much." Gabe slid an arm around her shoulders and pulled her closer. "That's part of *your* charm. But you need to remember that Jess is smart and she's tough in her own way. You don't need to fight her battles for her."

He was right, Summer thought. Jess was smart, stubborn, and independent.

She took a deep breath, looking out at the snow and thinking about a house with too many shadows and too much regret. It was hard to stop worrying about someone you loved, she discovered.

Summer was paid to take risks. She actually enjoyed the adrenaline rush and the challenge of pushing herself to the limit. But Jess didn't know that dark world. She still trusted in human honesty and the generosity of strangers.

And that trust scared Summer more than anything else.

When Gabe eased from the bed an hour later, Summer made a muffled protest, then rolled onto her side, burrowing into the warmth left behind him.

Quietly, the SEAL moved outside and punched a button on his cell phone.

Izzy Teague answered on the first ring. "Acme Car Wash. Hand polishing is our specialty."

"One of these days you're going to wise off to some Beltway big shot and find yourself out on your ass looking for a new line of work," Gabe said dryly. "I could have been the SecDef or head of the Joint Chiefs."

"Not on this line, pal. Only two people have this number." A chair creaked. "*Don't* ask who the other person is." Izzy was quiet for a moment, keys tapping at a computer. "You're calling about Jess, I take it."

Gabe watched a fresh curtain of snow veil the window. "You don't miss much, same as always. Tell me what you can."

"Jess wandered into the middle of . . . something. But that's it. Tell Summer there's nothing to worry about."

Gabe frowned. "I have your word on that? Summer's damned touchy where Jess is concerned. It's one of those twin things."

"Jess is fine. I'm watching out for any possible . . . complications."

"I'll hold you to that." Gabe's eyes narrowed. "If they arise, you'd better haul ass and deal with those complications," he said quietly.

"Trust me, civilians wandering around in the middle of work is not my idea of good mission planning."

So Izzy was on a mission, Gabe thought. "Anything you can talk about?"

Izzy cleared his throat. "Afraid not."

"If that changes, you know where to reach me."

"Roger that."

"Watch your six, Teague," Gabe muttered. After hanging up, he stared into the darkness, running through a list of possible contacts, starting deep inside the Pentagon.

Then he leaned back and dialed the first name on his extensive net of military contacts.

When Gabe finally put down the phone, his thoughts were far away from the quiet snow dusting the Philadelphia streets.

On the desk in front of him was a toy otter from the Monterey Bay Aquarium, a gift from Summer. Nearby was a photo of Summer with her proud superior after both had received special citations for their work on a high-profile kidnapping case.

Leaning down, Gabe opened a drawer of the desk and pulled out a plain blue rubber band, like thousands of others sold in cheap packages anywhere in the country.

But this rubber band had helped him through half a dozen operations after an accident in the line of duty. Because it had come from Summer's hair, he still regarded it as a powerful talisman.

Twisting the rubber band between his fingers, he stared out into the snow-swept darkness. Now that he knew Izzy's covert assignment, he had to assess how closely Jess was involved.

And the animal involved was more than a description in a secret file, because Gabe had spent the last month guarding the missing lab animal on its maiden voyage from Australia. The trouble had begun three months earlier, when the ultrasecret transgenic koala bear had developed unexpected heart problems, which had not responded to treatment.

The scientists in charge had immediately made arrangements to transport the animal to the United States for evaluation and stabilization. When the animal had shown no tolerance for air travel, Gabe and twelve other men had accompanied the female koala on its transpacific voyage.

Gabe had heard the recent news about the raid that had resulted in two dead government agents. Currently, one agent was still in guarded condition—and the animal was missing.

How in the hell had Jess Mulcahey stumbled right into the middle of the situation?

Gabe glanced down at his watch and thought about putting in a second call to Izzy, but when he looked up, Summer was standing in the doorway.

"Something wrong?" she asked quietly.

"Just a few calls I had to make." She was even more beautiful in the moonlight. Gabe hadn't thought it was possible.

Her expression turned tender. "You need to sleep, Navy, but first you need to eat some of my very excellent spaghetti. And if you don't like it, I may have to practice my Weaver stance on you," she said wryly.

"Don't worry, I'll love every bite." But because of what he'd learned in his calls, Gabe suspected his time with Summer was limited, and he didn't intend to waste one precious second.

He figured there were better things to do on a kitchen table than eat spaghetti.

# chapter 12

ave to go."

Hawk felt Jess turn, mumbling against his chest. "Go back to sleep," he murmured.

"Report's done. Can't stay—not safe now." She twisted without warning, one elbow digging at his ribs.

Stifling a curse, Hawk drew her away from his side. His jacket slid away, revealing her naked breast.

He couldn't stop himself, covering her with his mouth, enjoying the way her breath caught when his tongue ran over her.

"Hawk," she said drowsily.

"Right here." He couldn't stop his hands gliding over every inch of her as his jacket shifted and fell to the floor.

She opened her eyes, searching his face.

Without a word she arched her body, pushing against his hands, and made a sharp sound of pleasure when his fingers tangled in the slick curls at her thighs.

She made a little sound that could have been his name, then she rolled onto her side and pushed away from him. "You haven't—you don't want to—"

"I'm fine," he said harshly.

But she was fully awake now, her eyes shimmering with

questions. She took a breath, sliding on top of him, her hands tugging at his belt, then working awkwardly at his zipper until he couldn't think, couldn't breathe for the desperate need to be buried deep inside her.

"Jess." His voice was savage, his fingers locked hard over her wrist.

"Now." Searching, she drew him between hands that weren't quite steady. "My rules, Lieutenant. Here and now. Fair is fair, so shut up." She looked deep into his eyes, then circled his rigid length.

His control exploded when she traced him slowly, slipping one bead of liquid onto her finger.

Against her open lips.

His need flared white-hot.

His, he thought blindly. He whispered her name, spreading her legs while her smoky green eyes searched his face. She was sleek, tight.

Too damned tight, Hawk thought through a bloodred haze of desire. He would hurt her if he wasn't careful.

And right now he couldn't be careful, not pumped up with pills that churned through his blood, amping up his hormones.

She leaned down, wriggled side to side, moving to fit him inside her. Every motion left him hungrier. With a sigh she closed her eyes and brought him deeper.

But not deep enough. He was too big, the fit too tight.

Hawk gripped her waist, trying to ignore the angry demon of need that made him ache to shove her back and ride her blindly, without care or concern.

"Stop," he grated. "Don't . . . move."

She shuddered, then went still.

His jaw clenched. "Jess, are you protected?"

She frowned. "I'm safe."

"You need to be sure," he said tightly. He remembered the pill case in her purse but he wanted verification.

"It's fine. Don't worry." She watched him, color flooding her cheeks. "Trust me."

Him trusting her. Oddly, Hawk realized that he did.

She winced as she pushed against him, biting her lip. "Would you mind explaining why in the books and all the movies, this part is effortless? I mean, there are violins and gauzy scarves and everything fits perfectly. There's no cellulite in sight."

Hawk laughed darkly. "Surgeons make a fortune. So do filmmakers, honey."

"You're too big," she rasped. "I'm no expert, but I've never felt—" More color swept into her face. "So small. So tight."

Hawk cursed, his eyes closing as he felt her rock against him. "You damned well better not remind me, Jess. I can feel exactly how tight you are."

And it was killing him.

"Then do something. You're the expert." She sounded cross and embarrassed.

"What the hell do you want me to do, force you?" It was coming too close to being a possibility, Hawk realized grimly.

He decided that the medicine contributed by the Navy's top-secret research team needed to come with a detailed warning label. No women within twenty feet. No beautiful, stubborn, reckless women anywhere within range of sight or hearing.

Meanwhile, he had a major problem. The part of his anatomy that was between them felt like iron.

She worked her body back and forth, making no headway, then fell back, exasperated, her hands on his shoulders.

"Just *do* it. I'll be fine." Her lips twitched. "I'll think of Queen and Country."

If he hadn't been so gripped by need, Hawk might have managed a laugh. As it was, even the ghost of a smile was beyond him. "Hell if you'll be thinking about England or anything but me when I'm inside you."

"But you're not inside me," she muttered. "Not really. And I want you to be." She pressed against him. "I *really* want you to be."

So much for the violins and the gauzy silk, Hawk thought. She was so tight it felt like her first sexual experience.

His body went absolutely still. "This isn't your first time, is it? I'll be damned if I'm going to—"

She made a low, shaky sound and looked away. For an awful moment Hawk thought she was crying.

Then he realized the broken sounds were muffled laughter, her body shaking beneath him.

"I don't think the question's particularly funny," he snapped.

"It's not, but the way you asked—terrified—I can't help laughing. And no, it's not my first time. But you're so—" She cracked an eye open. "Okay, you're huge. And I'm not just saying that because guys love praise for their physical assets."

"What guys?" He refused to ask how many. It wasn't his business. This was strictly one-time sex, delivered on an emergency basis.

"Who? Every primate with a Y chromosome," Jess said wryly. "And, no, there haven't been that many. Three total. Actually, make that two and one-half, if you count the dentist."

Hawk bit back an oath. He wasn't sure how you could manage a one-half rating in sex, but he didn't want to think about Jess with other men.

It was bad enough trying to figure out what to do with her here and now.

"Actually, that works out right," she continued breathlessly, "because you're definitely one and a half in the endowment category, so that makes an even four." Her lids fell, framing smoky eyes. "Assuming that you stop complaining and get yourself inside me. Push harder or something."

*Push harder?*

God, Hawk thought, she was going to kill him yet.

He shook his head and their eyes met. Then she smiled, slowly, as if they shared some ancient joke that no one else could understand.

Hawk's body tightened.

He twisted, rolling her beneath him. Slipping her legs up around his waist, he arrowed down, rocking her, each movement driving him inside her in increments. She gripped him, hot and tight as a glove, her breath catching on a gasp as he filled her completely.

Then withdrew.

Her protest broke in a sigh as his hips knifed down sharply. Fully sheathed in her wet heat, he drove her over the floor, across his leather jacket until she dug her nails into his back.

She gasped his name. Her back arched. Hawk felt her hot, intimate contractions grip him tightly where he rode deep inside her.

As her nails scored his back, he took her up again, finding a fierce rhythm that left her gasping, plunging into waves of pleasure. This time he followed, spilling himself inside her with fierce abandon.

# chapter 13

**T**hunder cracked, rolling in the distance.

Hawk's fingers tightened in Jess's hair.

He smiled as she sighed, her hips moving against him with slow satisfaction.

His response was instant. In any other man, it would have been unnatural.

"Again?" Her eyes snapped open. The man was amazing.

Already hard, he answered with his body, pulling her on top of him.

Her nails dug into his back. "Wait just a minute. You can do that? I mean, most men—"

"*Forget* most men."

"Gladly."

Hawk coaxed her breast erect with his teeth, moving deep inside her until she closed her eyes and made a broken sound of pleasure, at the edge of another climax.

Without warning, static hammered through the elevator. A voice filled the silence that followed, raw and angry over the tinny speakers. "I know you're there, even though you covered the camera."

Jess's smile faded.

"You're there and you can hear me. Bitch."

Hawk's arms tightened. When Jess started to snap back an answer, he shook his head in silent warning.

"Just remember, you won't be anonymous after this, bitch. We know what you look like now. No more spying on peoples' lives and filing your damned reports. Someone will be watching for you."

Jess quivered in Hawk's arms and once again started to speak, but he cut her off with a finger to her lips.

"It would serve you right if we just left you in the elevator another few hours."

Hawk dug beneath the sleeve of his jacket, found a pen, and scrawled on the back of the ace of spades.

*Don't talk.*

Jess nodded tensely, her heart pounding.

*Recognize the voice?*

She shook her head.

Hawk's jaw was rigid as he pulled out his cell phone. He pressed a button and set the phone on the floor.

*I'm getting this on the recorder. We'll find him. Don't worry.*

She brushed his jaw gently with her knuckles and mouthed two words.

*Thank you.*

Jess turned her head, unable to listen to the hate-filled voice. She felt his fingers tighten on her shoulders, then loosen, circling with gentle comfort.

So gentle, she thought.

With so much violence locked inside him.

She made a low sound, brushing her face. Her tears felt cold on her skin.

As Hawk looked at her, he crumpled the playing card between his fingers.

Jess mouthed a word. *What?*

He stared at the folded card, his jaw working back and forth as he opened it tensely. *I'd like to kill him.*

He stared at the black outline of the ace of spades, then wrote something more.

*I thought you were exaggerating about the threats. That makes me one of those worthless shits I warned you about.*

She grabbed the pen and card, tossed them over her shoulder, and gripped his shoulders fiercely.

*No,* she breathed.

Above them the angry voice faded against the static. The silence inside changed, charged with need. Whispers replaced anger and leather rustled on silk while strangers forgot their distance, snared in an expanding universe of intimacy, beyond questions or answers.

Thunder cracked and growled as Hawk locked his fingers through hers, lifted her arms, and watched her as he drove into the dark places no man had ever filled before. His eyes were hungry, his body unsated as he claimed her with unnerving skill, one climax racing into another, until they were spent, exhausted.

When they were done, she lay staring up at the shadowed ceiling, his leather jacket caught in folds beneath her still trembling body.

Neither spoke.

What could words have added? Jess thought.

He was strong, generous, amazingly sensual.

Strangely, he had made her feel strong, too.

Her. Awkward and uncomfortable Jess, who counted only three men in her experience, not one of whom had left her body tingling neck to toe from his mouth and teeth and just a hint of beard burn.

She sighed and closed her eyes.

"Cold?"

She shook her head. He took time for small, wet bites that left her nerves zinging all over again.

"You're . . . very good at this."

His eyes narrowed. "A problem?"

"No. I just—" How many other women had fallen for his rough skill and dark charm? Jess wondered.

Not her business. No questions and no strings.

"Sorry. That came out wrong." She refused to be a cliché. For God's sake, it was sex in an elevator, and the idea had been hers, not his.

She'd practically forced him to finish.

Color filled her face.

She searched blindly and grabbed something lacy to cover herself. Since it turned out to be her underwear, it was a useless effort.

Gently, he opened her fingers, letting her lace panties fall. "Izzy will phone when he's close."

How incredibly easy to want more, Jess thought. *Isn't this another fine mess you've gotten yourself into?*

She shoved back the tangled weight of her hair and fixed a smile on her face.

The man deserved a smooth ending, an easy farewell, not a crushing wall of female hormones.

"Well," she said briskly, slipping on her right shoe. "That was . . . wonderful."

Without a word, Hawk pulled her shoe off and turned it in his fingers. "Wrong foot," he said quietly.

The air seemed to shimmer as he lifted her leg and bit the arch of her foot, while desire backed up in her chest and her body flared straight into full awareness of where they were and what they'd just done.

More than once.

And what his eyes promised they were about to do again.

He was naked and gorgeous, his muscles rigid as he rose

against her. Jess saw scars scattered over his chest and arms as he leaned toward her. With a helpless sigh, she flowed over him, unable to want less.

Neither recognized the creak of the cables high overhead.

Sudden static from the interior speakers flared above, muting the growl of the wind.

And then the elevator shuddered noisily to life and began to move.

# chapter 14

**O**ver, Jess thought.

Except that her fingers were clutching her blouse and her other hand was on top of his underwear.

Don't be a complete idiot, she thought blindly as she tossed him his underwear. "Not my style."

Heat filled her face as he drew her blouse over her shoulders, smiling faintly. Dear God, what kind of fool would he take her for? How hopelessly naïve did she seem to him?

She tugged at her skirt, trying not to watch him pull on white cotton and denim jeans with a ripple of taut muscles.

Forget your own underwear, she thought wildly. There was no time for small details.

She stabbed at her buttons with shaky fingers, then tossed him his T-shirt. As her hair swung into her face, she felt his hands finish closing her blouse and then tuck the silk into her skirt.

She passed him his belt as the elevator flashed down another floor.

Jess saw him shrug on his black sweater. The man had fantastic shoulders.

Third floor.

She jerked on her suit jacket, punched her feet into her shoes, smoothed her hair.

Wearing no stockings, no bra, no panties.

Wearing the taste and smell of a man she barely knew and would never forget.

The elevator chimed once and the doors flowed open with silent, flawless ease. Hawk was two steps ahead of her now, pulling on his backpack.

Jess realized he was blocking any view of her, giving her a few more seconds to prepare for prying eyes.

He leaned lazily against the doors, holding them open as his friend Izzy strode up in a gray uniform.

"About damned time," Hawk said calmly. "You'd think there was some kind of storm outside."

When he looked back, Jess was finally ready, her jacket straight, her face calm.

Her heart was rattling like a jackhammer, but no one could hear that. She wouldn't show it, wouldn't say anything. She would be calm and contained like the sister she'd always admired.

She straightened her shoulders, reaching for the hand Hawk held out to her.

And staggered as her heel caught in the metal track of the elevator door.

The two men were at her side in a second. To Jess's mortification, she couldn't move. Muttering, she wriggled her foot and finally stepped out of the shoe, hobbling out into an avidly curious circle of staff and guests.

Her skin crawled as she remembered the voice on the elevator. He was here somewhere, she realized, scanning the faces intently.

Then Hawk was beside her, one arm draped over her shoulders. "Keep walking," he whispered. "I'll handle your friend from the elevator."

She heard fast steps, a sharp voice. "Ms. Mulcahey?"

Jess stiffened.

"No," she said imperiously. "You must be mistaken."

The man stared after her, frowning.

Stocky. Small, trendy glasses. She hadn't seen him here before, but his face suddenly seemed familiar. Maybe she had seen him in Santa Fe. Or Chicago or Phoenix.

Hawk's hands tightened. He drew her closer, guiding her through the lobby, where rain painted silver trails over the windows and trees bent down before hammering winds.

After what felt like a century they reached the shadows beyond the front desk, away from the crowd of curious staff and guests. Izzy Teague hung back, speaking with two men in gray uniforms with Acme Elevator Repair badges in bright red letters.

They didn't look like any repairmen Jess had ever seen. They were tall and muscular, their eyes tracking a continuous flow across the lobby, noting those present and anyone leaving.

They were all wearing small earphones, Jess realized, and they moved with silent efficiency.

This was definitely goodbye.

But she could deal with that. She *had* to deal with it.

"I'll send someone with you," Hawk said quietly. His hand opened, picked a piece of granola bar off her collar.

"You don't have to do that."

"Like hell I don't," he said harshly.

She closed her eyes, wriggling. What she felt left her pale with embarrassment.

"What's wrong?"

She moved from side to side, flushed. "It's just—"

"What?" Hawk said urgently.

She swayed again. "I'm—I didn't have time to . . ." She wriggled from side to side. "Afterwards, I mean. From you."

His eyes hardened to slits, and something dark and possessive crossed his face. One of the hotel workers walked toward them, but one look from Hawk sent him scuttling away.

"The ladies' room is straight to your right." His voice was like gravel. "I'll wait here and see that no one goes in."

Jess swallowed hard, then walked away quickly, feeling his eyes bore into her back every step of the way.

"Are you okay?"

Hawk didn't answer, his eyes locked on the door where Jess had vanished. He couldn't get her last words out of his mind.

He couldn't stop wanting to touch her again.

"Mackenzie, are you listening to me?"

"Yeah." Hawk scowled at Izzy. "We'll leave as soon as Jess comes out."

"What happened in there?"

"She got a nasty warning. Have one of your team check that elevator, because you're going to find out the power problems didn't all come from the storm."

"No shit. So Jess was right about the retaliation."

"Dead right." Hawk watched the man in the designer glasses walk calmly to the far end of the lobby. "And I know the man behind it."

Izzy followed his gaze. "Night manager?"

"I recognized the voice, despite a few basic steps he took to disguise it. I want the man reported and fired. Ideally, I'd also like to gut him slowly and hang him up above the tennis court."

"Not standard policy," Izzy said dryly. "I'll put someone on it. How's Jess doing?"

"She's damned tough. Terrified of elevators, but she took it like a pro."

Izzy said nothing, staring at Hawk.

Hawk didn't turn around. "If you've got something to say, you'd better spit it out, Teague."

Izzy watched the door open to their right. Jess emerged looking serene and polished, like the princess she was supposed to be. Her gaze locked on Hawk, then skittered away, her face filling with sudden color.

Izzy cleared his throat. "I got nothing to say, Navy. Nothing at all."

"Good. Let's have the intel from the latest satellite fly-over."

As Jess watched Hawk and Izzy, a thin woman with very red lipstick and anxious eyes bore down on her.

"This is awful. No, this is worse than awful. You were stuck in there for all that time during the storm?" The woman shook her head, watching Izzy's team work in the elevator. "If you ask me, it sucks, but then no one ever asks me anything. By the way, my name is Doris." She stuck out a hand. "The manager sent me to see how you were doing." She looked at Jess. "You *are* Elena Grimaldi, aren't you? I mean, that's what the manager told me." Her voice fell to a whisper. "He also told me that you were . . . well, the inspector."

Jess waited a long time, then nodded slowly. Her identity didn't matter now. She'd decided she didn't want the job any longer.

"And if you ask me, which no one ever does, this place is a disgrace. We get a new night manager every week, the head of the beverage and catering department keeps quitting, and

our occupancy rate is way below national average." She
cleared her throat expectantly. "So are you?"

Jess felt like she had stepped right into the path of a
whirlwind. She was still trying to assimilate her nightmare
of being caught in the elevator, with the amazing experience that had followed.

She watched Izzy's team efficiently check out the wiring
in the elevator, while Izzy spoke quietly with Hawk. Neither man looked at her.

"I'm sorry, what was your question?"

Doris leaned closer. "Are you the hotel inspector? I
mean, the manager told us someone would be coming, so it
isn't a complete secret. From the way the upper management have been scowling, I figure you already delivered
your report."

Jess saw Hawk turn. A moment later he looked up.
When their eyes met, awareness sparked between them like
a downed power line, and Jess felt goose bumps snap to life
all over her body.

Then, very slowly, Hawk's mouth hiked in a faint grin.

Jess felt giddy with the reckless high spirits she hadn't
felt since she was a girl. She was still wearing Hawk's watch,
she realized.

Doris hadn't stopped talking, deep in the middle of a
monologue involving a dozen more questions and something about the night manager.

"Could you excuse me for a moment?"

Without waiting for an answer, Jess crossed the lobby
and held the watch out to Hawk. "I don't mean to intrude,
but . . . I didn't want you to forget this."

As he took the watch, Hawk's hand skimmed down her
arm. Neither spoke.

But Jess knew that they were both remembering.

Long seconds passed, and she heard Izzy clear his

throat. Jess recalled that they were in the middle of the lobby, surrounded by bustling people, and Hawk was clearly an important person who had been kept away from his work too long. "Well . . . I guess that's all. I just wanted you to have your watch back."

Pathetic to want to stay, she told herself.

Even more pathetic to want him to want her to stay.

She raised one hand and gave a little two-finger wave, keeping her smile casual. Nothing had really changed after their strange interlude in the elevator. Clearly, Hawk's colleague was impatient to reclaim his attention, while Jess had decisions of her own to make, starting with her line of work.

"Drive carefully." She smiled crookedly. "On your bike, I mean. In the storm and everything."

More pathetic than ever, she thought grimly.

She wanted to touch his face, but she didn't. She wanted to kiss the little scar above his right eyebrow, but she didn't do that, either.

The lobby was more crowded than ever. Now there were three men standing near Hawk, all of them clearly impatient to hold a private discussion.

"See you around," she said.

Oblivious to Doris and everyone else, she picked up her handbag and suitcase and walked quickly through the crowded lobby out into the storm.

# chapter 15

"**W**ant to tell me about that?" Izzy's voice was low, but not quite casual.

"About what?" Hawk watched Jess's slender body vanish behind a bellman and three hotel guests in bright yellow rain slickers. He wanted to follow her, to be certain that she was safe.

But that was out of the question. He'd already missed precious hours of work. "You'll put a man on her for the rest of the day?"

"He's waiting out in the parking lot. She won't have a clue. The manager was pretty certain the Neanderthal who pulled the stunt with the elevator was the night manager. He won't bother Jess again."

Hawk nodded, feeling some of his tension slip away. But he couldn't take his eyes from Jess's back as she strode with quick grace through the crowded lobby.

How had he ever thought she was a foreign agent, when every emotion raced through her eyes, and she couldn't lie to save her life? But he was paid to see traitors behind every corner. He was trained to smell guilt and manipulation. After a while you started seeing them even if they weren't there, Hawk thought grimly.

"So what happened between you two in that elevator?"

"None of your damn business." Hawk's words came out in a snarl as he watched Jess slip through the front doors of the hotel. Why did he care where she went or what she did? She'd been a pain in the ass from the first moment he'd seen her lathering her hair in his shower. Despite what had turned out to be decent sex, they had no possibility of a future.

Decent? Hell, it had been astounding sex, Hawk admitted. And as fantasies went, fast sex in an elevator with a stranger was right near the top.

He cleared his throat, hit with sharp memories of her nails digging into his back, her legs locked around his waist.

The soft, squeezing pull of her climaxes.

*Yeah, fine, Mackenzie.* But they *still* had no possibility of a future.

Suddenly the front doors opened. A slender woman in a tan raincoat walked in, an umbrella over her head.

But it wasn't Jess.

Hawk stifled a curse, remembering the smell of her perfume, the feel of her skin.

Which was about as stupid as it got.

"Let's move out," he said savagely. "Have you narrowed that list down yet?"

"We're down to six prime suspects. Three of them have relatives in the area, and I've got updated locations on all of them," Izzy said quietly. "I'll bring you up to speed outside, while we walk to your bike."

Jess had $87.23 in her bank account. Though she would have preferred to have one last meal courtesy of room service, staying was impossible.

Ignoring her empty stomach, she headed for her mud-spattered Jeep Wrangler. It had its quirks, but the car was her baby, and Jess figured she could nurse it along for another five or six years.

As she swung her suitcase into the backseat, she saw a news van pull up to the front of the hotel. She remembered what Hawk had said when he'd accosted her after her shower. It had something to do with the mesh laundry carrier he'd seen on the floor near her bed.

Had he thought she was a smuggler hiding contraband? Jess realized she'd probably never know.

She glared through the heavy rain. The sky already looked like midnight. The weather would make her drive south to Portland tricky, especially with all the downed tree branches and debris from the storm.

Jess sighed as her stomach growled noisily. She dug one of her staple granola bars from the glove compartment, then revved up the Wrangler's motor, pleased to hear that it had been perfectly tuned, just as Hawk had promised.

Her gas was topped off, too, she noticed. She hoped they'd used high-octane, since it made the motor run better.

On an afterthought, she checked the tires. The Wrangler was a little quirky, and she didn't want any problems on a deserted stretch of road.

Satisfied, she slid behind the wheel and rechecked her maps, then studied the hand-drawn directions Hawk had given her. Despite the weather, she planned to drive five or six hours before she took her first break.

Assuming that the storm didn't kick in with full fury again. Then all bets were off.

More news vans pulled up as she cruised through the parking lot, and she barely avoided two men with cameras who were interviewing eager hotel staff about storm damage and power problems.

She took one last look at the hotel. Hawk was probably still inside, deep in discussion with his friend. Whatever was on their minds seemed crucially important. Not that any of that mattered to her.

Her job here was done.

Jess took a deep breath and shoved away the memories, concentrating on the road.

After a swift briefing on the suspects and a transfer of the latest topo and aerial maps, Izzy vanished with his team. Hawk's new orders were to investigate the coast to the south, and ascertain if the assault force was still in the area. His main area of focus was to be a small town named Bright Creek.

He was crossing the grass, headed toward his motorcycle, when he saw a throng of people standing beneath bright lights. A press van was parked near a well-groomed reporter, who was talking excitedly on her cell phone.

*Press.* How in the hell was he going to get to his motorcycle?

Backtracking silently, he circled a minivan and waited impatiently, but the news crew showed no sign of leaving. Apparently they had just returned from an extensive report on local floods and a bridge wash-out.

Five minutes later, the press truck was still parked directly opposite his motorcycle. A huge halogen dome flicked on, casting searing light across the parking lot.

Hawk inched away from the news team. He was under tight orders to keep a low profile and stay well under the radar of the press, but he heard several crew members discussing the stalled elevator as a possible human interest story in connection with the devastating storm. The last place he needed to be was on TV, so he beat a retreat, scanning the parking lot. As he did, a battered Jeep Wrangler climbed the hill, headed toward the main road.

A Jeep would be just about right for his needs, Hawk decided. And this particular workhorse had big thirty-one-inch tires and some nifty off-road modifications.

He backtracked swiftly into the pool area, then cut into the heavy woods lining the road.

As soon as he was out of sight of the hotel, Hawk sprinted toward the highway, and when he finally broke through the trees, the Jeep was just climbing the hill.

He turned up his collar against the rain and moved out into the road. Jess wasn't going to like it, but right now Jess wasn't his problem.

# chapter 16

Jess gripped the wheel, squinting through the rain. She had already passed a big tree on its side and several cars stuck in the mud by the side of the road. There was debris everywhere and all the traffic lights were out, so she was taking every curve slowly while she watched for fallen power lines.

She tried to block out the memory of Hawk's body, the rough brush of his hands. Even the thought of his rare laugh made her heart catch.

His eyes had been hard, his hands achingly gentle.

But any connection between them was over, she told herself firmly. You couldn't have a relationship with a shadow.

And given the continued bad weather, she needed all her concentration for the road.

Suddenly she made out a dark shape in the middle of the road. Please, not a bear, she thought anxiously. Jess knew they were scattered over the isolated mountains and forests of the Northwest, but she hadn't actually expected to see one this close.

She flipped her lights to bright, peering through the rain.

Not a bear, but a man was standing squarely in her path,

waving his hands. As Jess slowed the Jeep, she recognized the line of his shoulders.

*Hawk?*

Why was he standing out here in the rain?

Quickly Jess pulled to the shoulder. Rain blew in her face as she rolled down her window and leaned out. "Hawk, why are you—?"

"I need your Jeep."

"You need my *what*?"

The man reaching for her door looked more dangerous than ever, with his hair wet, his backpack shrugged over one shoulder, and his face absolutely unreadable. "You heard me. I'm taking the Jeep."

She decided it had to be a joke—except there was no trace of humor in his eyes.

"Why don't you drive that expensive motorcycle?"

"The motorcycle is currently unavailable." He didn't look at her, his gaze focused on the road that snaked south along the coast.

"But I don't see why—"

His head swiveled. His gaze bored into her like gun barrels. "You're not listening to me. I need the Jeep now."

He was a cold, distant stranger who bore no resemblance to the man she'd just had reckless sex with. Twice.

But if he could be stone cold, so could Jess.

"Okay, you drive." She started to climb over the gearshift into the passenger seat, but Hawk's leather-gloved hands circled her hands on the wheel.

"I can't take you along. You'll have to stay here. You can wait under that tree over there."

"Under a *tree*?" Was he crazy?

Jess fought back a wild urge to laugh. Things like this *didn't* happen to her. Her life was orderly, predictable and mundane. She completed her investigations, wrote her detailed reports, then headed off to start her compliance research on the next hotel. She didn't get trapped by strangers in her room, have sex in elevators with big, commando-type guys, and then get carjacked by same in the middle of a rainstorm.

"Forget it."

"This is serious business, Jess. I need the Jeep. It will be returned to you."

"I'm not leaving."

His face was a mask as he opened her door. "Easy way or the hard way."

When she realized he would not be deterred, Jess grabbed her handbag and suitcase and shoved open the door, avoiding any contact with his black-clad body. "What now? I'm supposed to call myself a taxi to Portland?"

He tossed his backpack into the narrow backseat and swung up behind the wheel. "Someone will be by to pick you up in less than five minutes. I already made the call. Go wait under the tree."

And miss her ride? No way.

Jess put down her suitcase near the edge of the road, frowning. "How will I recognize them?"

Hawk revved the motor. "You won't have to. They'll recognize you. And don't get the crazy idea to start walking. Stay put."

She put one hand on the fender of her Jeep and glared at him. "This thing is quirky, so remember to baby it with high-octane. The fuel light comes on sometimes for no reason, and I've had some trouble with the prop shaft slip-joints."

There were other things to tell him about the Jeep, but Hawk wasn't paying much attention.

"I'll keep it in mind," he muttered.

He pulled the door closed and shot around in a tight

half circle, headed for a dirt road that wound straight up into the mountains overlooking Puget Sound.

"Be careful," Jess called. "With my car," she added quickly, even though Hawk was too far away to hear.

Five minutes passed.

Then ten more passed, while dense clouds rolled in from the ocean, and the rain increased to a hard spray. Squinting, Jess pulled out her umbrella and angled it over her head, watching the road.

No cars appeared in either direction.

Maybe Hawk's contact had gotten lost. Maybe there was a problem somewhere else. Feeling anxious and very alone, Jess scanned the road again, then pushed to her feet, grabbed her suitcase, and began the wet trek back to the hotel.

Stranded. Alone. Now soaked.

Truly, one of her better days.

A rusted green Explorer topped a hill behind her. Jess moved off the road and waited as the SUV slowed.

The driver studied her impassively. "Ms. Mulcahey?"

"Why?" Jess didn't want to give her name quite yet.

"Lieutenant Mackenzie sent me."

The man wasn't wearing a uniform, but he had *military* written all over him. He looked a little jumpy, too.

Jess watched him slide out, grab her suitcase, and stow it in the backseat, then hold open the passenger door for her. "If you don't mind, I'll drive. Lieutenant Mackenzie wants you to have an escort."

"Me?" An *escort*?

Jess had so many questions, she didn't know where to start. Besides, she was shivering. She needed to warm up before she could sort through what was happening.

There was something dreamlike about slipping into the

heated car, protected from the pounding rain. She'd been irritated with Hawk for taking her Jeep, but now more than anything she was worried about him and whatever dangerous business he was involved with. It was sobering to realize that he had pushed her out of his thoughts completely, treating her like a stranger as he commandeered her car.

She, on the other hand, was having serious trouble forgetting their recent intimacy and the little scar above his right eyebrow.

"Ma'am?" The driver was studying her curiously. "Are you okay?"

Jess cleared her throat. "I'm fine, just very cold." She brushed rain off the sleeves of her jacket, shivering. She was coming to the conclusion that she had made two major mistakes that day.

The first had been getting carried away with Hawk in the damned stalled elevator. The second had been when she dug out her cell phone and called her boss back in Virginia. She was tired of living under a false identity, tired of being on the road fifty weeks a year. So she had quit, just like that, and the relief had been astounding at first. Now that reality was setting in, Jess knew she'd have to scramble for new work, because her bank account was scraping zero.

And there were no fairy godmothers flying around this neck of the woods.

She winced as water trickled down her neck. "I'm going to Portland," she said firmly. "I'll get a flight there."

"Not a problem, ma'am. Lieutenant Mackenzie said to take you wherever you wanted to go." The driver seemed tense as he studied the road.

"Is something wrong?"

"No, ma'am. I'm just going along to keep an eye on things."

"What things?"

"Nothing in particular." His voice was polite, but there

was an edge to it that implied he would brook no further discussion on the subject.

Jess persisted. "You mean, like a bodyguard?"

"Not exactly."

"Wait a minute. Did Lieutenant Mackenzie tell you that I needed a bodyguard?"

"He said you needed a driver, ma'am. This storm has created dangerous conditions all over the state," the driver said quietly. "As you can see, the winds are still high."

But Jess doubted that he was worrying about the weather. She noticed him checking the wooded shadows along the road as much as the passing traffic, and she was certain the bulky shape under his left arm was a holstered gun.

What in the heck was going on?

*Target,* Hawk thought.

Alma Donovan didn't look dangerous or even particularly noteworthy, dressed in trim flannel pants and a fleece jacket. The last school bus had left hours before due to the storm, but the teacher was still in her room, hanging posters and art for the next curriculum change.

Looked like she was finishing a presentation on the Civil War, Hawk thought, scanning the room through high-power field glasses. The woman appeared to be a dedicated teacher. Judging by her smiles, she loved her job. But the question was whether or not to believe the report she had called in the night after the lab animal had been stolen.

Finding out was Hawk's current assignment.

Her call had been placed at 10:42 P.M. Every word was captured on tape by the local sheriff's department in Bright Creek. Hawk had listened to the tape a dozen times, checking inflection and tone for any wrong notes, but he'd found none. The woman sounded worried, confused, and even a little embarrassed to be bothering the police with what was probably not important. But the lights on state land, converging abruptly and hovering just below the ridge of the hill, had seemed out of place. Since the school was located on a promontory above an isolated stretch of road where there had been occasional problems with drifters, she thought she'd better report it.

You couldn't ever be too careful, she'd said anxiously.

Three teams of experts had listened to the call. Voice analysis had suggested that she was telling the truth.

But machines could be fooled.

And Alma Donovan's anxious description of motorcycles traveling fast dovetailed with Hawk's trail observations. The time and location matched, too, except that she had seen only *two* motorcycles.

Why the extra rider on the cliffs?

Hawk ran through several scenarios as he stowed his field glasses in the Jeep's glove compartment, pulled on a gray cap, then picked up a heavy box with tools. His orders were to assess the teacher's story and determine its credibility along with any possibility of her involvement.

Pacific Pest Control to the rescue, he thought grimly.

He let himself into the school with the key Izzy had provided, and once inside he flourished brushes, traps, and poison spray while heading toward the only lit room in this wing.

Alma Donovan was pinning up a four-color diagram of the Battle of Gettysburg when Hawk tapped at her door. She spun around, one hand to her chest. "Yes?"

"Sorry to disturb you, ma'am. The principal says there have been several mice sightings this week. I'm here to handle it."

"Mice?" Unconsciously she stared down at the floor. "I haven't seen any in this room." She noted the name embroidered on the front of his uniform. "You're Mr. Stanford?"

"Yes, ma'am."

"And who did you say called you?"

"Your principal, Mr. Rukowski." Hawk smiled a little. "You can call him and check if you'd like." He held out a fake business card. "Or feel free to phone my boss."

She studied the card carefully, then handed it back. "I don't think that's necessary. It's just that—we're all a little jumpy. The school was robbed about six months ago, so we were told to be careful during off-hours."

"Security is always a good idea," Hawk said calmly, pulling out a specimen bottle and a small brush. "Do you mind if I look around the room? It should only take a few minutes."

"That's fine with me." She watched curiously as he brushed along the floor near the far wall, then placed the brush inside the oblong bottle. "What are you doing exactly?"

"Looking for any sign of rodent droppings. We need to determine a dispersal pattern before we can come up with a good control program."

"Very scientific." She nodded in approval. "Well, don't let me interfere. I'll just finish up here."

"You're teaching Gettysburg, I see." Hawk's tone was conversational as he continued taking more "specimens." "General Lee made a big mistake in keeping his orders vague that day. He was probably trying to soothe the big egos of his key commanders, but it lost him the battle, probably the whole war." He looked up, smiling slightly. "I'm a bit of a Civil War buff. I've been to visit most of the key battlefields over the last five years. Antietam. Bull Run. Gettysburg." Since the story was a lie, he prayed she wouldn't press for many details.

But Hawk did remember tramping through the woods

in Virginia and spinning stories with his Civil War–fanatic brother.

"You have? What a wonderful idea. I try to make my students see the smoke and hear the shouts—rather like an immersion experience, though nothing compares with actually being there. Walking the ground and listening to the cries on the wind." She finished tacking up the big poster of the battlefield and stood back, looking a little embarrassed. "Some people don't understand how important it is to know where you came from. Otherwise, you can't possibly know where you're going, can you?"

"Sounds logical to me." Hawk took another fake sample and glanced outside, where clouds hugged the road. "Pretty isolated up here. Not surprised you've got a pest problem."

She crossed her arms, looking at the road. "When the school was built, plenty of parents opposed the location, but it was a question of cheap land, I'm told. Sometimes in the evening, I worry about being here all alone." She continued to stare out at the wooded hills that faced the Sound, as if lost in thought.

"I hope you've never had a problem, ma'am."

"Me? Oh, nothing really." She began to erase spelling words off the chalkboard. "Of course, there was that odd business on National Forest Land," she said slowly. "I saw lights up on the ridge about midnight."

"You must be a good teacher if you're still here working at midnight." Hawk shook his head, grinning. "You ought to get overtime pay."

"Not in this job. It seems the work is never done. Homework to check, reports to grade, lesson plans to finish. I came back for a recital that night and then I decided to stop by the room and pick up a book I'd forgotten. That's why I was here so late. But something about those lights just felt wrong." She moved the eraser back and forth against her palm, unaware of the white powder raining over her fleece sweater. "There was a Humvee, too. No one in Bright Creek has a Humvee. Down in Seattle, maybe. Not here."

Hawk leaned an arm against the wall. "Maybe it was tourists."

"In black uniforms? With automatic weapons?"

No one had mentioned *this*. "Pretty strange. But it had to be dark. I mean, maybe you saw something else."

The teacher shook her head slowly. "My ex-husband was a Marine, and I know a submachine gun when I see one. I'm certain these men had some kind of military background because they moved as if they'd trained together. With all the security concerns, I decided to watch them."

Why hadn't she included these details in her call to the sheriff? Hawk wondered. And why hadn't anyone checked her out personally until now?

"You probably think I'm nosy, but I didn't watch because of that. It was simply because . . ." Her voice trailed away.

"Ma'am? Was it something they did?"

"No, it was what they didn't do. They didn't keep their lights on; they didn't make much noise, and they kept stopping to look down at the ground. It was almost as if they were looking for tracks."

Hawk kept a look of polite curiosity on his face. "Maybe they were hunting."

"No hunting is allowed here, Mr. Stanford. They were on national forest land, and of course there's no hunting permitted on school grounds. No," she continued slowly, "these were no regular hunters. I told the sheriff that when

I called, but the operator was too busy to take down any details."

"I guess you'd know what you saw," Hawk agreed. "Not many hunters travel in Humvees, either. Sounds plenty high-tech to me."

"That's what I thought. Their clothes were odd for hunters, too. Black, not camouflage, with none of the reflective things that hunters wear. And their boots had big silver toes."

Hawk remembered the bootprints he'd found in the mud. Now he had confirmation.

He shoved his work cap back on his head. "You must see pretty good from up here," he said casually.

Color swirled through her face. "Actually, I used these to watch them." She opened a drawer and pulled out a pair of heavy black 12x field glasses with image stabilization.

Hawk had used those kind of glasses a number of times and knew they were powerful enough to pick up details out to five hundred yards. That part of her story fit.

He pulled out a new specimen bottle. "Funny that the sheriff's people didn't seem more curious when you called."

The teacher shifted restlessly. "I've seen things before." Her eyes narrowed. "Last month I saw one of the teachers meeting one of my female students up there in the woods," she said. "Another time I saw a janitor taking a computer. At least, that's what I thought. But it was only a box of broken lab equipment that he was hauling to the dump."

That explained the lack of follow-up. Someone figured she was just a lonely busybody and filed away her report under "Idle Gossip."

But one thing bothered Hawk. "So these people had lights on, did they?"

"Lights?"

"Flashlights. Car lights, that kind of thing. I mean, otherwise, how could you have seen what they were wearing and how they moved?"

She twisted a strand of hair between her fingers. "Funny, I hadn't thought much about it. I think the lights were very focused, centered on their hands mainly. That's how I saw their boots, when one of them dropped a light. After that all their lights went out at the same time, almost on cue, and that's what made me think they'd trained together."

"Sounds pretty odd to me." Hawk took another "specimen" and then stood up. "Since they were right across the road near the Sound, I guess you could see every detail."

"Oh, they weren't near the beach. They moved back and forth, but they were always inland, straight through those trees." The teacher pointed to a dense cluster of pine trees. "It still bothers me, but the sheriff's department didn't seem interested when I called, so I guess it's nothing."

"Probably not." Hawk studied the dark circle of trees on the ridge. He was already planning the best approach to the site so that he could protect any evidence. Meanwhile, this location wasn't safe for teachers or for students until the assault team was tracked down. Though Hawk was under strict orders to maintain secrecy, he couldn't leave without a nudge of warning.

"I hear there have been problems with illegal immigrants up here. They're landed at night by boat and then secretly transported south. These men could have been criminals."

"Do you think so?"

"Hard to say. But if they were, you were in danger simply because you watched them. Probably you shouldn't stay here at school alone after hours."

The teacher studied Hawk warily. "If something bad is

happening here, one of the children could get hurt. I could never live with myself if that happened."

Alma Donovan was on the level, Hawk decided, irritated that she and her report had fallen through the cracks.

And he was determined to scare her into taking adequate precautions. "You're all targets, as far as I can see. These men who smuggle illegal aliens—well, they're as cold as it gets, and you don't want to tangle with them. I've got an uncle on the force, and I've heard a few stories about the things they do."

Hawk closed his bottle and set it inside his toolbox. He'd already decided to have Izzy arrange for this school to be closed for several days, ostensibly because of storm damage. No teachers and kids were going to be mowed down in the cross fire when the government teams closed in on the area.

When that happened, both sides would be shooting to kill.

"I think I've got all the samples I need here. I'll make a few more stops along the hall in the other wing and call it a day. This storm's not going away, either."

The teacher followed him to the door, then grabbed her coat from a desk. "I think I'll be leaving, too. It's later than I thought." She glanced anxiously outside. "You never know what kind of things can happen."

"Nope, you sure don't." Hawk held the door as she carried out a pile of books on Gettysburg. "I'll walk you out."

As soon as she was gone, he dumped his tools in the Jeep and headed to the wooded spot where she'd reported the lights on the night of the theft. Another government team had already checked the general area, but now Hawk was narrowing the location. As he drove, he watched carefully for cars, lights, or any signs of activity. The Jeep's motor growled, occasionally misfiring. Hawk was relieved that so far it hadn't affected his speed.

After checking that he was alone, he pulled off the road and approached the target area from the higher slopes.

If there were any traces of evidence left, he wasn't going to compromise them with tracks from the Jeep's big tires.

It was a short walk through the dense woods to the location the teacher had described. Hawk took each step slowly, checking for tracks, debris, and fallen evidence. He found a cigarette butt and the cap from a water bottle, and both looked fresh. More searching turned up footprints and tire tracks, and this time the boot marks were clear.

They were the same ones he'd found on the cliffs to the north. But only two motorcycles here. Now one Humvee had entered the mix.

As he slipped to one knee, following the direction of the marks, he saw a few dark threads hanging from a small evergreen. Bending closer, he ran his light over the branches, lifting them to look beneath.

Grimly, he snapped two dozen photos with the macro lens on his digital camera, than carefully bagged the threads. One thing was certain. The team was moving with less caution now. Morale could be falling. What in the hell had happened?

Squatting near the Humvee tire tracks, Hawk studied the isolated hillside and the coast of Puget Sound in the distance, re-creating the scene. The way he saw it, the motorcycle team had regrouped here after the attack in Portland. They had met the Humvee for backup or supplies and possibly new orders. They might have transferred the stolen lab animal here—or received it from the other vehicle. Judging by the pattern of the tracks, and the limited number of footprints, the motorcycles hadn't stayed here very long.

Silently, Hawk followed the rutted earth through the woods. Fifty yards from the glade, the motorcycles had separated, one peeling off to the north, the other heading into the mountains.

Three riders on the cliffs. They weren't always travelling together.

Hawk frowned at the cloud-covered peaks looming inland to the west. With a little skill, a driver could hunker down and become invisible within minutes, lost inside miles of rugged terrain. But there was no place to shelter the animal in that isolation, so Hawk turned back to the other set of tracks, which vanished onto the highway.

The Humvee had headed in the same direction. Only one option was left, Hawk decided.

They would have to bring in the *real* expert, who could pick up a minute molecular trail *ten thousand* times beyond human sensing. Hawk smiled grimly at the thought of ninety-five tough pounds of unbridled energy able to climb ten-foot hurdles, scale metal ladders, and leap through hanging tires, while picking out a single molecule in a million different scents.

Pulling out his secure cell phone, Hawk headed back to the Jeep. Izzy would have all the arrangements completed within the hour, now that Hawk had verified locations for an intensive search.

Nobody could evade a scent-trained military tracking dog for long.

Jess sighed with relief when she saw lights in the distance. They had been driving for over two hours, but most of it had been spent circling around after reaching roadblocks due to bridges washed out by the storm. It didn't help that all the streetlights were still out.

She was starting to wonder if she should give up and

stop for the night. Through the rain she saw a sign for a restaurant and bar, advertising king-size steaks and stream-fresh salmon. The parking lot was packed with big cars, big motorcycles, and big trucks with huge tires. Country music vibrated in a throbbing bass over the loudspeakers.

She was also worrying about Hawk and her Jeep, truth be told. The engine was quirky at the best of times, and Jess had learned how to baby it for maximum performance. But Hawk didn't know about that. He also didn't know about her old problem with the fuel cap.

"Can you get in touch with Hawk—I mean Lieutenant Mackenzie?"

"Only if it's an emergency, ma'am."

Jess studied the darkening sky. Trees bowed and pitched in the wind and leaves skittered across the wet road. "It could turn into an emergency. There's a problem about the Jeep that I forgot to mention to him."

The driver frowned. "What kind of problem?"

"The fuel pump. If the plug gets dirty, he'll have to clean it."

"If not, what will happen?"

Jess rolled her shoulders tensely. "The motor could stall. He won't have much warning either."

The driver drummed two fingers on the dashboard, staring out into the rain. After a long time, he reached down for the cell phone on the seat beside him.

# chapter 17

Country music pulsated from the dance floor and men with shaved heads and graphic tattoos played pool beneath grimy lights.

Hawk stared with distaste at the greasy wedge of grayish meat next to a slice of soggy bread. He was hungry, but not *that* hungry.

Then the restroom door opened and Jess came out.

He'd been given her message about the fuel pump twenty minutes ago. Since she wasn't far away, he decided they should meet up here. He avoided thinking about why he would trouble to do that, rather than simply talk to her over the phone. Especially when he wasn't going to need the Jeep for very much longer. He pushed back his chair, doing a quick survey of the crowded room. He noted no one who looked familiar from his classified briefing, and his digital photos of the new Humvee and motorcycle tracks were stored on the camera in his pocket, ready to be turned over to Izzy.

He'd be ready to move out as soon as he ran through this fuel pump problem with Jess.

He hadn't taken three steps before their eyes met. She gave him a faint, almost ironic smile, and once again Hawk was struck with the quiet strength she radiated. If things had been different. . . .

*But they aren't, fool.*

Somehow the woman had morphed again. She didn't look like a princess any longer. Hell, she didn't even look like a career woman, not in faded jeans, midriff-baring pink shirt, and sandals. As she crossed the foyer past the bathrooms and pay phones, she looked tired, wet, and discouraged, even though she was working hard to hide it.

A man in tattoos and a cutoff denim vest halted in front of Jess, bent low, and whispered in her ear. Hawk saw her face fill with color as she shook her head.

Within seconds she had men on her like flies, and they weren't the kind of men who watched *Oprah* or took no for an answer. A big biker in a black T-shirt was leaning closer, next to his friend in the denim. Meanwhile his skinny pal with tattoos and a ratty ponytail was holding out his beer to her.

Where in the hell was the driver who was supposed to be watching her?

Jess backed up, wrestling with the skinny biker, who dropped his arm around her waist as he tried to make her drink some of his beer. Cursing, Hawk pushed a chair out of his way.

One minute she was alone, the next minute men were everywhere.

And they were really *big* men, Jess thought grimly as she grabbed a pool cue from a nearby table. For some reason they thought she was there to meet them, and they weren't big on listening to any refusals.

When the biker with the tattoos put his hand on her rear, she shoved the cue between his legs, and he went down hard.

His big friend threw back his head, laughing noisily. Since he looked wobbly on his feet and smelled like a distillery, Jess gave him a blinding smile, moved one step sideways, then stuck out her foot to trip him. Fortunately, she had changed clothes in the restroom or she might have had some problems doing that in her pink silk suit.

He wobbled, but didn't fall, grabbing a chair with one hand and Jess with the other. She staggered under his weight, going to one knee on the floor, and when he didn't release her, she kicked free and crawled under an empty table, emerging on the far side with a sea of legs in front of her.

New blue motorcycle boots with silver toes and big buckles moved past her. Next came a muddy pair of black work boots with thick safety soles. Jess raised her head and peered carefully over the table at the people passing by.

Everything seemed to go in slow motion as she registered faces and noise and curses.

Suddenly the biggest biker went down like a log, crashing into a table with salsa, salmon, and a dozen senior citizens. Pandemonium ensued as a white-haired man sprayed the air with ketchup and his sprightly wife pulled out a .22 target pistol. "I'm armed and I'm dangerous," she called over the din in the room.

Jess hoped she had good eyesight or they'd all be mowed down.

When the pandemonium stilled, Jess rose cautiously. Her harassers were circling as Hawk came around the table, his eyes glinting murder and his powerful shoulders outlined by a faded gray shirt. He looked tough and angry.

The fallen biker staggered back to his feet, cursing as ketchup dripped slowly down his face. "Where is she?" he muttered.

The man with the ketchup gave him another good spray,

and the biker stumbled into a different table, sending it over on its side. A frail woman in blue orthopedic shoes screamed as her purse opened and went flying.

A big handgun dropped out of an inside pocket and skated across the table right toward Jess. She spun the body, caught the grip, and pulled back the slide to check for a round in the chamber. The gun turned out to be her sister's model, a Glock 9 mm that balanced nicely against her hand. She aimed it for safety toward the floor, glad for the months of shooting lessons her sister had insisted on after a particularly grisly FBI case.

"Hey, that's my gun," the elderly owner called out.

Hawk cut through the excited senior citizens, took the Glock from Jess, and handed it back to its owner. "Better keep that someplace safe, ma'am."

He grabbed Jess's arm, his expression stony. "Let's go." He pulled her toward the door, scowling at Jess's driver, who was three paces behind them now. "After you show me that fuel pump plug, you hit the road. Understand?"

"It wasn't my fault that—"

*"Later."*

Jess nodded, trying to hear over the banging music. Her leg hurt where she had tripped the trucker. Without warning she stumbled against an overturned chair, then swayed, feeling Hawk's arm shoot around her like a vise.

She heard him curse and looked up to see a row of bikers in front of them, blocking their path to the door, with the head biker right in the middle.

Hawk pushed her down as a chair went flying over their heads. Holding her with his left arm, he weaved sharply, working his way toward the side exit.

The senior citizens were yelling around them, and two more had produced Glocks. In his excitement, one of them put a round through the ceiling, and plaster rained down like dirty snow.

Jess saw her driver turn and take down a biker before a potted ficus tree hit him squarely between the shoulder blades and he went down with a groan.

Hawk pulled Jess toward the door.

He didn't appear at all frightened by a brawl. In fact, there was a glint in his eye that suggested he might have enjoyed a little fight.

He held Jess tightly, moving backward. "The lady's feeling faint, boys. Give us some space."

The big biker scowled back at him. "She don't look faint to me. I say you're dragging her off, and I don't like it none." There were muttered assents all around him.

"You're making a mistake," Hawk said quietly. The door was less than eight feet away now. He nodded at Jess's driver, who had recovered and was fighting his way closer on their right.

The biker said something under his breath, and all four of the men stormed forward. Hawk spun Biker Man in a circle and sent him back toward his friends, flipped like a three-hundred-pound bowling ball. All of them went down hard, their heads crashing into a row of stacked chairs.

They were still shouting threats as Hawk pushed Jess through the door. Jess's driver guarded their wake as Hawk shoved her toward the Jeep and stuffed her into the passenger seat.

"I wasn't faint," she snapped.

"I know you weren't. I was trying to avoid a confrontation in there—not that talking was any help."

Jess took a deep breath. "I suppose I should thank you."

"Forget about it." Hawk fishtailed out of the parking lot and looked back. In the rearview mirror he saw Jess's driver fighting with three bikers.

"Shouldn't we help him?"

"He'll be fine." He was surprised when he felt Jess's fingers brush his cheek.

"You're bleeding," she said anxiously.

"Nothing important." He took the road south, pushing the Jeep hard, acutely aware that Jess was staring at him. "Still steamed at me for taking your car?"

"You did what you had to do, I guess. You still won't tell me what all the secrecy is about, will you?"

Hawk shook his head, eyes on the road. A police car raced past them, sirens screaming.

"I suppose you think I started that brawl on purpose, to pay you back."

"You may be angry, but you're not stupid." Hawk glanced at the beach running alongside the road. After that he checked the rearview mirror. They were stopping at the next turn, and he didn't want anyone following them. "Why weren't you with your driver?"

"His cell phone kept dropping calls." Jess pulled one leg up beneath her, turning in the seat. "When we got here, he asked me to wait outside the pay phones while he made a quick call."

"Of course you didn't wait," Hawk said irritably.

"Of course I *did*. But I had to go to the ladies' room, and when I came out, he'd vanished." She propped her chin on her hand, studying him closely. "You're sure you can't even give me a little hint? Is it some kind of sting operation? Mafia surveillance?"

"I can't tell you anything, Jess."

She shrugged, and Hawk made a mental note to ream out both Izzy and the driver for a lapse that could have cost lives. Clearly this operative was still wet behind the ears and shouldn't have been let free in the field yet.

"You're doing that thing again with the mirror. Is someone following us?"

"It's just basic driving skills. I'm not about to take chances with a collision in this weather. The roads are still a mess, in case you haven't noticed."

"I noticed. I also noticed that you're an expert driver. But you want to be sure that no one followed us." Jess continued to stare at him, a frown working down her forehead. "I could help you if you'd just tell me what to do."

Hawk bit back a curse. By now any other woman he knew would have been shrinking into the corner, terrified of his scowl and curt answers. He didn't try for the effect, but somehow it always seemed to happen with women. He had been told that his chitchat skills were nonexistent and his flexibility quotient sucked.

Training hard and living in a constant state of combat readiness had that effect on you, but as it happened, the women he spent his limited free time with had never showed interest in anything besides fast, impersonal sex.

For that matter, neither had *he*.

As Hawk turned off the road, he wondered why Jess was different. Why wasn't she afraid when he glared at her? Was he getting soft or something?

Right now she was digging in her purse, her expression thoughtful. She produced some kind of a bar in plastic wrap, which she carefully broke in two pieces, holding the bigger one out to Hawk.

"You eat it," he said gruffly. Seeing what passed for food at the greasy spoon back down the road had destroyed his appetite.

"Go on, you need the energy. It's a peanut butter caramel protein mix that I make myself. You'll be getting twenty-one grams of protein, four grams of healthy oils, and seven grams of fiber. Tastes pretty decent, too."

As Hawk reached out for the bar, their fingers met. Instantly he was jolted by the memory of her body in the stalled elevator.

*Just freaking great, Mackenzie.*

Erotic memories of amazing elevator sex were the last thing he needed in his head right now.

He took a bite of the bar, expecting the worst. "Not bad."

Jess smiled thoughtfully. "I tinkered with the ingredients for months. Now I send bars to my sister because she forgets to eat." Her lips curved. "Her husband and I have a secret pact. He stashes one inside her briefcase and sends it to work with her."

For a moment there was something wistful in her voice.

"Sounds like you two are pretty close."

"No doubt about it. Summer and I are blood loyal—when we're not trying to murder each other for reasons too petty to remember afterwards. What about you?"

Hawk frowned. No one he knew dared to ask him personal questions. If they did, he made sure they didn't do it twice.

"My parents live in Virginia," he said awkwardly. "I told you, I've got one brother."

"Does he do spy work like you?"

As it happened, his brother had a higher security clearance than Hawk did. But Hawk couldn't discuss that or anything else about his brother. "No, he runs his own software firm. Travels a lot." That was the cover story his brother generally used, anyway.

"You mean, he makes video games?"

"Not games. He designs commercial software for business and scientific use." *For military and strategic use, actually.*

*Among other things he trained to do.*

Hawk finished the bar. When he looked down, he was

surprised to see that Jess was holding out a small Thermos bottle.

His brow rose. "Hemlock?"

"Very funny. It's coffee, Mackenzie. I filled this and stashed it right before the fight broke out. If things got bad, I was going to throw boiling black coffee on the big guy."

The woman didn't miss a beat, Hawk had to hand her that. And when he took his first sip, he felt a little kick of surprise. She'd just added dry creamer, only a little, exactly the way he liked it.

Hawk glanced at her out of the corner of his eye. His first instinct was that she was trying to get something from him. Why else would a woman he barely knew bother about details like that?

Jess seemed oblivious to his train of thought, carefully packing up her bags, cups, and powders.

If this wasn't some kind of subtle manipulation, what the hell was it? Women simply didn't take care of him. Women usually didn't even talk to him.

They generally didn't bother to hang around for good-byes on their way out of his bedroom, even if they were smiling in satisfaction.

She didn't look up as she continued digging inside her purse. "Sorry I only had the dry dairy powder. I usually try to restock when I'm at a hotel. With everything going on today, there wasn't time, but I remember you don't like much."

Hawk frowned at the road. Why did a stupid thing like her making his coffee just right feel so damned important all of a sudden?

He didn't have a clue, and he didn't have time to waste thinking about it. As soon as he got the quick demo on her car problem, she was getting dumped.

End of story.

Jess studied her mud-streaked sandals. "Forget fashion trends. What I need is major, kick-ass motorcycle boots like that guy at the diner."

"I beg your pardon?"

"You know, like that man's in the bar. He had the right idea wearing those really tall ones with the cool metal things on the toes." Jess pulled off one shoe and shook her head in disgust as a piece of dried mud fell onto her lap. "Just as well that I quit my job before I left. No one is going to believe that I'm minor royalty from Europe or anywhere else."

Hawk stared at her. "Say that again."

Jess was busy picking mud off the bottom of her shoe. "You mean, that I quit my job? Don't worry, I've been planning it for weeks. I'm tired of lying to people for a living." She took a deep breath. "I need to get back home and start looking for something else."

Hawk pulled off the road and cut the motor, judging each word carefully.

She looked up and seemed to register his tension. "It had nothing to do with you or what happened at the hotel, Mackenzie. It was way past time that I quit. Most inspectors burn out after two years, and I've been doing this for nearly four. If you go on pretending long enough, you start forgetting who you really are."

Hawk had known that feeling on occasion, working undercover for long stretches. Funny how well she'd pegged the feeling.

But he couldn't focus on personal matters. "I meant what you said about the motorcycle boots."

"Only that considering all the rain and mud, they seemed like a smart choice of foot gear." She glanced around at the quiet hillside where they were stopped. "Do you want me to show you how to clean the fuel pump plug now?"

"In a minute. You definitely saw a man wearing motorcycle boots inside?"

"Electric blue." Jess shrugged and slid out of the car. "He was near the table when I crawled underneath." Without slowing down, she lifted the hood and propped it open. "I'd better check everything while we're stopped."

"Where was he headed?"

"Across the room." She fiddled with a hose. "The guy appeared out of nowhere. It was right after the biker dude did his thing with my butt and I stumbled."

"What thing with your butt?"

"Oh, he didn't get very far. But he seemed to be determined to touch anything and everything that he could."

Hawk gave his head a little shake, fighting the pleasant image of jamming a pool cue down the man's throat. He refocused grimly. "This man you saw. Can you describe his boots?"

"I suppose so. They had a blue leather design and big metal buckles, like the kind on ski boots. They looked really expensive. I saw them right in front of me when I was on the floor, and the toes had some kind of round metal tips with a wavy design. Silver, I think. There may have been some lettering on the buckles, too."

Hawk kept his voice casual. "Did you see what it said?"

Jess stopped fiddling with the wiper hose and looked across at him. "TEC, I think. Or maybe it was TEK with a K. The man vanished pretty fast." She stood up slowly. "This is important, isn't it?"

Hawk dug in his pocket and tried his cell phone, but picked up nothing but static. "Yes. Maybe the most important thing that you or I ever do."

Jess was still frowning at him. "And you can't tell me why?"

Hawk didn't answer. He was already close to saying too much.

"How can I help?" she asked quietly.

"The fuel pump can wait." Hawk tossed the cell phone onto the seat, then steered her back to the car. He drove without speaking, turning up a narrow gravel road that wasn't listed on any map. By now Izzy would know what had happened at the bar, and he would have resorted to their fallback plan.

"Grab that notebook on the backseat. I need every possible detail you can remember about the man who was wearing those boots," he said tightly.

# chapter 18

Jess sat tensely, reminding herself that this wasn't a dream. As they bounced up the boulder-covered hill, the Jeep lurched, and she grabbed the roll bar. "You'll get better traction in four-wheel low."

Without a word, Hawk shifted to neutral, engaged the four-wheel drive, and picked up speed. "Been a while since I've been bouldering in one of these things," he said, scanning the hillside. As they emerged from the trees, Jess saw an A-frame building with two dark sedans parked outside. On the other side of the building, microwave towers bristled over the ridge.

"I'm breaking about fifty rules by bringing you here," Hawk said quietly, "but we need your help."

"No questions, I promise."

Hawk stopped behind the two sedans, and his friend Izzy emerged from the house, walkie-talkie in hand. Jess thought he looked tired as well as surprised to see her.

"Listen carefully." Hawk took her arm. "You're going inside with me. You don't look around and you don't ask questions. Can you do that?"

She nodded warily.

Hawk grabbed his knapsack, then reached across and

opened her door, his face grave. "This is no game, Jess. Do it my way or you'll be in a car headed out of here before you can count to three."

"Don't worry about me."

"I do. That's part of the damned problem," he muttered.

"Cell phones are out and I need a situation report," he snapped, not breaking stride as Izzy approached.

"Inside." Izzy shot a glance at Jess. "I assume you have a good reason for bringing her here."

"I do, but hell if you're going to believe it. There was a brawl at the diner. Jess slipped away from your man and got into some trouble. When the fighting broke out, she landed under a table. That's when she saw a pair of motorcycle boots."

"So much for flying under the radar," Izzy said grimly. Jess was certain that his eyes narrowed slightly, though his face revealed very little.

"You got a description?" he asked Hawk.

"She's working on it now."

Izzy held open the front door and waited for them to go inside. Jess looked around curiously at the large living room, currently occupied by a dozen desks with high-tech computers. Maps filled one wall and a fax machine hissed in the corner. Some of the maps had red circles and words scrawled on them, but she couldn't see the place names.

A medical textbook lay open on the desk in front of her.

As Izzy walked by, he closed it.

Jess didn't ask any questions, though the curiosity was killing her. Mindful of Hawk's warnings, she sat down in the closest chair. "Do you want me to finish my description of the man in the boots?"

There were four other men in the room. They looked up, frowning when they heard her question.

Izzy motioned the men into the neighboring room and shut the door. "I'm listening," he said tightly.

Hawk sat down in front of one of the computers and punched in some words. "Are these the boots you saw, Jess?"

She walked behind him and studied the screen. "No question. They were covered in mud, and I think there was a tear in one of the fasteners at the ankle. He was wearing a windbreaker with a dark hood, and he had a pair of worn leather gloves shoved in his pocket."

Izzy looked at Hawk, then vanished into the neighboring room.

"Do you want some coffee?" Hawk was already filling two mugs at a nearby pot.

"No, thanks. I'm already a little jittery as it is."

"Take it easy, honey. You're doing fine." Hawk looked up as Izzy reappeared, carrying a pile of papers.

"We need you to pick out the man." Izzy sat down at a desk and motioned Jess to sit beside him. "It's very important."

Jess suppressed a wave of anxiety as Izzy put a pile of photos facedown in front of her.

"I'll give you five seconds with each one. Look at them and answer quickly. Don't think about it." He pulled off the top photo and flipped it over. "Was this the man?"

The face in the photo had dark hair and a straggly beard. "Not him."

"How about this one?"

The second man was older, with drooping eyelids and a scar across one cheek. "Not him either."

Izzy flipped through three more photos. The men all looked tough and dangerous, but none of them was the right one.

Jess shook her head. She could feel the heat of Hawk's body as he moved closer.

"How about this one?" When Izzy turned over another photograph, Jess shot forward.

The hair was different. So was the beard. But the eyes were the same, narrow-set and cold. "That's him. The eyes are right, but he didn't have a beard when I saw him. His hair was a lot shorter than this, too."

"You're sure, Jess?" Hawk leaned down, his hand on her shoulder. "This is definitely the man you saw?"

Jess stared at the photograph, memorizing the eyes, the thin nose and thin mouth. "That's him. I'm sure of it."

Without a word, Izzy gathered the photographs. His expression was tight as he walked outside, motioning to a man with a sniper rifle.

"Damn good job, Jess." Hawk leaned down beside her. "How can you remember his face so well? You couldn't have seen him long."

"Faces are part of my job. In order to assess key management, I have to memorize photos in advance. That way I have an edge when I arrive at a hotel on assignment. Summer taught me some tricks to isolate facial features like eye shape and lip size, things that are hard to disguise. All it takes is a few seconds."

"Remind me to thank your sister when I see her." Hawk's hand traced her cheek and his jaw tightened.

Abruptly he took a step back. "I have to get moving." He raked a hand through his hair. "I'll see that an experienced member of Izzy's team travels with you to Portland. We should be done here in a few more minutes."

Jess felt a sudden, sharp emptiness.

She wouldn't see this man again. They had met through a giant quirk of fate, something unplanned, never to be repeated. If they tried, it would only be tawdry and awkward.

*Time to move on,* she thought grimly.

"I appreciate that, but it's really not necessary. I'm sure I'll be fine. I'll just need a car."

"You'll get back your Jeep *and* a driver," Hawk said flatly. "No more mishaps."

She turned away, reaching for her handbag. "Be careful out there. Wherever you're headed."

"Count on it."

The maps on the wall seemed to blur, and she lowered her head quickly. The last thing Jess wanted was for Hawk to see any sadness or regret in her eyes.

"Are you okay?"

"Sure." Jess didn't turn around, staring at the blurred row of maps. "Thanks—for the elevator. You know."

"Hell, I should be thanking you, honey." His voice was rough. "I'll never forget a second."

She wanted to turn around, but she didn't. *Right man, wrong time. The general story of her whole, stupid life.*

"Jess, hang on a second. I have to do something. Just wait here, okay?"

She heard his footsteps cross the floor. The maps shimmered brightly as the door closed behind him.

"Those were the boots, all right. The description matches the tracks I found on the ridge, and those are unusual boots. Jess said he was there for only a few minutes." The rain had finally abated, and Hawk stood next to the Jeep, holding a plastic bag with the items he'd found in the woods. "Our pals were in a hurry, I'd say."

"They're getting nervous and nerves make them sloppy." Izzy rubbed his jaw. "I've sent your report to all teams. If this guy in the boots is who we think he is, you'll have more surveillance tonight. The man's got a dozen current warrants in three different states, plus the Canadian authorities want to chat about an armed robbery in Montreal two years ago. He's a real motorcycle nut. Used to live in the area and still has an ex-wife in Bright Creek."

"Could she be involved?"

"Too soon to say."

"If these people are in the area risking public exposure, it's because they're looking for the same thing we are. Which means they don't have it," Hawk added quietly.

"That's the way I see it, too." Izzy's voice fell as he tapped the map. "The ex lives about here."

"How about I go talk to her?"

"We sent two male agents, but no luck. Now the local police tell us she hates men." Izzy frowned. "It seems her father abused her, and her husband left her flat broke with a baby. She may be a little unstable."

"Did you try using a female agent?"

"She washed out in three minutes. This woman Luellen's got a real bullshit meter. She runs a Laundromat down in Bright Creek and deals with loggers and a lot of rough types, so she knows when she's being conned." Izzy folded the map carefully. "But I've got a plan. We're going to—"

The door whipped open behind them, and both men turned.

"What's wrong?" Hawk snapped.

Jess pointed behind her, through the open door. "You'd better get in here." The little TV near the coffeemaker was on, blasting local news. "That man I told you about? He's there, right on the news."

# chapter 19

**A**pparently, a local brawl was big news in the area. Hawk grimaced as the grainy footage cut to two bikers hovering around Jess.

Without warning the camera angle shifted across the table to him, and then Bubba and his two friends went flying on their faces.

"Nice view of your ugly mug, Mackenzie."

"That's not professional footage. Look how the camera is weaving."

"You probably have one of the senior citizens to thank. Someone must have had a video camera."

Hawk shook his head. The video footage made him look like some kind of kung-fu superhero. He'd spun the big guy off his feet without apparent effort and sent him flying.

"Wow," Jess said. Then she cleared her throat. "Hold on. He should be on again any second." She leaned forward, flushing at a quick shot of her grabbing the Glock. "Look, there he is." She tapped the corner of the screen excitedly. "He's wearing a windbreaker, and he's trying to cut through the crowd."

"Well, I'll be damned," Izzy breathed. "Bull's-eye." The

man frowned at the camera and backed up. Two seconds later, he was gone.

Hawk turned down the volume on the set. "We need that footage."

"I'm on it." Izzy headed for the door, then stopped. "I'll be ready to leave here in five minutes." He rubbed his neck. "Make that ten. And one more thing, Mackenzie." His eyes narrowed. "You've been seen," he pointed out quietly. "Judging by that film, you're no everyday Joe, and they'll be watching for you."

As the door closed, Hawk considered what Izzy hadn't said.

Anyone with a military background would know that Hawk was using expert aikido moves. Thanks to the footage, he would be recognized immediately, and since he'd left the bar with Jess, she could become a target, too.

Jess stared at him. "You don't like being caught on tape, do you? I'm really sorry about all of this."

"Forget it. You gave us a good tip, so it was worth it."

Jess smiled uncertainly. "So I really did help?"

"More than you know." Hawk poured himself a fresh cup of coffee, considering their next move. Izzy had already scrambled teams with an updated description of their suspect in the motorcycle boots. Now Hawk's focus would be Luellen Hammel, the man's ex who managed the Laundromat in Bright Creek.

Unfortunately, Hawk couldn't go near her because he had a special habit of unnerving women.

All except Jess, who didn't frighten or back down an inch. The woman was like a damn bull terrier, and for some reason the thought pleased him keenly.

He scanned the TV channels, picking up two other reports of the melee at the diner, both times catching a glimpse of their suspect. Hawk had finished his coffee when Jess moved toward the window.

"There's someone out there waving at you. She's over by the Jeep."

*"She?"* He opened the door and went out.

The woman had to be about eighty, with permed blue-white hair, white gloves, and an ample chest hidden beneath a crocheted shawl. Her body was misshapen, bent over a rough wooden cane.

Why was the grandmother from hell motioning to *him?* Irritated, he studied the heavily made-up face, certain he'd never seen the woman before.

Then she stuck out one foot, revealing size thirteen ostrich-inlay cowboy boots underneath her full skirt.

Hawk snorted. "Damn, Teague, you're downright scary."

Izzy hiked up his skirt, revealing spandex bike shorts and hairy legs. "I didn't have time for panty hose. Not that it's easy to find them in a size 2X tall." He slanted Jess a cool look. "I'm confident that you're going to forget you ever saw me, Jess."

She nodded slowly, as if unable to believe her eyes. "That's amazing." She walked closer and pointed carefully. "But one of your—that is, your chest is a little off balance."

Izzy looked down and dug irritably beneath his shawl until he straightened the padding at his bosom. "Damned breast inserts never stay where they're supposed to. I knew I should have used the duct tape."

Hawk headed toward the Jeep. "Thanks for all you've done, Jess. One of the men will be here shortly to drive you to Portland."

"Good luck," she said gravely.

"Luck is a highly overrated commodity. We'll be using reasoning power, field experience, and superior intel." Izzy slipped a big red purse onto his arm and gave another tug at his chest, where the breast insert had begun to slip again. "Trust me on this."

Hawk shook his head. "Something tells me we're going to need all the luck we can get if *you're* our secret weapon."

Izzy's eyes narrowed. "Then be glad that I'm only one of them."

"I've never driven this model of Jeep before. It's nicer than I thought."

After a little wrangling, Jess and her driver agreed to split their time at the wheel. Jess was on deck, savoring the pleasure of having her car back again. It might be battered and quirky but at least it was *her quirky*.

"No doubt about it. Unfortunately, one ride will spoil you for sedans."

They were on a flat stretch of road with Puget Sound to their left and mountains to their right. Fog was drifting low, and the driver concentrated on passing cars.

The man assigned to her didn't say much, scanning the road with apparent randomness, but Jess knew he missed nothing. He'd even brought sandwiches and coffee along, so they wouldn't have to stop until late that night. Apparently Hawk didn't want to risk any more incidents in all-night roadhouses.

Now if only they could avoid any traffic problems, a distinct possibility since the traffic lights were still out in this part of the state.

As they rounded a curve, Jess saw a short man in a blue postal uniform standing in the middle of the road, waving. A silver Jeep Rubicon was parked just off the shoulder with its hood raised.

Her driver didn't slow down.

"Aren't you going to stop and help him?"

Her companion didn't answer, scanning the steep wooded

slope beside the road. As he slowed down slightly, Jess's skin began to prickle at the back of her neck.

The man in the uniform headed toward them, smiling, and made a motion for the driver to roll down his window. "Got a battery problem," he called, moving toward the car. "Stuck on the way home from my shift. Think I could borrow some jumper cables?"

The driver kept his pace, shaking his head.

"Hey, wait! I need help here." Angry, the man trotted alongside the car. "I got a wife at home who's six months pregnant."

"We're in a hurry. I'll have a repair truck come out from the next town. I believe it's only six miles away."

"Damned phones being out don't help." The man in the uniform frowned and reached down, patting his shirt pockets. "Never have any cigarettes when I need them. I don't suppose you—"

"Don't smoke."

The worker flashed a gun from his pants pocket, its muzzle trained on the driver. "Stop the car, hands up, and get out. Do it now."

The driver floored the Jeep and jerked the wheel. Jess heard bullets drill into the passenger-side door.

"Down," her driver yelled. He kept accelerating as the passenger-side window exploded in a hail of glass fragments. A small bridge rose in front of them, covering a shallow inlet off the Sound. He headed straight for it.

A man in a green jumpsuit ran out from behind the silver Jeep, leveled a shotgun at his shoulder and pumped out five shells. Jess's door shook. He kept firing, running at the same time as if he'd done it many times before.

As they drove over the bridge, the driver glanced at Jess. "When I come down, jump out. Hit the water and stay out of sight. They won't be able to see you from here." A bullet raked the front fender. "We're six miles north of Bright Creek. Take my cell phone from the seat and keep it on. One of the team will find you."

The back window exploded, glass filling the car.

"Go."

With shaking hands Jess yanked open the door and jumped out. She hit muddy ground, lost her footing and staggered down the slope, then sank into a high wall of reeds beneath the bridge. Shivering in the cold, she heard the Jeep moving on past her. Footsteps hammered across the bridge, followed by gunshots at close range.

The driver let out a harsh curse.

Jess closed her eyes, her fist pressed against her mouth.

"Where's the other one?"

"Doesn't matter. We've got a car, so let's get the hell out of here." A door slammed and the Jeep's motor roared. Another door slammed and the Jeep barreled away.

Moments later, there was no sound but the hiss of the wind on the reeds and the wild hammering of her heart.

Her Jeep had certainly been a popular item recently. Storms had a way of doing that, Jess thought grimly.


"I thought we were going to pick something up?"

"It's waiting for us in Bright Creek."

Hawk shot a glance at Izzy as they sped through the rain. "Do you have any idea how dog-ugly you are, Teague?"

Izzy gave his blue-white wig a tug. "Up yours, Mackenzie." As Hawk drove, Izzy's smile faded. "No soap or perfume," he said quietly. "Don't handle anything with distinct smells."

Hawk's brow rose. "Afraid it will clash with your eau de bag lady?"

"No, because it will disturb the search dog we're going to pick up in five minutes."

A little town was coming up in front of them, and

Izzy pointed to a ramshackle storefront with a huge FOR RENT sign in the window. "Park around back behind the Suburban."

"I hope this is going to work."

"Trust me, this dog will make your hair stand straight up."

As they got out of the car, the back door of the building opened. A tall man in a dark business suit emerged with a dog on a leash.

The animal didn't look like much, Hawk thought. Just a big brown mass of dog that stood alertly, watching them approach.

"Meet L.Z."

"As in Landing Zone? You're telling me that this dog can jump out of an airplane?"

Izzy's eyes narrowed. "And a hell of a lot more than that, Mackenzie." As they crossed the pavement, the big Belgian Malinois barked once, his whole body going tense. "Nice to see he remembers me," Izzy muttered. "Things like makeup and a costume change won't fool L.Z. for a second, and that's only part of what makes him so amazing. Come on, I'll introduce you."

*What was she supposed to do now?*

Jess shivered in the cold wind, soaked to her waist. Time seemed to slow down as she staggered forward, her damp hair pasted against her face. She hit the power button on the agent's cell phone, scrambling up the slope toward the bridge.

All she heard was static.

What had the agent said? Was it six miles to the nearest town?

She reached the road and saw her driver facedown, motionless. Blood pooled around his head and shoulders.

*Oh, God.*

She shoved the phone into her pocket and sank down beside him. He groaned as she gently turned him over.

The front of his chest was a solid red stain, but he opened his eyes and managed a faint smile. "The phone?"

"No answer."

"Afraid . . . of that." He managed to touch her arm. "Good work. Told me you were . . . tough." He winced a little and seemed surprised to see his hand covered with blood. "Should have run the bastard down."

"You couldn't have known what he had planned."

"Tired. Going . . . under." His eyes closed.

Jess crouched beside him and managed to pull him off the road into the grass. The cold wind hissed over the marshes, a low, sad sound, as she waited for a passing car.

But no one passed, and the driver's lips were turning blue-white. She'd covered him with her leather jacket, but she wasn't sure how much longer he had.

Shivering, Jess ran down the hill toward the silver Jeep Rubicon left abandoned by the road. The key was still in the ignition. Candy wrappers and newspapers covered the backseat.

She leaned under the hood and scanned the engine quickly.

Fuel line.

Radiator.

Spark plugs all tight.

She checked for all the easy problems and came up with nothing.

She was still wet, freezing without her jacket, and her hands were stiff. Then she saw the small leak from the radiator. When she checked the chamber, the water was half gone.

She grabbed two discarded soda cans from the front seat

and ran to the marsh, filling them quickly. After patching the hole with gum and making three more trips, the radiator was full again. The motor sputtered, then broke into a delightful roar.

Jess jumped out, closed the hood, and saw something glint on the ground. She shoved it in her pocket. Then slid behind the wheel and raced back to the fallen agent.

He was losing consciousness again when she crouched and slid an arm beneath his neck. "I got the Rubicon running. Now we've got to get you inside."

He blinked at her, looking disoriented. "Not doing so good. Sorry."

"You have to help me. You're going to die here if I can't get you to a doctor."

He took a sharp breath and put one hand on her shoulder. It took them ten minutes, but he managed to stagger to the Rubicon, where he collapsed into the seat.

Jess sped off toward the town called Bright Creek.

"How'd you fix it?"

"Radiator leak. I patched it with gum and refilled the chamber. The idiots have driven this car right into the ground, and that's not easy with a Rubicon. Heck, they didn't even know what to look for."

"Radiator leak. No . . . shit." There was a glimmer of a smile on the agent's ashen face as his eyes closed and he went under again.

Wind tossed the big trees in the main square of Bright Creek beneath a sky filled with gunmetal clouds.

"Run through that again, Teague. He's scent-trained for both weapons-grade plutonium and all major biohazards?"

Izzy scratched the big dog's head. "He can detect scent trails that the most sophisticated lab equipment misses. We'd be ten years behind without animals like this."

"I believe it. The dog looks smart enough to talk."

"The Navy's working on *that,* too," Izzy said tightly. "But if you ask me, I'll deny it. L.Z. has been scent-trained to our missing bear, and when I leave, the dog will go with me. If there's any scent connection with Princess, L.Z. will signal. Then I'll take Luellen into custody while you and the team rush the place."

"What if she's got backup in there?"

"If so, they're silent and invisible. My people have been watching the place for the last twenty-four hours."

Hawk studied the Laundromat across the street from his vantage point of a vacant building they had commandeered for this purpose. One of the Laundromat windows was boarded up and the *D* was missing on the neon sign. A tall woman was counting change near the front desk.

"I'd still like to ride shotgun, Teague."

"Forget it. If there's a man within a hundred yards, she'll clam up. Given what's happened to her, I guess she's entitled to hate men." Izzy finished sliding a line of duct tape in place across his chest, rearranged his dress and picked up his cane from the floor of the Jeep. "How do I look?"

"Don't ask." Hawk gave a tight grin. "The makeup's pretty good, I have to admit. Just look flustered and helpless. And remember to hide the cowboy boots."

"Everyone's a fashion critic." Izzy patted the big brown dog in the backseat. "Ready to move out, L.Z.?"

Instantly the dog sat up, ears raised.

Hawk felt like he was watching an ultrasecret weapon go into full combat readiness, and it was an awesome sight. "I'll be listening to the relay from your mic. If you run into trouble, just say *kiwi.*"

"Say what?" Izzy turned. "A fruit code, Mackenzie? You couldn't come up with anything better than that? Hell, I at least expected *tango-two* or *code bravo.*"

Hawk crossed his arms. "Keep it simple, stupid."

Izzy straightened, giving his ample chest a shake. "Ain't nobody simple around here, is there, L.Z.?"

The big brown dog barked once.

Izzy hiked his purse up onto his arm. "Time to go to work, boy. Let's go track down our princess," he ordered.

# chapter 20

**H**awk touched his earphone as Izzy and the dog crossed the street. He worked the transmit button. "You read me, Teague?"

"Clear as Tina Turner pounding home the national anthem," came the low answer.

"Nice image. Bet her legs are better than yours."

Izzy muttered a few choice words as he hunched over his cane, moving slowly. Anyone watching would have sworn he was at least seventy.

The door to the Laundromat opened, and the owner looked out, studying Izzy warily. Hawk listened to every word that followed, impressed with Izzy's performance, which appeared to be working like a charm. When he mentioned his arthritis, the woman offered him a rolling cart. Then Izzy explained that he had to bring a load of dirty clothes in from his car, and the woman even offered to help. Izzy apologized haltingly for causing her any bother and said he'd handle the clothes himself.

So far there had been no response from L.Z., but it was still too soon to be conclusive.

Hawk tried to be patient.

"How is he, doctor?" Jess waited anxiously, pacing the waiting room of the Victorian house on Bright Creek's main street. It had taken her less than ten minutes to make the drive and another five minutes to find the doctor's office. Now the wounded government agent was on an I.V., waiting for medevac transport to the county hospital. After all that had happened, Jess was feeling a strange sense of anticlimax.

"He'll be well taken care of. Beyond that I can't say. I'm only a general practitioner, and surgery is far from my specialty."

Jess glanced at the row of maps on the wall and then noted the framed medical school diplomas. University of Washington. UCLA. Ohio State. The wounded man was in good hands, she decided.

"Pardon me, but you look like you could use some rest yourself."

Jess looked down, startled to see that her pants were still wet, streaked with mud. "It's a long story." Remembering Hawk's warnings, she decided the less she said the better. "We had an accident. I'd rather not say more until I speak with the local police."

"I'll have to report the gunshot wounds, of course."

Jess nodded, her eyes moving back to the framed maps. She frowned when she realized one of them looked familiar. "Can you tell me what that town is?"

He glanced up and shrugged. "It's Bright Creek. Our whole area, actually. Now I'd better get back to work. You're welcome to rest here as long as you like. By the way, you dropped this paper bag when you came in."

Jess reached out for the bag, which she'd found wedged under the front seat of the Jeep Rubicon along with old newspapers and food wrappers.

"If your friend is taking any of those medicines, I'll need

to know that. Some of them are highly experimental, not approved for general use."

"Medicines?"

The doctor frowned. Opening the bag, he shook half a dozen bottles on the table. "None of these have patient names, so I assume that they are being used for a double-blind clinical trial."

"Not that I know of." Jess turned one bottle in her hand.

"Very well, I'll get back to work now." The door closed.

As she stood staring out at the street, a wave of exhaustion hit Jess.

Her fingers closed over a piece of metal she'd picked up from under the tire, forgotten in her pocket. Without thinking, she traced the smooth outlines and then went very still.

It was a boot buckle, she realized.

Wavy lines crossed the half-circle, with the letters TEK etched in the middle. Just like the boot ornaments she'd seen in the pictures Hawk had shown her.

She dug her driver's cell phone out of her pocket and hit the redial button on the chance that the driver's last call had been work-related.

"Central."

"Central *what*?"

After a pause, the man on the end cleared his throat. "Where is Worthington?"

"Agent Worthington is in Bright Creek receiving a transfusion. He was shot about twenty-five minutes ago."

"What is your name, ma'am?"

"Jess Mulcahey."

"I see." Papers rustled. "Would you please hold?"

Jess sighed and sat down in a chair facing the big picture window. Two cars parked. A bakery van lumbered past.

"Ms. Mulcahey, where are you now?"

"In Bright Creek at the doctor's office on Main Street."

"I see." Again she heard the hesitation in the man's voice. "I'll have someone sent over as soon as possible."

"There's something else you need to know. The men who attacked us had a bag full of special medicine. It may be important to Lieutenant Mackenzie. Could you call him and tell him that I—"

"Hold, please."

Jess tapped her foot impatiently, glaring at the street as the minutes ticked past. Abruptly the line went dead.

"Very funny, pal." Angrily, she stood up, hitting the redial button as she paced in front of the window. The phone rang a dozen times, but no one picked up.

She was redialing when she noticed one of the dark sedans across the street was the same one she'd seen at the house where Hawk had driven her earlier. The old lady walking toward the car looked oddly familiar.

She leaned closer, watching the slow, shuffling feet. The blue-gray hair.

*Izzy.*

Jess shoved the phone in her pocket, shifting the paper bag from hand to hand. She couldn't walk away until she was sure that Hawk had these medicines. They had to be important, and since no one seemed to care about what she had to say, waiting around wasn't an option.

She opened the door and walked cautiously toward Izzy.

Hawk scanned the street, one hand on his earphones. L.Z. was out of the car now, and Izzy had just picked up his bag of "dirty" laundry, which had been placed in the backseat earlier. As he listened, Hawk continued to scan the roof and the nearby alley, assessing threat possibilities.

A flash of color drew his eyes back to the street. He cursed at the sight in front of him.

"Something wrong in there?" Izzy asked quietly.

"This isn't possible. Jess Mulcahey is walking out of the house behind you. Damn it, what is *she* doing here?"

When Izzy kept walking, Jess trotted across the street, cutting him off.

"You shouldn't be here," Izzy said curtly.

Hawk touched his low-profile earphones, picking up every word.

"I had to talk with you. Your agent was shot by two men in a broken silver Rubicon. He's at the doctor's now. They're sending him off via medevac helicopter."

"Are you hurt?" Izzy demanded.

Hawk realized his hands were clenched. What in God's name had gone wrong?

"No, I'm fine. The men took my Jeep, but I got out in time. Then I found this bag that they'd left behind in their car." Jess held out the brown paper bag. "When the doctor told me that these are some kind of experimental medications, I thought it might be important. I tried using the agent's cell phone, but they hung up on me."

"I'll take them," Izzy said tensely. "Now you'd better go. I'm a little busy here."

"I understand. There's just one other thing," Jess added quickly. "I found this buckle beneath the Rubicon. It's exactly like the one on the boots that man was wearing in the diner. See the lettering? It says TEK. And they both have that wavy design on the edge."

"Okay," Izzy said shortly. "I'll relay that information on to the relevant parties."

"Consider it relayed," Hawk said tightly, aware that only Izzy could hear him. "Now get Jess the hell out of there."

"Jess, you need to go back to the doctor's office and wait. Someone will be by shortly."

"Sure." They were almost outside the Laundromat, and L.Z. seemed restless, ears forward, sniffing the air.

Hawk saw Jess look down. "Is something wrong with your dog?"

"No, he's fine," said Izzy.

"Get her *out* of there, Teague." Hawk saw the manager, Luellen, come around the counter holding a floppy nylon purse. She raised a dirty metal blind and looked out at the street.

Izzy bent his head toward Jess. "You need to go, Jess."

"Okay, I'm out of here." When Jess turned around, Hawk breathed a sigh of relief. Things were getting too damned complicated without her being added to the mix.

The Laundromat door opened, and the manager gestured to Izzy. "Honey, you sure you don't need help with that laundry?" She glared at Jess. "Why don't you grab the other end? Can't you see that bag's too heavy for her to handle?"

"Oh. Sorry." Jess glanced uncertainly at Izzy. "Do you want me to—"

"No, no. I'll be fine." Teague's voice had suddenly morphed back into grandma mode.

Luellen sniffed and swung her big purse onto her shoulder. "Like hell am I letting a nice old lady like you carry all that laundry." Sweeping past Jess and the dog, she grabbed the heavy bag away from Izzy. As she did, L.Z. growled and went flat on the sidewalk.

*Holy, holy shit.*

Hawk's jaw clenched. The dog was signaling a scent trail for the missing lab animal.

A door opened behind him. "A call just came in for you, Lieutenant. It was a woman named Jess Mulcahey. She said that—"

"Not now. We've got a positive alert from L.Z. Get the

other teams over here." Princess could be locked inside the Laundromat or hidden in the woman's car, maybe even stashed by Luellen Hammel in a different place entirely. It required only a few molecules to trigger a positive response from the dog. Izzy's job would be to narrow those possibilities so that Hawk could take the animal alive.

Mistakes weren't an option.

"I need you to scramble two teams," Hawk ordered. "One for the Laundromat and one for the manager's house."

"When—?"

Hawk held up a gesture for silence. Outside on the street, Luellen was staring at L.Z.

"Your dog definitely looks sick," she said.

Izzy bent down and stroked the dog sitting at attention. "No, she's just resting, honey. It's been a long day for both of us."

*Amen to that,* Hawk thought grimly.

"Well, I'll be going now. You take care." Jess gave a little wave to Izzy. "It was nice to see you again." She cleared her throat. "Honey."

"Just get out of there," Hawk muttered irritably.

"Hey, wait a minute." Luellen spun around. "You're *her,* that woman from the bar. I saw you on TV today." The manager pushed open the door with one foot, still holding Izzy's laundry bag. "Honey, I can't tell you how many times I've wanted to give one of those creeps a pool cue right at ground zero. Who were those guys hitting on you?"

"Well, I never actually found out who—"

"What's your name?"

"Jess, but—"

"Look, Jess, why don't you come on in so I can buy you a Coke? I want to hear this story from beginning to end."

Jess moved from foot to foot uncertainly. "You mean now?"

Hawk had a sudden glimpse of Jess's pale face as she glanced across the street. When the manager put down the laundry bag and pumped her hand, pulling her toward the door, Jess smiled some more, murmuring that her husband was waiting and she really had to go.

Luellen looked around. "I don't see anyone. What's a few minutes in here going to bother him anyway?" As she spoke she withdrew a gun from her pocket and gestured in the general direction of the street.

"Oh, he's parked down the street," Jess said vaguely, staring at Luellen's gun and allowing herself to be herded into the Laundromat. "He had to get gas."

"So you two know each other?"

"It's been awhile." Izzy laughed brightly. "You know how it is."

"Damned right I know. And you can let your husband stay worried. Screw all of 'em." Snorting, the manager leaned down and flipped over the big red sign on her front door. "As a matter of fact, I'm going to close early tonight. Anybody else who comes by can just take a hike. I like things nice and quiet in here. No distractions."

Something in the woman's tone disturbed Hawk. Judging from the slur in her voice, she had been drinking.

He studied the topo map of the area near her residence and calculated times and distances. Then he hit a button on his walkie-talkie without moving his gaze from the figures inside the Laundromat. "It's Mackenzie. Here's what I want you to do."

He continued to speak quietly, looking at the map.

L.Z. was now sitting by Izzy's leg, his body rigid. His keen eyes were locked on Luellen as Izzy gripped his cane and hobbled toward the nearest row of washing machines. "I think I'd better get started on this laundry."

"I've got a better idea." Luellen glanced outside, then began to nod. "Yeah, that's exactly what we should do."

Jess backed toward the door. "Actually, I need to go. I really, *really* need to go."

"Don't move." Luellen lurched in front of Jess and slapped one hand over the door. Hawk heard L.Z. growl, followed by the snap of a round being chambered in a gun.

Jess tried to ease away, a smile pasted on her face. "Is s-something wrong?"

"Damned right. There's a man across the street. He's been over there watching us ever since you two came in here."

*Shit.*

The manager was clearly nuts, but she was also shrewd and seemed to have eyes in the back of her head. Jess and Izzy would be history if they weren't careful.

"Izzy, anytime."

"Oh, I'm sure you're mistaken." Calm as always, Izzy hobbled across the room, trying to wedge his padded body between Jess and the angry manager. In the process, he drew Luellen's attention, so that she shifted the gun a few inches away from Jess's head.

"I'm not imagining anything. He's there, damn it."

Hawk saw Luellen's gun twitch. He watched the muzzle waver, still dangerously close to Jess's head. "Izzy, get that gun away from her. We need to find out if the bear is hidden inside her trailer. I don't want to storm the place unless it's necessary."

"Honey, you'll probably want to put that gun of yours away now." Izzy smiled sheepishly and shook his head. "I don't want to see anyone hurt by mistake, and I'm not half ready to die." He spoke as if he were addressing a child.

"Hurt?" The woman looked down and sniffed. "Sorry, I guess I'm a little jumpy. Fact is, my ex staggered in here drunk last week and tried to slap me around for old time's sake." Her voice hardened. "There's only one way to get rid of a mean, sorry bastard like that, and you're looking at it right here. As in kiss my .45." She held up the gun and made a loud popping sound. "Know what I mean?"

# chapter 21

**D**amn, damn, damn.

Out of the corner of her eye, Jess saw Izzy move between her and Luellen.

"Your ex is giving you problems?" he asked casually.

"From the first second I met him. If he gets in my face again, I'll shoot him."

"Being a woman can be a trial, by all that's holy. But that gun is making me nervous, honey."

"Sorry about that, but I'm taking no chances. If you're weak, you're a target." Luellen's eyes were cold. "I'm not going to be weak ever again."

Jess had to admit that Luellen made a crazy kind of sense. She almost felt sorry for the woman.

When Luellen lowered the gun slightly, Izzy nodded. "That's better. Not that I don't sympathize, honey. The best day of my life was the day my husband got blind, stinking drunk and fell off a bridge," he said casually, putting a few more inches between Jess and the delusional manager. "I didn't even go to the funeral. Told everyone I was overcome by grief, but I was too afraid someone would see I was laughing."

"You go, girl," the manager said, bumping hips with Izzy.

Jess watched in mute disbelief. Izzy was completely convincing in his role as a bumbling old woman.

A loud thump echoed from the first row of washers. "Don't tell me something's broken." Izzy fluttered his hands, looking distressed.

"Hell, something's always happening to this rotten equipment, not that it gets replaced." The manager scanned the room and shook her head in disgust. "Matter of fact, this whole place gives me the creeps lately. I could swear that stinking ex of mine has been prowling around here at night."

"Any idea why?" Izzy asked casually.

"Hell no, but I keep seeing lights outside and cars going past at a crawl. Then I get all itchy behind my neck, like somebody's out there watching me."

"Why would they do that?" Izzy spoke very clearly, once again giving Jess the impression that he was speaking for the benefit of people outside. Of course, with Izzy tricked out as Whistler's mother, and the Laundromat manager acting as if she wanted to harangue every female in sight about the evils of unscrupulous men, the whole experience was becoming a little surreal.

But the gun in Luellen's hand was definitely real, Jess thought grimly. So was the urgency she sensed in Hawk's secret mission.

"Things have been pretty damned weird around here the last few days. Lotta strangers in and out of town." Luellen reached across the counter and gripped her handbag with her left hand, keeping the gun in her right. "I've gotta go see my kid," she said flatly. "If that man is bothering her again—"

"Well now, why don't I come along, dear? Ride shotgun, you know?" Izzy spoke slowly, leaving Jess no question that Hawk or someone on his team was listening.

"What do you mean?" Luellen asked suspiciously.

"I thought if your ex was making trouble, I could be a witness. You could have the bastard arrested."

Luellen's mouth stretched into a slow, nasty grin. "I never thought of it that way. You'd be a witness for me?" She swung around toward Jess. "You, too?"

"Well, I wish I could stay, but—"

"If you want to stay, then *stay*." Luellen's face took on a mulish look. "After I pick up my daughter, we'll go get something to eat. Ruthie can go along with us."

Izzy fingered the shawl that covered his chest. Jess waited silently.

"Honey, you have got yourself a date." Izzy picked up his red purse. "I guess my dirty socks are just going to have to wait." He met Jess's gaze, as if he were talking to her. "Didn't you say your husband was waiting for you, Jess?"

"Um, right down the street."

The manager snorted. "That man comes barging in here trying to order you around, I'll shoot out both his knees." She waved the gun for emphasis.

The woman was running on three cylinders, Jess thought. "I can handle him, trust me."

"You can never trust them." Luellen paced the room. "They're supposed to pay alimony, but do they? No. They're supposed to pay child support, but do they? *No*."

Izzy touched Luellen's shoulder gently. "I'm feeling awfully hungry. Maybe we should go."

"Yeah, we should." The manager shifted the gun to her other hand, frowning. "I'm worried about my kid, you know? That creep has been bothering Ruthie. She said he comes out to the trailer when I'm not there. But I got a restraining order after the last time he knocked me around, so I could use two witnesses."

Jess didn't move. "I really can't come with you right now because . . ."

"Why the hell *not*? My car is parked right outside. We won't be gone much above an hour." Her hand twitched as she spoke, and the gun waved in the air.

Jess looked at Izzy, waiting for some hint as to how to proceed. "Well, if she's coming with us, she should tell him first." Izzy sniffed. "Otherwise the stupid man is liable to go off without her."

Jess gave Luellen a little wave, backing across the room.

Luellen snorted. "Dumb as cows, most of 'em." Her eyes seemed glazed and unfocused as she motioned them toward the back door, where a dusty Bronco was parked. "My car is parked right over there. Just call him on your cell phone while we drive." Her gun was still gripped in her hand.

Jess was afraid to throw more oil on the fire. Every time she spoke up, the woman's gun hand got twitchy.

"Well?"

Jess cleared her throat, wondering who she was supposed to call, but before she could speak, Izzy dug deep into his purse. "Why don't you use mine, honey? I swear, I never leave the house without it." Looking down, he covertly punched two buttons before handing the phone across the seat.

"Thanks." Jess slid into the car and took the phone, surprised to hear Hawk's quiet voice.

"Jess?"

"Um, hi, honey."

"You need to get out of that car now," he said tightly.

"My friends and I are going out for a while, just up the road to my friend Luellen's house. Don't worry, honey. I'll be fine."

"Get out of there, Jess."

"I don't think that's possible."

"Why? Is she drunk?"

"No, I don't like Chinese food. If you want to stop, let's get barbecue—you know how crazy I am for that."

"She's crazy?" Hawk cursed softly. "Is anyone left inside the building?"

"No . . . honey. And I won't be long."

"Is the dog, L.Z., sitting up, looking stiff?"

"Yes, I'd say there's no doubt about it."

"Jess, I need you to put Izzy on the phone. Do it now."

"I will, honey. See you soon." She pretended to power down the phone and held the lit screen toward Izzy so that he saw it clearly.

"All done? No problems?" Izzy looked at the screen, then carefully slipped the activated phone into his purse.

"He said it was fine. He'll just wait." Jess was certain that Hawk was either tracking them through the cell phone or recording their conversation . . . or both. He'd used his phone as a recorder in the elevator when the threats had come over the speaker. There was no question that he and Izzy were using state-of-the-art technology.

Luellen gave a cold laugh. "Glad that's done with. Ladies, start your engines." She rested her gun on the dashboard as she fishtailed out of the parking lot.

The Bronco went into a skid, and beads of sweat trickled down Jess's neck.

"Is he good in bed?"

Jess stared at Luellen. They'd been driving for almost fifteen minutes, and Izzy had carried most of the conversation during their drive. Afraid of saying the wrong thing, Jess had volunteered only one-word answers so far. Staring at Luellen, she wriggled in the seat, moving her feet restlessly. "Is who good in bed?"

"Your husband—that man I saw you with on the TV. So is he good in the sack?"

Jess cleared her throat. "Uh . . . pretty good, I guess." Her toe brushed something hard under Luellen's seat. Moving aside her purse, Jess searched the floor and pulled out a folded towel that felt unusually heavy.

When she opened the towel, Jess realized why.

Inside the dusty cloth was a Colt 45. The 1911 model was loaded with a full magazine judging by its weight. Jess's sister had the same model Colt for use as her non-service weapon, and she trained with it once a month at a private gun range in south Philadelphia, even dragging Jess along several times for reluctant and very uncomfortable lessons.

Jess sat back stiffly. Was Luellen so paranoid that she had weapons stashed wherever she could reach them in an emergency? God help them all, if so.

One thing was certain. Jess couldn't possibly give the gun back to Luellen. The woman was running on empty in the logic department, and a second loaded weapon was the last thing she needed.

Taking small movements, she rewrapped the Colt and slipped it down into her purse where Luellen wouldn't notice it. "You mean he's no better than good? Now, *that's* a damned shame." The manager blew out a sigh. "You ask me, there's nobody half as hot as Paul Senior on *American Choppers*." She grinned, tapping her gun against the steering wheel. "Damn, that man has one prime body." She gave a ragged laugh. "He can clean my carburetor plugs anytime he wants." She grinned back at Jess, and barely missed a garbage truck lumbering in the opposite direction.

Izzy inched over the seat, as if he were bracing to grab the wheel.

"Almost home." The manager slowed down abruptly. "If I don't crash because of Ruthie's stuff down here on the floor." She reached down and tossed a book onto the dash. "That kid leaves books everywhere."

Beside Izzy, the big dog sat up straight, body rigid.

"Damn, but there's something real wrong with your dog."

Izzy stroked the dog's back. "It only happens around strangers, part of the training. So your daughter reads a lot?" he asked.

"Thanks to that no-account boyfriend she hangs around with. I saw him come out of the public library with twenty books one day, filling Ruthie's head with his crazy ideas about college and traveling." She turned the wheel with a nerve-wracking jerk. "If I find out she snuck out to see him tonight, I'm going to lock her in the tool shed."

Jess swallowed. "You wouldn't really do that?" Her fingers curled into her palms and she flashed back to panic and disorientation. She scowled at Luellen, hating the memories of her own blinding fear.

"Damn right I would." Luellen took another curve dangerously fast. "There's my place. And that ex of mine better not be anywhere close."

Through the dense trees Jess saw a weathered gray trailer with three smaller buildings, no more than sheds, spaced out along a muddy path.

"It must be peaceful out here," Izzy said quickly, as if he sensed Jess struggling with her anger.

"Part of the reason I like it. That and I can see someone coming in time to protect myself." She braked hard, her gun tapping on the wheel. "Any other cars in sight?"

"None that I can see," Izzy said after a casual check.

"Good. Okay, ladies, you can hit the bathroom, and I'll find my kid. After that, we'll go get ourselves some truly heart-stopping barbecue. Beer's on me."

---

FUBAR, Hawk thought grimly. He had heard every word of the conversation in Luellen's car. Now that Jess had been shanghaied to join Luellen's crazy expedition, the whole op was spiraling from bad to downright nasty, courtesy of Mr. Murphy and his screwed-up laws. If they hadn't needed Luellen to give quick access to her trailer for L.Z. to track the bear, he'd have ordered that she be taken out by a quick, nonlethal use of force. But now that L.Z. had signaled a positive scent they needed Luellen, crazy as she was. Hawk didn't want to risk any harm to the animal.

He walked through the Laundromat, past half a dozen agents who were busy combing every inch of space for evidence. So far they had found nothing to suggest the lab animal had ever been there, and without L.Z., their job would take hours, not seconds.

He motioned to a man in a flight suit. "Is the chopper ready?"

"All set, Lieutenant."

"Then let's move."

"Lieutenant, I need to speak with you first."

Hawk picked up an aluminum case from the floor and turned to the woman waiting in the doorway. "Yes?"

"I was told to report to you or Ishmael Teague as soon as I arrived, sir. I drove straight up from California."

"You've been fully briefed?"

The woman nodded. "Code name: Princess, sir. I had extensive lab and medical experience before I joined the agency, and I'm ready to take custody of the bear as soon as it's located. My identification has been verified by your people outside."

"Hold on." Hawk adjusted his earpiece as he received the thumbs-up for the new arrival. "I don't have time to talk." He glanced down at her ID. "Agent Lindstrom."

"Yes, sir. We've been checking out Luellen Hammel and

her twelve-year-old daughter, the way you requested. The girl is an honor student, sir. No discipline problems in school. She keeps animals and seems to be pretty quiet."

Hard to figure out genetics, Hawk thought grimly. You could tinker with whole animals, but you couldn't hope to understand a human family.

"Anything else I need to know, Agent Lindstrom? I doubt you came all the way up here to brief me on the suspect's model family."

"No, sir." The agent hesitated, fingering the badge clipped to her jacket. "You need to know two things. One, Princess has had only female handlers, so she may become agitated around males. She has a very sensitive sense of smell due to her genetic programming, so she will pick up subtle hormonal differences." She glanced off to the south, where a bank of gray clouds straddled the mountains.

"And?" Hawk prompted. "Give me the rest."

"Princess is sick," the agent said quietly. "She exhibited some organ malfunction during her transport from Australia, but it didn't appear to be significant. Now that we've studied the lab work, it's clear that her organ problems are growing more severe. These problems are compounded by a highly advanced aging process, which is common in transgenic mammals."

"So you're saying the clock is ticking?"

"In a nutshell."

Wind furrowed through the azalea bushes near the town square. Even with the window closed, Hawk could hear dead leaves skitter along the deserted sidewalk. "How much time do I have, Agent Lindstrom?"

A muscle tightened at her jaw. "Less than twenty-four hours, sir. After that, the deterioration of Princess's organs will be irreversible."

# chapter 22

Jess's nerves were stretched to the breaking point. She had to keep reminding herself that Izzy knew what he was doing, and that Hawk was somewhere nearby, tracking them via cell phone. Meanwhile, she was determined not to trigger Luellen to more reckless behavior. Jess wasn't sure if the woman was desperate for friends or if she was psychotic.

Izzy studied the gravel driveway and gray trailer that perched awkwardly at the top of a denuded hill.

"Nice, isn't it?" Luellen swung open the car door.

"It must be quiet all the way out here."

"You bet, and that's just the way I like it." Luellen slung her purse over her shoulder and stomped up the wooden steps to the trailer. "Come on, you two. I'll get Ruthie and then we can go."

Izzy fell back and leaned close to Jess. "Stay here," he whispered. "Once she's inside, sprint for the woods."

Luellen turned and glanced back at them. "What are you two waiting for?"

Izzy smiled uncertainly. "Are you sure you want us to come inside?"

"Of course I'm sure."

Jess waited tensely as Luellen opened the front door of the trailer, the gun still gripped at her side. "Ruthie!"

"Mom?" Bushes rustled at the back of the trailer. A girl in a red sweatshirt pushed through a row of azaleas. "Just wait till I tell you who came—" She stopped when she saw Jess and Izzy. "Who are you?"

"They're my friends, that's who." Luellen glared at her daughter. "Have you been with that no-account boyfriend again?"

The girl swallowed hard. "Of course not, Mom. You told me not to, remember?"

"I know what I told you, and if I see that boy around here again, I'll call the police on him. You're both under-age, and damned if I'll let you sneak off into the woods so he can fumble at your clothes."

"But, Mom, I don't—"

"Hush. We've got company. Say hello."

"Hello," Ruthie said stiffly. "Why are you carrying that gun, Mom? You promised me you wouldn't do that any-more."

Luellen sniffed. "Too many people driving past the Laundromat late at night, honey. Something damned strange about it." Luellen patted her daughter's arm awk-wardly. "Look, I don't want to fight with you. Go get your sweater because we're all going out for barbecue."

Ruthie eyed Izzy and Jess uncertainly. "Are they from town, Mom? I mean—they don't look familiar."

Jess shot a glance at Izzy. Strangely, Ruthie seemed to have more sense than her mother.

"Just met them today, but they're real nice people. C'mon. Let's go."

Ruthie fingered her big bookbag. "Sure, but first I gotta feed my animals. I'll only be a few minutes."

She didn't wait for permission, but raced toward an un-painted wooden shed with a single high window and vanished into a side door.

Luellen snorted. "Her precious animals. As the Lord is my witness, that girl treats those animals like they were her best friends." She frowned. "I guess she gets lonely, living all the way out here. Her creep of a father keeps trying to take her back to Seattle, but I won't let him have her. Not as long as I can draw breath."

"She looks smart," Izzy said. "Real nice, too."

Ruthie appeared at the door of the shed, locked it carefully, then ran across the grass. "All done, Mom. Let me dump my books." She raced up the steps and into the house.

Luellen's mouth curved. "Smart as a whip, that's a fact. Got straight *A*'s on her last report card. Lord knows, she doesn't get her brains from me. All I gave her was spunk."

Jess struggled not to gape, surprised by Luellen's show of maternal pride and insight. Then she heard L.Z. bump Izzy's leg, whimpering low at the back of the throat.

Luellen backed up slowly. "There goes that dog of yours again. You sure she isn't sick?"

Izzy stroked the dog, but L.Z. remained rigid. "She just gets upset around strangers, or she might smell Ruthie's animals. It's protective instinct." Izzy's voice was calm, but his shoulders were tense, his eyes carefully scanning every inch of the terrain around them.

It had to do with the dog, Jess realized. Whenever the dog reacted to something, Izzy seemed to go on alert. And he looked wired now, as if braced for hostile action.

Ruthie rushed back minus her bookbag. "Mom, I forgot to tell you. Your friend came through here a few minutes ago on a motorcycle."

Izzy's eyes narrowed. Jess saw his stance shift subtly.

"What friend?" Luellen asked irritably. "You're not supposed to talk to men, Ruthie."

"He had these way cool boots and a camouflage jacket and—"

"You mean, your father was here?"

"No, not Dad. I don't know this guy, but he had boots sort of like Dad's and he said he was a friend of yours from the Laundromat. He wanted to know where you were and when you'd be back."

*Boots.*

Fear dug into Jess's chest.

Izzy turned slowly. "Sounds kind of scary. Is he a friend of yours, Luellen?"

"No one I know." Luellen punched out an angry breath. "I told you there've been all kinds of people driving around here at night. When I go out to check, they cut off their lights. Probably that turd husband of mine is putting them up to it," she said in disgust. "Anything to get out of paying child support, not that he pays more than once a year." She scowled at a bent sycamore tree behind the trailer. "At least he makes a good sight for my target practice." She gestured toward a picture of a man's face tacked on the tree trunk. Bullets had left ragged holes across the forehead and drilled out both eyes and cheeks.

Jess took a sharp breath as Luellen moved around Ruthie and put two bullets right between the man's eyes. And there was no doubt that the face on the tree belonged to the man she'd seen in the diner, the same man she had seen briefly on TV.

"That's your husband?" Jess asked anxiously.

"Richard Dickman, aka Richard the Dick," Luellen said with a sneer. "Mean, nasty sonofabitch that he is. If he comes around here again, I'll drill him in the head for real this time."

"Mom," Ruthie said anxiously, "did you take your medicine today?"

"I don't need that stuff anymore. It makes me feel crappy, like my thoughts are all scrambled up."

As if they weren't already scrambled, Jess thought.

"That man told you he was a friend of your mother's, Ruthie? Not a friend of your father's?"

"Yeah, that's right."

"Was he alone?"

"I guess so. I didn't see anyone else around."

Izzie shifted his bag to his left arm. "Ruthie, maybe you should show Jess around while I use the bathroom? I see you've got quite a garden in back."

Ruthie glanced at her mother for permission.

"Go on," Luellen said impatiently. "Show her your animals while you're at it. I know all about having to pee." She winked at Izzy. "It's hell getting old, isn't it?"

"But, Mom, I really don't think—"

Luellen shook her head. "Always arguing. Just like your father—may his mean and stingy soul rot in hell."

"I'd like to see the garden," Jess said quietly.

Ruthie glanced slowly from Jess to Izzy, then trotted over the damp grass. "Just watch your step. It's real muddy back here."

Halfway down the hill, Jess heard the low whine of motors coming from the trees behind them.

At the sound, Izzy halted, one foot on the trailer steps. He dug into his red handbag and stared at the three men on motorcycles winding along a muddy track that climbed up from the foothills. "Luellen?"

"Don't know them." Luellen was staring down the hill with narrowed eyes, her fingers clenched on her Colt.

"They're probably not here to pick up their dirty laundry." Izzy pulled a phone from his purse. "Get Ruthie and Jess into that storm shelter behind your trailer." His voice was low and harsh. It was also unquestionably male now.

"Wait a damned minute." Luellen took a step backward. "You're not a woman. You're a frigging *man*."

The drone of the motorcycles grew louder.

"Do it, Luellen."

"Damn, you really are a man." Luellen was still struggling to get her thoughts around the fact that Izzy had completely duped her. "Why the hell are you dressed that way?" The gun twitched in her hand as if it had a life of its own.

"Look, I'm a good guy, Luellen." Izzy's voice was a low growl. "But right now we're all in danger. So get them out of sight and don't come out until you hear me call you. Understand?" Izzy scanned the slope while punching in a number on his phone.

"It's that husband of mine, isn't it?" Luellen hissed. "I thought I saw him on TV today. What's he done now? Armed robbery? Illegal gun sales?"

Ruthie had halted just ahead of Jess and was looking back uncertainly.

"Ruthie, you and Jess head back." Izzy motioned curtly. "Hurry." He didn't look at Luellen. "As for your husband, I can't say."

Suddenly, the girl turned and bolted down the hill.

"Ruthie?" Luellen started after her daughter, but Izzy caught her arm.

"Get into the shelter. Take Jess with you."

"Not without my daughter." Luellen dug at his fingers, her expression mulish.

A sheriff's car fishtailed up the gravel drive as Izzy spoke curtly into his cell phone. "Teague here. What's your ETA?" He scanned the hillside. "We've got three motorcycles from the northwest and a sheriff's black-and-white. No sign of the princess, but L.Z. has signaled a direct scent. I say again, we have a direct scent signal. No open gunfire."

Jess realized what he was saying. Whatever Hawk and his people were tracking had to be nearby.

Jess turned and saw Ruthie disappear into a shed behind a row of young corn plants. Ruthie's garden was lovingly tended, with no weeds anywhere. As Jess cut through the thick green rows, slipping in the mud, her sandals stuck, and she kicked them off. She was breathing hard by the time she reached the shed.

"Ruthie, it's Jess. Are you okay?"

Something big clattered in the darkness. Gripping her purse, Jess lunged for the door, lost her balance, and slipped down the muddy slope on one knee. Her jeans were streaked and wet when she grabbed the door and peered into the darkened shed.

A clump of fur drifted past her face and she bit back a sneeze. "Ruthie?"

Another *clunk* came from the shadows inside. Cold air brushed her face.

She heard Luellen arguing up the hill, followed by Izzy's voice snapping orders. With the motorcycles coming closer, Jess knew there was no time to waste. She moved gingerly through the darkness, seeing two rabbits in a cage beside a hamster running on a big wheel. Only a thin line of gray light slanted through the single high window.

Jess nearly tripped over a rake and a shovel leaning against the wall.

Something skittered behind her, and she spun around. "Ruthie?"

The door slammed shut.

"Ruthie, what are you doing?" A lock rattled outside.

Jess grabbed the door, panic slashing through her. She was locked in.

Fear gathered, a tight ball in her throat. Outside in the deepening twilight, she heard the sheriff's car pull into the yard near the trailer, radio squawking. Footsteps crunched across the gravel.

Jess remembered the last order that Izzy had given.

No gunfire. Any harm to the princess—whatever that was—would be unacceptable.

She realized that Hawk and the team were fully prepared to die to carry out their orders.

Hawk stood at the open hatch of the Pave Low chopper, buckling on a Kevlar vest. The target zone was on the far side of the hill, only seconds away, but from what he could hear, the op was already going to shit fast. He'd have to insert ASAP, without cover.

The big bird thundered along the curve of the hill within feet of the treetops. Hawk knew that by drawing fire, he'd buy Izzy time to find Princess and take countermeasures.

As the bird cleared the tree line, Hawk closed his vest and secured his snub submachine gun. He picked out the sheriff's black-and-white near the trailer and what had to be at least seven other men running through the muddy yard toward the big tree where Luellen was standing.

Izzy had vanished.

"Down in twenty seconds," Hawk snapped over the din of the chopper's motor. "Notify Teague."

"Yes, sir." One of Izzy's team hunched over a walkie-talkie, squinting against the throb of the motor.

The chopper stopped, hovering twenty feet above the ground. Hawk gripped the heavy rope suspended outside the door and swung into the air. As he shot down the rope, his hands closed and his feet twisted, braking his descent.

Bullets zinged around him, clattering off the chopper's armored body, but his team didn't return fire. Their orders were crystal clear.

No harm to the animal. No matter the personal cost.

Dimly, Jess heard the sound of a helicopter approaching.

Sweat covered her face, trickling between her shoulders. Locked in waves of panic, she took gasping breaths, forcing her head down between her legs as dizziness threatened to overwhelm her.

*This is what I fear most,* she thought. *This is the nightmare, the thing that wakes me up whimpering. But I understand it now.*

All she had to do was control it.

Her nails dug into her palms. Dragging in a deep breath, she forced her body to relax while she counted down from ten.

Musty darkness stretched around her. The shed was filled with broken tools, watering cans and rusty shovels. None of them would help her get outside.

Jess took another deep breath, avoiding the sight of the closed door.

She'd beaten her fear once in the elevator with Hawk. She could damn well do it again.

She sneezed, frowning at the musty edge to the air. To distract herself, she ran her fingers over the work surface beneath the window, wincing as she met splintered wood. A stack of broken plastic lawn chairs leaned against the window next to an old garden hose and several empty feedbags.

She forced her hands open, coaching her body to relax,

muscle by tense muscle. No one but Ruthie knew she was locked in. No one would come looking for her.

She was on her own.

She stared into the shadows. Musty air filled her lungs as she grabbed a rusty shovel and began to dig.

# chapter 23

**U**p on the steps, the deputy shoved back his uniform hat, scowling at Luellen. "What the hell is going on here? Who are those men?"

"My daughter's missing. I have to find her."

He swept a glance down the muddy hill. "Why are they—?"

"I can't talk now." Luellen's voice was tight with panic. "She's in trouble. He told me."

"Who?"

"The man. The one who's dressed like a woman. He's some kind of soldier."

The sheriff nodded. "Where did he go?"

"Down the hill. Into the woods, maybe. Hell, I couldn't see. Now I have to find my daughter before—"

The sheriff pivoted sharply, gripping her arm. His eyes were icy. "Shut up."

"What are you—?"

A Colt nudged the hollow beneath her throat. "I said *shut up*. Otherwise I'll put three rounds into your neck. You know what a Colt can do at close range, don't you?"

Luellen nodded mutely.

"Where is the animal?"

"I don't know—"

He slapped her twice, hard enough to knock her back against the wall of the trailer. *"Where?"*

Her eyes snapped from one side of the yard to the other. She licked her lips. "I—Ruthie put it outside."

"You're lying."

"No. I swear it's true."

He slapped her again and spittle dripped down her chin, mixing with her tears.

"It's out in the shed. I swear it. I'll take you there right now and you can see for yourself. Just l-let Ruthie go."

He shoved the Colt against her forehead, and she gave a little moan of fear as she looked into pale eyes the color of broken spring ice. "Lie to me and I'll kill you. But I'll kill Ruthie first, and I'll do it to her while you watch."

"It's the God's honest truth. *Please.* I'll show you."

He looked at her, his lips thinning with distaste. "I lost it once, but I won't lose it again. I know the animal is here somewhere." He shoved her, kicking her. "One scream and I'll cut your throat. One lie and I'll do the same to your daughter. You have that straight?"

She gave a low whimper, nodding.

"Good. Now show me the shed."

He was right behind her as she stumbled down the steps, his hand clamped around her throat.

Exhausted from shoveling dirt, Jess huddled in the darkness, dust motes tickling her nose. She tried not to think about the rodents lurking in the gloom. As her eyes grew accustomed to the darkness, she studied the narrow window above her head.

That could be a better escape route than digging a tunnel. There was no reason to shudder and feel the walls close in. She'd handled her fear once before, and Jess swore she'd do it again.

Izzy was outside.

Hawk was outside.

*And you're still locked in.*

Her heart hammered against her ribs, so she took a deep breath and held it, summoning all her willpower and control. Feeling her hip throb, she searched the ground and found that she was sitting on the fallen shovel. She gripped the handle, grateful for the sharp pain, which had shaken her from the past and reminded her that she was an adult, no longer a frightened teenager. She had no time to linger in a place of sad memories.

Her fingers gripped the worn wood as she stared up at the narrow window. The old fears shivered, closing around her and threatening to leap back with all their full, ugly power.

There were tears on her cheeks as she peered into the darkness, sniffing at the musty smells of dirt and rust. Something brushed against her arm, and she bit back a yelp of surprise.

Fur pressed against her, part of a warm, round body. Some kind of dog, Jess decided, though she couldn't see the floor clearly. The round body leaned against her, nuzzling her arm, then climbed up into her lap. Blinking, Jess looked down into a pale oval face with huge eyes, a dark nose, and big, soft ears.

Not a dog. It had to be some kind of a bear. A slow, careful bear that seemed friendly and completely familiar with people.

Jess remembered Hawk's harsh question the first time she'd seen him. *Where is it?*

The answer screamed through her mind. The animal—whatever its value and secrets—was right here beside her.

Goose bumps rose all over her body. Jess knew in that moment that she absolutely had to keep the animal safe until Hawk arrived.

There was a sudden hail of angry shouting outside, and men ran past the shed, their feet drumming. "I got the girl!" one of them called.

Jess heard a scream. Ruthie.

She looked around wildly, but all she could see was a pile of old cardboard boxes, some gardening tools and various bags of fertilizer. She still had her purse, but there was nothing in it that could get her safely up to the window. Luellen's gun, taken from under the car seat, wouldn't help her escape.

The bear tucked its head against her shoulder, and Jess stroked the soft fur, working desperately at the problem.

"Bring the girl here," a man ordered, his voice coming from a distance.

There was no answer.

"Tonio?"

More silence.

"Damn it, Tonio—"

"Ruthie! I'm coming, honey. Stay where you are and—" Luellen's voice broke off in a sudden grunt of pain.

"Come, Ruthie. Otherwise, I'm going to cut your mother up while you watch her bleed."

Wind hissed through the trees. The chopper was gone. No answer came from Ruthie.

Jess listened with desperate intensity, trying to imagine exactly what was happening outside as more men ran past the shed. She reached into her purse and withdrew the gun she'd found in Luellen's car.

Suddenly gunfire exploded in the air, seeming to come from all sides at once. Jess clutched the bear, curling protectively toward the wall as noise thundered around her.

She shuddered as a round ripped through the roof and another split the thin wooden wall.

The window shattered, and glass rained down on her face and shoulders. By instinct she put her body between the animal and the window, as pain burned down her cheek from the rain of glass slivers.

Someone hit the door. The lock shook, and then light filled the space, blinding Jess.

"I told you she was in here. I saw her looking for the girl."

Terrified, Jess watched a dark shape loom against the light with a gun leveled.

"Get the bear, Tonio. Chavez promised us a million in reward money, remember? We'll split that million on a nice beach in Acapulco, with good tequila and some prime ass for the rest of our lives, no?"

Laughter spewed toward Jess.

"Come on out, honey. Bring your little friend over here to Tonio. We'll take good care of you."

As Jess frowned at the looming figure, a deep, almost unknown part of her brain took charge, recalling her shooting lessons with Summer.

*Grip. Sight. Fire.*

She cradled the Colt with both hands, flipped off the safety. Without squinting, she lined up the sights. The man named Tonio was still laughing as she squeezed off three quick shots.

# chapter 24

Hawk hit the ground running, and in seconds he was hidden beneath the trees. He had pinpointed the location of the men on the ground and wove through the woods until he came out behind the big sycamore tree near the trailer. He took the first target out before the man could feel the prick of his knife. A second target was crouched behind a derelict Ford truck with a rifle trained on Luellen.

Hawk dispensed with him via a single blow to the neck.

Neither man had time to whisper a cry of warning.

The man beside Luellen called to someone out of Hawk's range of sight, and feet pounded past the truck. Silently Hawk faded into the rows of corn, crouching between green leaves that hissed in the chill wind.

He fingered his earphone. "Izzy, do you copy?"

There was no answer.

Hawk didn't allow himself to dwell on grim possibilities. Until the missing bear was safe in government custody, he didn't have time for emotions of any sort.

He peered around the rusty fender and saw Luellen's daughter, held captive by a man in wraparound amber shooter's glasses. The girl's face was white with fear.

Hawk calculated a quick shot to the man's temple, but realized there were buildings behind them. He couldn't risk harm to the lab animal.

Or to Jess and Izzy.

Where were they, and where in the hell was the government's missing bear?

He heard the crack of three bullets fired in sharp succession. The sound appeared to come from a dirty shed halfway down the hill.

"Tonio, what the hell is going on down there?"

Hawk recognized Emilio Chavez in spite of his sheriff's uniform. The man just kept turning up like a bad penny wherever stolen technology and illegal weapons were involved. Now he shoved Luellen in front of him in a tight grip as he walked through the yard near the trailer.

Quiet as smoke, Hawk crept between the rows of corn, crawled around a pile of old tires, and came up on Ruthie's captor from behind. He saw her mouth work as she struggled with her terror.

The man jerked Ruthie up the hill, cursing when her feet slipped in the mud. "Hurry up, you fool." He glanced up the hill, cursing. "Where's Tonio, Chavez? Why doesn't he answer?"

Seconds later Hawk's big K-Bar knife blade snicked through the man's neck and blood sprayed the grass.

Hawk grabbed the girl as she swayed, one hand across her mouth in case she screamed. It was a tough break, he thought grimly. The kid was barely twelve and she'd just seen a man killed in front of her.

He took a quick glance up the hill. Izzy slipped around the trailer, crouched behind a discarded recliner, then nodded at Hawk and pointed silently down the slope.

Hawk gave a quick nod and turned to Ruthie. "Listen, honey, I'm going to get you hidden inside this truck, okay?" His whisper was low at Ruthie's ear. "I'm going to help you and your mother, understand?"

The girl was shivering, but she managed to nod jerkily.

"Okay. Now I'm going to take my hand away from your mouth, but I need for you to stay absolutely silent. Do you understand?"

She nodded again. After Hawk removed his hand, he carefully opened the rusty door to the truck and helped her climb inside. When she was curled up on the floor out of sight, Hawk covered her with an old seat cushion. "Where's Jess?" he whispered.

"In the shed. I l-locked her in. I was afraid that she was here for the bear my father brought me."

A pulse began to pound at Hawk's temple. "Your father, Richard Dickman?"

"Yeah. That's why you came here, isn't it? That's why the others came here—the bear has to be really valuable or my stupid father wouldn't want it." She swallowed hard, tears slipping down her cheeks. "When he asked me to hide it, I said sure. I mean why not? It was so nice, so cute. Even my mom didn't know it was here until this morning." Ruthie sniffed. "I begged her not to tell anyone."

"Where is the bear now?"

"In the shed behind the sycamore tree, down the hill from my garden. The lady's there, too."

"You mean Jess?"

Ruthie nodded. "I thought she wanted the bear, and I freaked. I mean, it was so helpless, so alone, and really hungry. My friend and I read about what they eat, and we finally found some eucalyptus at the florist's today. It was fresh and she ate a lot of it."

"You did a good job, honey."

"I don't want it stuck in some zoo. I was afraid that Jess and that other old lady might be trying to take the bear away, like maybe they were investigators from the state or something."

"Don't worry, the bear won't be put in a zoo," Hawk said. "But you need to stay here. Don't move, no matter what."

At Ruthie's nod, Hawk closed the truck door carefully.

Outside, Chavez's men were on the prowl.

Jess stared at the body on the floor. The air was filled with the sour, metallic smell of blood. Her stomach twisted with waves of nausea and the gun shook in her hand. She'd killed a man. His blood covered her jeans and darkened her arm.

Shuddering, she forced her gaze away from the floor, back to the bear that still gripped her chest.

It was too much to take in, so she put everything but survival out of her mind.

With the bear secure in her left arm, she pulled the dead man's body farther inside, then closed the door. Her body shook as she sank against the wall, hidden behind a worktable. Her fingers curled around Luellen's handgun, gripped rigidly in front of her.

Feet raced past outside. Angry shouts echoed across the clearing, followed by a volley of gunshots.

Something scratched against the door, and Jess leveled the pistol for a second time.

The door latch moved.

"Jess, are you there?"

Her fingers shook. She didn't answer.

"Jess, it's Hawk. I'm outside. Are you okay in there?"

Relief punched through her, but even then her arm stayed level. Voices could be faked, after all.

A crack of light outlined the door, widening slowly. Sunlight slanted into Jess's eyes, blinding her, and she heard the male voice break off in a curse.

"Are you hurt, honey?" Hawk stepped over the bloody body on the floor of the shed. "Talk to me, Jess."

She let her arm fall, keeping the bear tight against her chest. The air felt heavy, and she couldn't seem to breathe.

Hawk's shadow fell over her. "My God, you found Princess." He knelt beside her on the dusty floor. "Why don't you let me take her now?"

Jess couldn't register what he was saying. As he reached out, the bear pushed closer against her. *"No."*

"Okay, then she goes with you. But we have to move out now." His voice was absolutely calm, as if bullets weren't cracking nearby and a man wasn't lying dead at his feet. "Can you stand up, honey?"

Jess pushed upright, feeling a stab of pain above her eyes. But the sensation faded as Hawk motioned her to the door, checked outside, then pointed down a muddy path.

"Go. I'll be right beside you."

Her feet were bare, Jess realized. Her legs hurt.

Funny, she hadn't even noticed.

Hawk glanced across at Jess. Her face was streaked with blood, her clothes torn, her eyes dilated. She was probably in shock, and she looked like hell. But for the moment she was up and mobile, and he couldn't stop for anything until the bear was safe.

He flicked the button of his walkie-talkie, scanning the hillside. A Humvee transport was waiting back in the trees, but getting there wasn't going to be a picnic.

He tapped Jess's arm, pointing behind the rusted truck where Ruthie was hidden. Nothing moved around him as Hawk clicked the TRANSMIT button again, this time two quick taps, a prearranged signal to his team to indicate the discovery of their "package."

He touched Jess's shoulder. Her gaze locked on him and he saw her struggle to focus.

Shock and possibly worse. He couldn't stop to find out if she was bleeding. He had to get them out of harm's way.

With the bear still cradled at her chest, Jess swayed, then followed him over the muddy grass toward the woods.

As they ran, three members of Izzy's team emerged from cover, making a human shield with their Kevlar-clad bodies. Without a word, the group ran in a tight wedge toward the dark wall of trees. They were only a few feet from safety when they heard Luellen scream.

Hawk didn't slow, though he heard Jess's gasp.

"Keep going," he ordered.

Behind him Emilio Chavez's shout exploded down the hillside. "Bring the animal to me. If not, the old woman is the next to die. Two bullets in the stomach, slow and painful."

"The old woman?" Jess faltered, her eyes cutting to Hawk's. "He means Izzy."

"You have until I reach five," Chavez shouted, his voice tight with fury. "I begin now."

Hawk grabbed Jess's arm and forced her forward, his face expressionless. There was no sound from Izzy, but Hawk didn't expect one. The man was a pro and he would have expected nothing different.

Jess stumbled and Hawk pulled her the last few yards until the shadows closed around them. When she looked up, Hawk saw that her face was wet with tears.

"One," Chavez shouted, his voice echoing in the sudden stillness.

The Hummer was waiting. Two men jumped out, surrounding Jess. One of them reached for the bear, but Hawk shook his head silently. He leaned close to her and touched her cheek. "Go on, honey. Take good care of Princess for me."

She nodded, the bear still clutched protectively in her arms. Hawk didn't stay to see her climb stiffly into their transport. He was already racing through the woods, headed for the slope at the back of Luellen's trailer.

# chapter 25

Someone shouted a question. Chavez screamed back. "Two," he cried, the sound a roar over the wind. Energy backed up through Hawk's body as he ran, and every muscle seemed to uncoil, eating up the muddy yards in loose, powerful strides. Heart pumping, he jumped a boulder, cut through waist-high reeds, shot over a fallen log.

"Three!"

He sprinted out of the trees at the only point where Chavez wouldn't see him and slid to a crouch. Chavez was on his left, standing under the big sycamore tree, holding Luellen captive with his left arm. Izzy was six feet away, roped hands caught at his back, guarded by three men with submachine guns.

"Four, damn it!"

Hawk went flat against the wall of the smaller shed, pulled a scoped rifle from his webbed vest and laid it on the ground in front of him. He sighted on Luellen with the sniper rifle and aimed carefully.

Luellen went down, followed by two of the men near Izzy.

Izzy went down last, red staining his back and neck.

Grimly, Hawk studied the hillside through his scope, then sprinted past Luellen, who was moaning on the ground

a few feet away from the tattered target of her husband's
face, her left shoulder covered by a circle of crimson.

One of Chavez's men emerged behind the old truck, and
Hawk took him down with a round kick and a hook to the
throat.

Chavez was halfway down the slope, almost to the motorcycles. Shouting curses, he looked back and squeezed
five quick shots over his shoulder.

Hawk felt one of the bullets rip through his side, but he
didn't slow down. Chavez was his second mission priority
after rescuing Princess. The man had been hunted over
four continents, wanted for terrorist assaults and plutonium smuggling from Istanbul to Bangkok. Hawk's orders
were to bring him in alive or bring him down permanently.

As Hawk crawled over the muddy slope, hidden by one
of the sheds, he heard Chavez cut through the rows of corn.
Abruptly, the killer changed direction, veering toward the
truck where Ruthie was hidden.

Hawk shot to his feet. "Here!"

Gunfire raked the ground around Hawk, and then
Chavez dropped back into the corn that swayed in ghostly
green trails. He was too much of a professional to lose any
time taunting Hawk. Instead he answered with another
explosive burst from a Bulgarian-made AK-47.

Bullets tore through the mud. Hawk returned fire, and
his second burst caught Chavez as he rose, cursing, to
throw a grenade.

The grenade spun to the ground, pin unpulled. Chavez
staggered and followed it down, his face against the mud.
His feet twitched violently and lay still. The wind sighed,
slipping through the dark, dancing corn.

L.Z. whimpered as Hawk sprinted up the hill. The dog had
stayed hidden exactly where Izzy had ordered all through

the assault, but at Hawk's call, he bounded out of hiding, fur matted with mud and grass, tail swinging wildly.

"Good work, pal. Mighty damned fine nose."

L.Z. barked once.

"Yeah, I know. Let's go deal with it."

Luellen was leaning against the sycamore, her arm cradled against her chest, cursing like a stevedore.

Hawk ignored her, running toward Izzy, who was sprawled flat, motionless near the trailer steps. L.Z. followed and pressed his nose against Izzy's face, whimpering.

Hawk scanned the area, then dropped beside Izzy. "Come on, Teague, you big, ugly gorilla. Don't even think about checking out."

Luellen waved her free arm. "You shot me! I'm gonna sue your ass from here to Sunday, buddy."

Izzy didn't move.

Hawk ran a hand along Izzy's neck, cursing when his fingers met fresh blood, not the red ink from the paintball "bullets" he'd fired at Izzy and Luellen to confuse Chavez. L.Z. butted Izzy with his head and licked his face from one side to the other.

"Get the hell up." Hawk's voice was tight. "Come on. Move it, Teague."

"No need . . ." Izzy's body shook. "No need to kiss me, Navy."

Hawk took a sharp breath, and relief left him grinning. "Give it a break, Teague. That's not me, it's the wonder dog."

Izzy sat up slowly, one hand at the back of his neck. "Must have hit a rock when I fell. My whole head hurts like a bitch." He squinted at the red stain covering his chest. "Nice shot." He picked up a big circle of red-stained foam from the ground and tossed it over his shoulder. "Damned breast inserts never work, no matter how much duct tape you use, but they do help pad against a paintball bullet."

He reached down and scratched L.Z. gently between the ears. "Extra dog bones for you tonight."

The big Malinois barked excitedly as Izzy stood up and walked down the hill.

"Hey, what about me?" Luellen called angrily.

"Ruthie's in the truck," Hawk said, walking past her. "She's safe, but she's frightened. Go take care of her."

"Ruthie?" Luellen looked down the hill, then rubbed at her shoulder, which was covered with red dye from Hawk's paintball bullets. "You mean, I'm not hurt?"

"You'll have a big bruise tomorrow," Hawk said calmly. "Nothing serious."

Luellen shook her head as Izzy dropped his skirt and shawl on the grass, stripped down to spandex biking shorts and a gray T-shirt. "I can't believe she was—well, a *he.*"

"Lately, neither can I," Hawk muttered.

Two motorcycles wound through the mud and down the other side of the hill. Three miles later they met up with a black Humvee, following it through the storm-littered town of Bright Creek.

Jess was in the backseat, Hawk saw. She still had the bear in her arms, and her face was the ashen color of death.

She'd killed a man today. It was something you never forgot. She'd need help after this. Maybe a lot of help.

Hawk figured he'd call her sister and fill her in. Even though Jess's responses had been the right ones, they might not feel that way for a long, long time.

Hawk knew that from personal experience.

The Humvee sped past Bright Creek and pulled off the main road onto a gravel drive that appeared to lead exactly nowhere. Beyond a sharp curve, the road opened to a flat expanse of grass that bristled with communications trucks, microwave towers, and several dozen all-terrain vehicles scattered in front of a fenced communication complex.

Four of the highest-ranking members of the Joint Chiefs and assorted other officials were standing outside, cell phones in hand, and Izzy's team was lined up around them, along with a dozen government scientists.

Princess was finally coming home.

The Humvee stopped. One of Izzy's men opened the back door and started to help Jess out, but she brushed away his hand and stepped down, frowning. The bear was pressed against her chest, furry head to her shoulder, as Jess walked up the muddy path toward the cluster of people at the top of the hill.

She was quite a sight, Hawk thought. Her feet were bare, her hair a tangled mass at her shoulders. Her jeans were torn, and a dead man's blood streaked her legs and face.

She looked like living, breathing hell.

All talking ceased. Looking neither right nor left, she walked wearily toward the man who appeared to have the most bars on his chest, while the uniforms parted in a silent path in front of her.

Tattered and shell-shocked, she managed to look regal, and the men around her straightened, eyes forward, responding as if she were their queen.

She stopped in front of the Secretary of the Navy, taking a deep breath, cradling the bear with fingers that shook slightly. "I think my friend here belongs to you."

Someone began to clap behind her, then others joined in until the whole hillside was filled with the echo of applause.

Jess seemed startled, glancing around gravely as the Secretary of the Navy joined in the enthusiastic applause. "I didn't do anything," she said. "Nothing special."

If she wasn't special, then Hawk didn't know who *was*.

Walking up the path behind her, he grinned at Izzy. "Told you she was going to seriously screw up this op."

"Or rescue it." Izzy high-fived Hawk. "Face it, bro. She got game."

Hawk would have liked to stay and congratulate her himself, but he saw his C.O. gesturing at him. There was still work to be done, Hawk knew. He wouldn't have any personal time for weeks.

Maybe months.

He heard the drone of a motor and looked up to see a chopper skimming the trees from the south. He took a long time studying Jess, seeing the determined set to her shoulders and the way she stood, oblivious to her ripped clothes and bare feet. That was one tough, kick-butt lady, he thought. She was nothing like the pampered princess he'd assumed her to be in his shower.

Which just went to show how worthless first impressions could be.

The last of his uneasiness vanished as the chopper landed down the hill, and a figure jumped to the ground. Now he knew that Jess was in good hands. The FBI had sent in their best agent as liaison.

She happened to be Jess's sister, Summer.

Izzy tossed his wig into the nearest Jeep and nodded to Hawk. "Let's reload and then go hunt down the rest of Chavez's nasty hive."

# chapter 26

**T**he beach was deserted. Only a crowd of noisy birds circled, diving for their lunch.

Jess was tired—and tired of pretending that she was not. But for the last three and a half months she'd kept busy with a passion. She'd cleaned out her old apartment, tossed out all the papers from her hotel career, and moved here to the beach two hours north of San Francisco.

In the weeks after she'd found the government's priceless koala bear, she had received messages, phone calls and visits from a dozen quiet, tough Navy men who'd been friends of her father. The whole truth had finally emerged, how they had tried to contact her and her sister after her father's death, and how her mother had blocked all contact, blaming the Navy for his death. Over the years after that, they had lost track of the two girls.

Jess frowned at the restless wedge of ocean glittering through the window. In a strange way her mother's pain and anger made sense. Her father had been involved in Navy intelligence, Jess had learned. Though no one had given her

any details, she was certain that he had been meeting someone as part of a covert assignment when he'd died.

Not on a simple trip to the store for milk, as she and
Summer had been told.

A tough crew of ex–Navy chiefs had stepped in without
notice, checking that she was eating enough, sleeping
enough, relaxing enough. They didn't argue or accept any
evasions. Instead they took quiet charge, bringing food,
carrying boxes and furniture, rotating her tires and washing her Jeep.

Jess shook her head as the sea wind ruffled her hair.
What an amazing thing, to discover a whole set of surro-
gate fathers when you were grown enough to really appreciate them. Even her sister, low-key as always, was enjoying
the impromptu visits and gruff concern. Summer's husband, the Navy SEAL with the gorgeous body, felt right at
home among the crusty crew.

Jess finished folding a pile of freshly ironed linen nap-
kins and sat down in a rattan chair overlooking the harbor.
A lanky teenager was hauling boxes of flowers up from a
rusted pickup truck, and the colors made Jess smile with
delight. A dozen shades of red smiled back at her. When
the teenager saw her looking, he doffed his baseball hat in a
quick gesture of chivalry.

Jess waved back, then lowered her hand to cover her
stomach. She took a breath and closed her eyes, enjoying
the heat of the sun on her face.

Trying not to think about shadows or death, about what
had been and what would be.

For now, this moment was enough.

A few minutes later the bell in the front foyer tinkled. A
man with graying red hair walked into the hall, carrying a
basket of cut roses.

"More flowers for you. Some man was upstairs painting

your door, too." Her boss was a tall ex-Marine whose gruffness couldn't hide a marshmallow heart, and Jess loved him dearly. "I asked him why, and he said he was paid, that's all."

Jess felt a flutter in her chest at the latest in a string of unexpected gifts. "What color?"

"Santa Fe blue. Your favorite color." Her boss tried to look disapproving. "Another young woman brought a red hammock to hang out in the back under the olive trees."

"Dutch, did they say—?"

"No more than any of the others did. Must be that secret admirer of yours again."

Except they both knew that Jess's admirer wasn't a secret.

"About time you got off your feet," the old soldier muttered, sticking roses in a big porcelain vase by the window. "You were up before dawn fixing the curtains in the dining room and after that you just had to go down and tinker with the Sunday brunch menus."

"I'm fine." Jess hid a yawn. "In fact, I've never felt better."

Oddly, it was true. Each day she woke up smiling, brimming over with more energy than she'd had in her life. And of course she was eating like a pig. Pretty soon none of her clothes would fit.

She smiled radiantly at the thought.

"Never mind that. I'll stay and fix those flowers, Dutch." She stretched contentedly.

"I can manage them just fine." The ex-Marine had gentle hands for a man who was nearly six, six, and he enjoyed working with them. "Here's some herbal tea for you." He set a steaming pot carefully on the table. "Don't spill it."

"I'm not that clumsy." Jess cleared her throat. "I only spilled something once, and that was because your dog tried to do dog Olympics on my feet."

Sudden barking thundered through the first floor of the

little hotel, and a black mass of fur and legs roared like an express train down the picture-filled hallway, braking hard and spinning in a circle at Jess's feet.

"Speaking of the devil," she murmured.

The huge German shepherd barked again, then nuzzled its way beneath her arm, whimpering with pleasure when she leaned down to scratch behind his ears.

Jess stared at the dog for a long time. "Did he call me?"

The big man hid a look of worry, crossing the room with a noticeable limp. "Once last night after you went to sleep. Once this morning around five." His mouth tightened as he arranged clean silver on the nearby tables.

"Twice?" Jess's fingers tightened on the arm of her chair. "Why didn't you wake me up?"

"Because you need your sleep, blast it." The ex-Marine cleared his throat as he arranged crystal glasses on tables with pristine damask tablecloths. "I told him that, too."

Jess bit back a sigh of disappointment. "Where was he calling from this time?"

"Last night I heard one of those European sirens. You know—up and down, shrill as hell. This morning, I heard Big Ben."

So Hawk was in London, Jess thought. Last week it had been Thailand. The week before it had been India.

She forced a bright smile. "Join the Navy, see the world."

Dutch said something beneath his breath. "I'll finish up here. You go upstairs and rest for a bit."

"But the flowers—"

"It's my hotel, honey. Argue with me, and I'll just have to fire you." Concern filled his eyes even as he fought to hide his tenderness. "I'm almost finished here, anyway. Take Monster with you."

Hearing his name, the big German shepherd shot around Jess's back and barked loudly, clearly hoping for a walk.

Jess stood up slowly, one hand on the chair. The other touched the slight curve that was already visible at her stomach.

Hawk's baby had been conceived during a raging storm in an elevator that had stalled—touching Jess's heart and changing her life.

A baby was the last thing she had expected. Because of her longstanding hormonal problems, her specialist had finally prescribed birth control pills, and Jess had just begun her first month's supply when she'd gone to Washington In her stress and confusion there, she had missed two pills.

The news that she was carrying Hawk's baby had been the most wonderful surprise of her life. Jess had confided in her sister as soon as the pregnancy was certain, and now Summer was excitedly researching strollers and cribs, even planning a big baby shower that she thought Jess knew nothing about.

"I'm going, I'm going." She smoothed Monster's shaggy hair. "If Hawk calls me again . . ." She stared at Dutch, trying to seem calm and collected when she was anything but.

"I'll get you. I swear it." The big man cleared his throat. "You'd better tell him this week."

"As soon as I get my last blood test back." Jess's hands curled protectively over her stomach. "If I pass, everything will be fine. And you know that I feel disgustingly healthy."

But the cells nourishing the tiny miracle inside her could fail at any moment, causing her to lose her child. Neither one of them mentioned that, though both were thinking about it.

A car honked outside. Monster thundered down the hall, barking.

"That's Henri with the wine delivery. I'll take care of it." Dutch studied the sunny room, the polished wood and the gleaming crystal, shaking his head.

"What's wrong?"

"It's the crystal, I guess. It hits me like that sometimes. A 4-star bed and breakfast on the beach is a damned strange spot for an old, beat-up Marine. I surely never expected to get friendly with a bunch of ugly old Navy farts, either."

"It's hard to know where life can take us," Jess said quietly. She rested her hand on his callused fingers. "I've inspected hotels all over the country and not one was better managed or more beautiful than this."

The big man smiled, studying the room with pride. "With your help. I may even have to give you a raise. I don't want that big resort on the hill stealing you away."

Jess grinned. "As if."

Monster barked wildly at the back door.

"Yeah, yeah, I'm coming."

Jess watched Dutch limp slowly toward the back door. He smiled more now, she thought. One of her father's Navy buddies had recommended her for the job of manager and concierge at Dutch's small enterprise on the rugged northern coast. After one look at the charming pink guesthouses nestled in lush landscape beside the ocean, Jess would have signed on to scrub toilets. Within two months, she had doubled occupancy rates and secured a file full of glowing reviews, and business had never been better.

Dutch was exuberant, though he managed to hide it.

He was also as protective as Monster when it came to Jess and her advancing pregnancy.

But bless the man, he didn't plague her with questions the way her sister had. He'd only asked the name of the father once. Though Jess was pretty sure he'd gone off to make inquiries among that tight-knit military circle of his, he never mentioned another word to her.

It was Summer who called once a week to see if Hawk had come to see her yet. Jess explained that he was busy, still involved in the mission. The silence afterward said what Summer wouldn't.

That she knew her sister was hurting and she couldn't bear it.

Trailing her fingers along a row of framed watercolors, Jess climbed the stairs to her sunny room at the back of the top floor. She stopped at the landing, a silly grin on her lips.

The door was bright blue, just the way Dutch had described. The paint was still drying.

Another gift.

Her room was a small, sunny space large enough for only a bed and a tiny reading alcove, but the trade-off was the balcony with tall French doors. Jess gazed through the glass now at the blue-green panorama of deep coves hugging steep, rugged cliffs.

After one more blood test, her specialist would give her a clean bill of health. Like her mother, Jess had been diagnosed with a luteal-phase defect that meant miscarriage was a definite possibility. So far the baby growing inside her racked up full points for vibrant good health and growth rate, but anxiety made Jess clam up every time Hawk called.

She tried to remember the odds, tried not to desperately want the child she and Hawk had conceived in reckless passion, but no amount of logic and sense made her want the baby less. Within seconds of learning she was pregnant, she had wrapped her heart around the idea with no regrets or reservations. She already had plans to teach her daughter—or son—to make soap from scratch, change a Ducati carburetor, and bodysurf in the Pacific.

Summer would teach the Weaver stance, the rumba, and how to avoid identity theft.

But first Jess had to tell Hawk about his baby.

The week before she missed three calls because of time differences as he roamed the far corners of the globe. Another time their connection had failed. Last week she'd told him to set aside time for a long talk tomorrow. Anxious or not, she meant to call him immediately after her last and most crucial medical checkup.

Inside her room, Jess studied a huge vase of flowers, a gift from Summer and Gabe, who were coming for a visit the following weekend. Several of her father's Navy buddies were due soon too, ready to dish out tall tales about the father who'd died too young.

Jess opened the French doors and savored the salty air. Her body was pulsing with energy, and she had a sudden urge for strawberries and an almond milkshake.

With a side order of Dutch's homemade pickles.

But first she was going to take a walk on the beach. Grabbing a hat and sweater, she headed down the winding front stairs through the flower-filled lobby.

She didn't hear Monster bark as a sleek motorcycle pulled around back into the service entrance.

"Where is she?"

"Beg your pardon?" Dutch put down a case of domestic champagne.

The man in the black leather jacket had stubble on his cheeks and his eyes looked tired as he slid off the gleaming Silver Ducati. "I'm looking for Jess Mulcahey."

Dutch leaned back, studying the man. He noted the muscled shoulders, the careful eyes.

The hidden restlessness.

This had to be Hawk Mackenzie, the man he'd tracked across Europe and Asia. The man whose military file he'd raided and researched.

He was a hero and a loner.

He was also a heartbreaker.

Damn the man. If he broke Jess's heart, Dutch and three

of his buddies would tie the SEAL down and cut out his tongue.

And then they'd do something *really* bad to him.

"She's not here," Dutch snapped.

"Then where?"

"Out." Defiantly. "Not that it's any of your business."

"You her boss?"

Dutch nodded.

The man in the motorcycle jacket glared at him. "That better be all you are."

Dutch would have decked the man if he hadn't seen the pain in his eyes. "Mister, the woman's the same age as my granddaughter." He moved across the courtyard, painfully aware of his limp. "Give it a rest."

Hawk Mackenzie cursed, rubbing his neck. "Yeah, well—sorry. I just wanted to be sure. She doesn't answer my calls. She doesn't answer my letters."

Dutch crossed his arms. "Because you call at gawdawful hours, boy. And because your letters never have return addresses."

"I left an address in San Francisco." Hawk jammed a hand through his hair. "Probably the mail takes a while to forward. I've been on the move."

"Care to tell me what you've been doing?"

"No."

Dutch nodded. "That's what I figured."

The SEAL glanced at Dutch's leg. "Vietnam?"

"Tet offensive." Dutch's eyes narrowed. "January 31, 1968. Right before dawn."

"I've heard some stories."

"None of them come close, believe me." Dutch stared across the sunny courtyard, his head ringing with the echo of mortar fire and incoming Huey's over the city walls. He forced away the flashback. He'd had enough practice at it by now. "I get by. The leg feels just like the real thing." He sniffed. "How long are you staying?"

"Not long enough. So how is she?" His mouth was tense, his eyes scanning the room. "Does she like it here?"

"Loves it. Took to it like a fish to water. Never seen anyone who's better with the guests and the staff."

"She was damned good at her old job. She always had an eye for schedules and organization. Not afraid of anything either."

"I've heard some rumors about that. I hear she shot a man. Don't suppose you'd be more specific," Dutch said.

"No, I wouldn't."

Dutch stared at Hawk for a long time. "She's upstairs, third door to the left. I told her to take a nap, but she probably won't."

Hawk smiled faintly. "That sounds like Jess." He slung his helmet and a small knapsack over his shoulder. "Thanks."

"Don't thank me yet. If you hurt her, boy, I'm going to cut out your heart and eat it for lunch," the limping hero of Hue City said calmly.

Jess was staring out at the water when she heard Monster bark behind her. As usual, the big dog had insisted on accompanying her down to the beach, determined to protect her against sand crabs and kites and anything else that got too close. Jess smiled as she heard Monster scuttling over the sand. Probably chasing another crab. The dog was decimating an entire species single-handedly. "Leave the poor creature alone, Monster. Otherwise, I'll have to tell Dutch to—"

She turned—and all the words dried up in her throat.

The sweater she'd tied around her shoulders fell. "Hawk."

The word was a whisper, a caress, then a breath of overt panic.

"I've only got forty-eight hours," he said hoarsely. "I jumped a transport at Gatwick, grabbed another one in Virginia, changed in Houston, and—"

His knapsack fell. He caught her hard against his chest, his eyes closing as he was battered by unbearable emotions.

She was as beautiful as he remembered and more, but God knows, he wasn't good at emotions. He still wasn't used to thinking in terms of two instead of one. As a soldier, his focus was on burying his emotions, not facing them dead on.

He was trying his hardest, damn it. One of these years, he might even succeed. Meanwhile, he felt like a fish with legs.

"I forgot this." He pulled her closer. "How good you always smell." He buried his hands in her hair, dragging in the rich earthy scents. "Lilacs, cedar and sea salt."

"It's a shampoo I make for Dutch's guests." Her head was turned against his chest, and her voice shook. "He wanted something different for their rooms, something they could take away with them to remember the hotel."

"Any man would remember that smell," Hawk said roughly. "Dutch's one tough coot."

"Tough or not, he's been nice to me."

"Yeah, well, the old fool loves you."

Jess shook her head. "He's just worried about . . . things."

Hawk lifted her face with his hand. "What kind of things?"

Jess took a deep breath and tried to pull away, but Hawk tightened his grip, needing to feel her warmth and strength. Her smile was the cure for too many cold nights and too many bleak dreams. She promised laughter and belonging, things that Hawk had given up hope of ever finding.

"I would have come sooner. Hell, I would have stayed if I could. But there were threads to tie up, Jess. I had my orders."

"Don't apologize. Your work wasn't done." She studied his face. "You're tired."

"I hit the runway in San Francisco, then rode straight up. You look amazing. You're almost glowing."

"Must be the sea air." Jess touched his face. "I hope you got all of them, including Luellen's husband."

"Nabbed him that same day. He hadn't gotten more than five miles away when we found him. He won't be bothering Luellen and Ruthie again for a long time."

"And that man in the sheriff's uniform?"

"He won't be scaring anyone ever again."

"What about those men of his? Will they be freed?"

Hawk smiled grimly, thinking of the list of charges that Emilio Chavez's men faced. "Not a chance." The female FBI agent hurt in Princess's capture had finally recovered consciousness, but two other agents had died. "Not for about three hundred years. And that's if they're lucky."

"That's a relief." Jess looked down at the sweater clutched between them, covering her waist. "Hawk, I need to—"

His hands slid up her back as he molded her against his body. "Can we go somewhere, Jess? I can't stop remembering your taste on my mouth, the little sounds you make when you come, and I want to make you come all night." His hand opened, nudging her nipple beneath her bra. His jaw hardened as he opened her blouse and savored the beauty of her naked skin.

His fingers weren't quite steady, but he didn't care. He had so many things to ask.

So many belated promises to keep.

"Hawk." Her breath was ragged. "Someone will see us."

"We're alone, honey. Just that damned dog, and I doubt he'll mind a little discreet nudity." Hawk freed her breast and ran his fingertips across the dark red crest that tight-

ened instantly. "You're different. Hell, I can't remember
that much, but I could swear you are."

Jess made a lost sound as he pulled aside her sweater,
then lifted it while his lips closed around her breast.

She sucked in a breath. He tasted her slowly until her
fingers closed, digging at his hair. He tugged her blouse
open, looking at her.

The need hit him so hard he almost forgot where they
were. Finally, he pulled away with a curse, buttoning her
blouse quickly. "Come with me, Jess. I rented a room right
up the beach." Desire had burned all the soft, gentle words
out of his throat, threatening to overwhelm him. "Say no
and I'll leave. If you don't want this, I'll be back on a plane
to Europe tonight and I'll never bother you again."

Her fingers smoothed his hard jaw, brushed the new
scar above his right eye. "You'd do that?"

"If you're not interested, I'd understand. We had two
hours in a dark elevator, a drive in a Jeep." His voice hardened. "Time in a firefight, too. That hardly qualifies as normal courtship," he added grimly.

"You want to court me? To get to know me?" Something
came and went in her eyes, but damned if Hawk could
figure what.

He shrugged, all his rehearsed speeches swept away. He
wasn't used to facing his emotions, much less talking about
them.

"You sent those people, didn't you? The boy with the
roses. The woman with the hammock. The man who
painted my door."

"Bright blue." Hawk smiled crookedly. "I figured you'd
like that. I read somewhere that women like gifts."

"Women do," Jess said. "I do."

"I want to do everything right, Jess. I want to start where
we should have started. I don't know if I can wait, but I'll

try." His body was taut, his mind restless with the fantasies that had plagued him for long months. "I can't forget the way you felt against me that day in the elevator and how you looked when I left." His voice tightened. "You told me you could feel me. Hell—dripping down your leg. From the amazing sex we'd just had."

"It was amazing, wasn't it?" Her voice was surprisingly grave. "Two hours. Two strangers. Funny how fast things can change."

"We aren't strangers now, Jess, and we've got a lot more than two hours." He traced her breasts, watching her eyes darken. "Let me take you back to my hotel." He had a sudden moment of uncertainty that made him stop, take a deep breath. "Unless—"

Her smile was like sunrise on water, skipping from wave to wave, lighting the small shadowed places where he'd pushed down his fear. "No 'unlesses'." She reached into the back pocket of his jeans, dug a little, then pulled out the plastic key card he'd shoved there. "Room 179. Let's make it someplace we'll always remember."

The relief rocked him back so hard that for a moment he couldn't speak. His head tilted, resting against her forehead, and a long shudder ran through him. They'd work out their lives, find a way to be together. And when she was completely sure of him, when he'd gotten her stubborn sister to stop hating him, Hawk would take her to a beautiful little hideaway up the coast, make love to her for about fifty hours, then pull out the small, emerald-cut diamond he'd been carrying around for weeks now.

And if she turned him down, he'd probably shoot himself.

Her hair drifted over her shoulders as she stood in the wind, her thick, wool sweater caught between them. "So what are we going to do about Monster while we're having

wet, delirious sex?" Her eyes searched his face. "There may
be barking involved."

"Only by me," Hawk said roughly. And he wasn't sure
that he was kidding. Even the casual brush of her hand on
his zipper had him roaring inside.

Jess's fingers touched him again. Her eyes went dark
when she felt his taut jeans. Suddenly she rose on her toes,
her hands circling his neck. "Don't worry, Navy. I always—" She stopped, her breath catching. "No."

Hawk looked down, frowning. "What is it, Jess? Did
you hurt your ankle?"

She was staring at her sweater, now caught between their
bodies. "Not now." Her face was pale. "Please, not now. . . ."

"Honey, what *is* it? Tell me what's wrong."

Hawk saw something darken her white skirt, saw her
sweater fall to the sand, a bright blue pool suddenly spot-
ted with red.

He didn't understand.

She gave a little sob of pain. "I'm so sorry, Hawk. I was
going to do this right. I tried to tell you so many times." She
bent over, biting back a moan. "There was a mixup with my
pills. My stupid mistake with the storm and the elevator.
But now it's too late to explain because you're here and I'm
afraid—so afraid that I'm losing our baby."

# chapter 27

S teel nails clawed at her stomach.

Jess took deep breaths as the pain tightened and grew sharper. She'd known what could happen, known exactly what symptoms to watch for.

Contractions. Lower back pain. Spotting.

Now she had all three. She'd heard the statistics, and she'd assured Summer she was prepared for whatever happened. In the end she'd managed to fool everyone but herself.

She wasn't prepared, wasn't even close.

She saw Hawk rub his eyes, saw him fight to take in the shock of her news, but before she could explain, pain gripped her and she bent double, hands pressed to her stomach. As she closed her eyes, she was struck by the wild thought that if she pressed hard enough and long enough, she could fight fate and hold the precious baby inside.

The sudden wetness between her legs told her she was wrong.

"Hawk," she said hoarsely. "I'm bleeding."

His fingers touched the dark stain on her dress. With a curse, he pulled her up into his arms and began to run. "Hold on, honey. Just stay with me."

---

There were people everywhere, phones ringing, and equipment carts rattling by. Elevators came and went while more people swam past.

Hawk registered it all dimly, like part of somebody else's dream. All he could see was the closed doors to the emergency room, where Jess was lying on a white bed, hooked up to tubes, fighting for herself and her baby.

Their baby.

He closed his eyes, felt a moment's fury. His baby. Damn it, she should have told him as soon as she knew. If he'd known, he'd have found a way to get back, even if briefly.

If only he'd known. . . .

He drew a hoarse breath, closed his eyes. There was no one to hate, no one to curse. He'd never had more than a few minutes on the phone with her, and looking back he remembered how many times her voice had caught, then trailed away. Every time she did, he'd changed the subject, afraid to act too serious. Afraid she'd misunderstand.

He'd screwed up, not Jess.

He felt a burning behind his eyes as people jostled him, chattering about baseball, pizza or stocks. She'd been in the room for almost an hour, and no one had come to tell him anything. He knew that when the news was bad they delayed it as long as possible.

He wouldn't let that matter. They would try again, he swore. They'd make a dozen healthy, laughing babies.

But Hawk couldn't get rid of the vision of Jess's body, still and pale on a hospital gurney. What if the bleeding wouldn't stop?

"Hawk?"

He closed his hands to fists, slammed them against the wall, unaware that he had moved, even when the pain splintered up his arms. Why hadn't he come *sooner*?

*"Hawk."*

When he opened his eyes, Jess's sister was staring at him, her hair tangled as if she'd been running. "Jess—where is she?"

"In that room down the hall. She's been there for about an hour. The baby—something happened. There was blood." He cleared his throat, ignored the burning at his chest. "I asked the nurse for an update ten minutes ago, but I haven't heard anything yet. If I lose her, by God, I'll—"

"Hawk, listen." Strong fingers closed around his fists. "I just spoke to Jess's doctor."

She kept talking, but he didn't hear. All he saw was her mouth moving slowly and the worry in her eyes.

He frowned, trying to hear the words. "Can I see her?"

"Not yet. They're watching her for the next twenty-four hours. They're concerned about the luteal problem."

Hawk shook his head. "Wait—a what problem?"

"It's a hormone imbalance. Jess knew she might lose the baby, in spite of the medication she was taking."

He realized there were other people scattered around the waiting area now. Summer's husband, Gabe, a SEAL Hawk had met twice in training. Dutch was there too, flanked by five or six crusty types who had Navy written all over them.

They were all watching him silently. Hawk figured they had every reason to hate him. "She was sick?" he said raggedly. "I should have come back sooner."

No one said anything. They didn't meet his eyes.

"She didn't tell me," he whispered. "Didn't trust me." He leaned against the wall, feeling the cold tile at his back. "Damn it, I want to *see* her."

Summer reached out awkwardly. "Don't do this, Hawk. It isn't your fault. There had been some sudden changes in her bloodwork a week ago. Her doctors didn't tell her because they weren't sure what it meant."

"She's in danger then?"

Summer closed her eyes and nodded. "I won't lie. It happened so fast and she's still losing blood. They can't figure out why." Summer's voice broke. "They're getting her ready for surgery. We can't see her now."

Hawk turned away, walked down the hall and out the doors to a little courtyard, embarrassed by the tears that cut past his iron control. He put one arm against the wall as his knees threatened to give way.

"Hawk."

He was still in the courtyard, a cup of coffee forgotten beside him. The stone bench was cold, but he barely noticed.

"Hawk, please look at me."

*Bad news.*

He couldn't bear it. All his steel was gone. His world had shrunk to a single question and his sanity danced on the outcome. "Go away," he muttered.

If he didn't hear, it wouldn't be real. He could sit here in the twilight and feel the wind on his face and keep on pretending.

Jess's sister sat down beside him. She put her hand gently on his shoulder. "Hey."

"Don't say it." His hands shook as he groped for the coffee cup. "Go away."

"It's done, Hawk. She's stable." Summer leaned against his shoulder, her careful control breaking as she gripped the front of his leather jacket. "Damn it, listen to me. Jess wants you."

"She . . . wants me?" He dropped the coffee and swung around, studying Summer's face.

She was crying. Smiling. "Inside, pronto, pal. Never argue with a Mulcahey."

*She was stable.*

Hawk's hands locked, and he shaped an awkward prayer of thanks in silent words that were far too rusty.

When he stumbled to his feet, a nurse was walking toward him, her eyes gentle with understanding. "Lieutenant Mackenzie? My patient is asking—no, demanding to see you. You have three minutes, no more. We've given her something to sleep, so she may nod off."

Hawk lunged around her and sprinted down the hall.

Her face was pale, her hair damp. She looked up, whispering his name when he pushed open the door.

Hawk leaned down and locked their hands, worried at how cold her skin felt. "Hey there, beautiful."

She began to cry, slow, silent tears that shook her body while Hawk pulled her against his chest and ran his hands helplessly over her hair. "I wish I could change this, Jess."

Her fingers shook against his. "We never talked about what happened. When I—I messed up my pills back in Washington. I figured I was safe. . . ."

"It's not important now, Jess."

"It *is* important. The mistake was the best thing that ever happened to me, Hawk. Now I keep trying to find someone to blame for having a body that just isn't right."

He cupped her neck gently, brushing a tear from her cool cheek. "There's no one to blame. I've accepted that. We'll have another baby, honey. Ten or fifteen maybe. We'll start our own baseball team."

Jess smiled tentatively at him. "You want ten or fifteen?"

"For starters."

She placed his hand gently on her stomach. Her smile grew. "Then why wait?"

Hawk stared at her, then down at the blanket that covered her. "What do you mean?"

"Everything is good." She gave a shaky laugh. "Don't ask me. The blood tests were bad, then they were good. That's all the surgeon told me. The bleeding started, then it stopped when they were prepping me for surgery. That's all anyone seems to know."

Hawk didn't move. "You mean we've got ourselves a baby?" He couldn't hide the gentle wonder.

"Looks that way." She reached up and traced his cheek. "I hope she looks just like her father."

"She?" Hawk swallowed, beyond overwhelmed. "It's—definite?"

"The doctor told me I'll need to eat right and continue my hormone therapy—but yes. It's definite."

Hawk fumbled in his pocket. "You're going to have to marry me now. I've had this ring for weeks, waiting for the right moment, but since there *never* seems to be a right moment, I want to put it on your finger now." He cleared his throat and held out a small box, locked in his hand. "Marry me, Jess."

She drew in a breath as she opened the box. A single perfect diamond glinted against black velvet. "It's beautiful."

"No, but you are." The door opened behind him, but Hawk didn't look away from Jess's face. There was new color to her cheeks, and he clutched at his courage to finish what he'd been rehearsing for weeks. "I've made plans, pulled in some favors. After next month I won't be traveling so much, and I have some leave coming." He laid the ring on her palm and closed her hand around it. "I can't promise I won't make mistakes. I can't say I'll be any good at this relationship stuff. But I'm sure as hell going to try."

She made a soft little sound, and Hawk realized it was

his name. She caught his hand and his ring, bringing them both to her lips. "Yes."

"You mean—"

"Yes, with my whole heart. Why don't you put this ring on my finger, Lieutenant?" She held up her hand, smiling through tears. "Then I'm going to kiss you."

"Sounds like a damned good battle plan to me, honey."

The door closed behind him.

"What's going on in there?" Dutch stood protectively outside Jess's door, staring at Summer.

"He just asked her to marry him."

"What'd she say?"

"Yes. The kissing was about to start, so I left."

"About damned time they finally did something that made sense." The big man pulled out a handkerchief and wiped his forehead. "I'm too old for this shit. Begging your pardon, Summer."

"Not a problem." She managed a thin smile. "I think I am, too."

"What did she say when he asked her?"

"I didn't hear the details, but she was kissing his ring and his hand, so I figure that meant an unconditional *yes*." Summer sighed. "I tried to keep her safe from so many things over the years. Ever since our parents died, I thought she was the soft one. But I was wrong, Dutch." Summer shook her head. "It takes guts to be an optimist, guts to believe that people are generally good. More guts than I ever had, at least."

She looked up as Gabe slid an arm around her waist. "What would you say to getting a brother-in-law?"

"Sounds good to me."

"About frigging time." Dutch strode off with a wide grin, eager to bring his Navy pals up to speed. Right after that, they all adjourned to the courtyard for cigars and handshakes.

There were going to be plenty of babies from those two, the way Dutch saw it, and the old crew of quiet, decorated heroes from Vietnam decided to get in some practice with their Havanas right now.

Hawk stayed with Jess for the three days she was in the hospital, leaving only to shower and wolf down bad coffee and food that he didn't taste. He bullied her to eat every morning and held her hand while she fell asleep each night.

On the morning of the third day, Summer cornered him in the hall when he was buying more awful coffee from a machine that required exact change.

"You look pitiful, Mackenzie." Summer shook her head and straightened his collar. "On the other hand, three days of stubble kinda suits you. My sister is clearly going to have her hands full."

Hawk rubbed his neck uncertainly. "That's okay with you?"

"Yeah." Summer blew out a breath. "I was too busy being a jerk to give you any sort of chance. I guess I always had a problem where Jess was concerned. Only a few minutes difference in our age, but she's still my little sister. I've been so busy babying her for so long that I couldn't see it was the last thing she needed."

"She's tough," Hawk agreed slowly. "If you could have seen her that day in the shed, you'd know how tough. She was covered with blood, and a gun was locked in her hand. No one would have gotten past her."

"I saw her afterward," Summer reminded him. Even now the memories made her shiver. "I never thought she paid enough attention when I gave her those shooting lessons. I'm glad I was wrong."

"So am I." Hawk stared down at the dirt-colored coffee.

Summer touched his arm. "What's wrong?"

He swirled the muddy drink around in his cup, frowning. "I keep wondering if this was even partly my fault. Maybe something I did or the shock of my coming here so suddenly. It's eating at me, Summer. Even the hint of a possibility."

"That's crazy." Summer took the coffee from his hands and tossed it in the nearby trash can. "There was nothing that any of us could have done to stop this. Jess knew what might happen, and she had a lucky break. End of story. We don't get to play God, Hawk, no matter how much better it would feel."

"I should have come back sooner." He rolled his shoulders. "I should have cornered Jess and worked all the details out of her."

For the first time in three days Summer broke into real laughter. "I can see you don't know Jess as well as you think. She's like a pit bull when she thinks something's important." She held out three quarters to him. "Live dangerously, Mackenzie, but buy yourself some tea. That coffee could kill you faster than one of those secret ops you and Izzy run."

He chose his tea and shrugged. "If I'm going to be a father, I'd better start doing a lot of things differently. I'm going to make her happy, Summer. I love her the way I love breathing, and it feels just that natural. Funny, I always thought that sappy stuff happened to other people."

Summer linked her arm through his. "Only the lucky ones like us. She's crazy about you, by the way. Has been ever since she nearly ran you over with her Jeep."

"She told you about that?"

"Every detail. She said you look pretty hot on that bike of yours, too, especially in black leather."

"Yeah?" Hawk tried to hide a grin. "It's one sweet ride."

"She can't wait to get inside the motor. She's been nuts

about engines ever since she was old enough to hold a Phillips screwdriver. You two have a lot in common." She walked down the hall, then turned. "Just don't make her cry, Navy, or I'll have to seriously kick your butt."

By the end of the day, Hawk had been told the same thing, in various different ways, about twenty times. Dutch and each one of his Vietnam buddies made sure that Hawk knew he got points for being a SEAL, but that the jury was still out on his qualifications as a husband.

But when Jess called them all into her room to display her engagement ring, they beamed in quiet approval. Dutch even slapped Hawk on the back.

He hadn't gained a bride-to-be, Hawk realized. He'd gained a whole Navy team, and a crusty old bunch of heroes they were.

Hawk couldn't think of any better company to be in.

# chapter 28

**T**wo feet stuck out on the ground, wedged under Jess's Jeep.

    With yelps and wild barking Monster raced up and began to slobber on Hawk's toe. "In a minute, boy. Let me finish checking this fuel line."

The dog barked again. This time teeth closed on Hawk's foot.

"Damn, Monster. I told you—"

"Leave the fuel line, commando man. I have an errand to run."

Hawk slid out from beneath the Jeep. Smiling, he grabbed Jess's ankle, moving slightly until he could look up her bright-blue skirt. "Nice legs. Nice underwear, too."

"Nothing special."

"Anything's special on you, honey."

"Very slick." She smiled, her eyes slanting down at him. "How about you come up here and French kiss me, sailor."

"I'm sweating, Jess. I'm covered with grease and sweat and—"

"Aaaah, no more. You're making me go all hot and tingly. I *looooove* a guy covered in grease."

Hawk pulled a rag from his pocket and rubbed his

hands, never taking his eyes from her face. "What kind of errand do you have in mind?"

"A drive up the coast to drop off a package for Dutch." She lifted a basket. "Picnic halfway. The weather's supposed to be gorgeous today. Blue skies and only a hint of clouds."

Hawk finished cleaning his hands and stood up slowly. "I'm game."

Jess ran a hand over his jaw. "Nice stubble, Mackenzie. Very sexy. So are the pants."

His worn jeans were frayed and ragged, riding low at his hips, and he didn't have a clue what she meant, but he liked the shimmer in her eyes just fine. "So this picnic thing—you cleared it with Doc Wilson?"

"A-OK with him. He says I'm good to go on all accounts. French kisses and . . . anything else we want."

Hawk was perfectly aware that it had been four weeks since her near-miscarriage. But he still couldn't seem to relax. "Your appointment wasn't until tomorrow. Damn it, I wanted to go with you, Jess."

"The receptionist called an hour ago and said there was a cancellation, so I went in earlier." She crossed her arms. "I needed to go alone, Hawk. Can you understand that?"

"Because you're tougher than I think you are. And because you think I need to back off, is that what you're telling me?"

Jess's eyes narrowed. "That about covers it." One hand settled on the slight curve of her stomach. "As it happens, Doc Wilson gave me his full medical seal of approval, blood tests, physical exam and all. No conditions of *any* sort." Her voice turned husky. "If you see my drift."

Hawk saw the drift, all right. It was making his brain turn fevered. He'd been handling her with kid gloves ever since her near miscarriage and the awful hours that followed in the hospital. Over the last weeks he had done nothing more than kiss her—no matter how much he wanted to do more.

"So you mean. . . ." He slid his fingers into her hair. "We could go somewhere and fool around."

"Forget fooling around. I'm planning on wet, delirious sex. I want you inside me, Lieutenant." She moved into his arms, her hands sliding into his back pockets so that she could pull him suggestively against her thighs. "And barking would *definitely* be involved."

Hawk slanted a look up to the sky.

*Thank you, God,* he thought.

The day he wouldn't want this woman was the day he would be stone cold dead. But some instinct of worry still lingered, making him pull away gently. "Maybe today isn't such a good time, honey. Summer and Dutch are waiting for you. Something about roses for the backyard, they said."

Jess stood staring at him, a frown crossing her forehead. Then she turned and strode into the house, her face thunderous.

Hawk stabbed a hand through his hair and wondered what the heck he'd done wrong this time.

"Stop *handling* me."

Jess glared at Summer and Dutch, who were bent over a gardening catalog on the back porch. "I won't break. I won't fall apart. I had a near-miss with the baby, but I'm fine." She reached across the table and grabbed the catalog, flipping it shut. "You two are both dear and close to me, but you're not my keepers, understand? And just so you heard me clearly, I'm disgustingly healthy, all systems go. Doc Wilson gave me the official news today."

Summer cleared her throat.

Dutch whistled softly beneath his breath.

"I mean it, you two. Back off. And lay off Hawk, too. Stop warning him that he has to treat me like expensive crystal or I'll shatter."

"We never said—"

"Yes, you did. And just for the record, we're getting married sooner than you expected. If you're very good, you'll both be invited to the wedding."

"You are?" Summer sat up straighter.

"We will?" Dutch said.

Jess glared at Summer, said a rude word, and stormed out.

He couldn't find her anywhere.

She wasn't in the kitchen. She wasn't in the backyard, dozing in the red hammock he'd bought for her.

She wasn't even shmoozing with the guests out on the sunny patio.

Starting to get worried, Hawk sprinted up the stairs to the little apartment they shared at the back of the top floor, courtesy of Dutch.

They had finally agreed on a date for the wedding. They had even started to discuss the guest list. Jess wanted three people. Hawk had about two hundred Navy buddies and family friends that he couldn't wait to introduce her to.

He grinned, wondering if he had lost his mind.

More than likely.

If so, it was the best thing that had ever happened to him.

He pushed open the door of their room. "Jess? Honey, are you—" His breath cut off in a harsh rush of surprise.

She was standing in the middle of the rug, smiling at him in a hot-pink thong and not a stitch else. "Yes?"

"I—" He cleared his throat. "That is, you weren't—" He heard noises down the hall and kicked the door shut with his foot. "Damn it, Jess, you can't stand there wearing a few pink ribbons."

"Why not?" She bent down and picked up her sunhat, giving him a brain-scalding view of her perfect legs and nearly naked butt. "What's wrong with being comfortable?"

She stretched slowly, in the process presenting a spectacular display of full, round breasts.

Saliva backed up in Hawk's throat and he made a manful effort not to look. "Because. . . . " He didn't have a single sane answer to give.

"There was one funny thing I found out today. One of my scars from that day in the shed is completely gone. And Doc Wilson said my last ultrasound showed that my appendix might be starting to grow back. He said it happens sometimes, but that it was still kind of unusual."

Hawk made a note to check with the medical geeks at the secret Walter Reed lab where he got his meds. The lab happened to be the same place where Princess was living the high life these days, well fed and lovingly tended by round-the-clock experts. Hawk wondered if Jess's contact with the bear when she was wounded in the shed may have had some subtle physical effects. Blood or saliva mix, resulting in some kind of genetic transfer?

Hell if he knew. He was a SEAL, not an egghead. But the reason Princess was so valuable was her amazing ability to heal wounds and regrow all her major organs. Which meant that—

Hawk couldn't focus on all the ramifications and possibilities now, not with Jess stretching, on the edge of being gloriously naked, a foot in front of him.

Still smiling, she picked up a bottle of her homemade moisturizer and rubbed some slowly over the beautiful curve of her stomach, then up over both taut coral nipples. Her body was changing week by week, and he was noting each detail with huge pride. Pretty soon she'd need to wear different clothes. Hawk couldn't wait.

As she reached over her shoulder to stroke cream on her back he felt a heat wave tackle his brain. He was all too aware that he hadn't touched her intimately since she'd come out of the hospital.

And now she was smiling at him, killing him brutally, and he realized he would be on his knees any second. But since he was a big, tough SEAL, retreat simply wasn't an option. Instead, he calculated the terrain, estimated enemy reserves, and assessed his tactical options. "You want to have wet, noisy sex, is that it?"

"Could be. If you're lucky."

"You called me commando man. You said it that sexy way you have." Hawk's throat was dry, like it or not. Maybe he wasn't such a big, tough SEAL where Jess was concerned.

"Sexy?" She ran her tongue slowly across her lips. "Who, me?"

He bit back a groan, but by God, two people could play this particular mating game. He locked the door, his eyes on her face. Slowly he pulled his damp T-shirt over his head.

Her cheeks filled with color. She watched his hands clench over straining denim.

As Hawk unsnapped the top button of his jeans, he decided that getting naked for a woman was a real kick—just as long as it was the right woman you were stripping for.

He unsnapped the next button on his jeans and heard her breath catch. She had just realized he wasn't wearing anything underneath.

"Hawk, you're not wearing any underwear."

"I was in a rush this morning. I thought I might go down to the beach at dawn for an early swim, but I didn't have time." He didn't tell her that his icy morning plunges were the only way he could recover after long, restless nights with her soft legs wrapped around him in sleep.

Payback would be pleasant.

Smiling calmly, he opened one more button, feeling the denim go even tighter.

His hand froze as she shot toward him, knocked him back onto the bed and straddled him in her tiny pink thong until he thought he had died and gone to Navy SEAL fantasy heaven.

"By God, I love you, Jess." He took a hoarse breath. "No more kid gloves either." He pulled a field knife from his pocket, slid the blade beneath the pink silk, and cut off her thong in two neat strokes. His eyes were on hers as he tossed the closed knife to the floor and lifted their bodies while he stripped off his jeans.

He kissed her slowly, wet and long with lots of tongue until she moaned his name. She was slick against his palm, warm as sunlight, and his brain was on fire. He wanted to go slow, licking his way over hot skin until he found her silky center, aroused and ready for his mouth.

Yeah, he really, *really* wanted to taste her until she went crazy and drove her nails into his back. It was one of his fonder fantasies.

But he was caught between her thighs and she didn't seem ready to let him go anywhere. He drove his body against hers, groaning when his erection nestled within her thighs, cradled high against her wet heat.

No icy swim today.

No more pale fantasies either. He was going for broke, for something they'd both never forget. There were all kinds of promises, he realized, and his body buried deep within hers had to be one of the best.

When she rose, arched her back, drove her hips down against him, Hawk felt sweat cover his brow. His hands opened on her hips, guiding her down to meet his powerful thrusts.

Decisive psychological advantage was necessary in urban combat situations, especially on complex terrain, he thought dimly.

She came in a rush, with a scream of surprise and pleasure that echoed through the room and out over the balcony.

He couldn't fight a smile of dark, near-Neanderthal pride at his unconditional conquest of her body. When her quick, tight contractions stopped, he brought her up again, high and hard, until she dug her nails into his shoulders and screamed all over again.

When her eyes finally opened, she glared at him. Her mouth set in a mutinous line. "Proving something, Lieutenant? Like how hard and sexy you Navy guys are?"

"Could be." The new medicine that the Navy was giving him had some seriously strange side effects, Hawk had discovered. In addition to promoting the healing of his ribs to the point where he rarely felt the pain anymore, he was starting to be able to control his body in ways that bordered on sheer voodoo.

But control had its advantages. He was enjoying every brain-jolting second of this erotic foreplay with Jess. He was still hard, pressed as far as he could go inside her when he moved his fingers, stroked her wet, silky skin, making her come all over again.

She clawed him, raising long red welts that made Hawk grin. That was his Jess, all fight and spunk.

"Now you're starting to get me *really* mad."

"Sorry to hear it, honey."

"No you're not."

Hawk's grin grew even wider. "You're right, I'm not." *Not for one damned second. Seeing you naked, sated and happy is too amazing.*

"I want you inside me. It's been weeks," she snapped. "I'm dying to feel you." She reached down, her fingers wrapped around him. When they tightened, stroked his length, they squeezed most of the sanity out of his brain.

She was going to get her way any second.

"Ever notice how you're astride my line of tactical communication?"

She licked her lips, her voice husky with desire. "Are you suggesting a large scale withdrawal, Lieutenant?"

"Like hell." Hawk rolled over, gripped her hips, and nudged her wet folds. "Wrap your legs around me," he said hoarsely.

When she did, Hawk groaned and drove her under him until the bed shook. Inch by inch with every thrust she crossed the silk quilt and then her hands were at the iron headboard, gripping tight. Her back arched, and their eyes met in reckless understanding.

"Do me now," she whispered. "Do me hard, Hawk." She gave a broken moan. "Love me. No more kid gloves—"

"I do, honey. Now and forever. As hard as I can make it, Princess. Because it looks like I'm going to be your damned captive forever, body and soul."

He let his body drive home the final promise while their bodies met and strained, and the sex was wet and delirious, exactly like she'd said. Then he followed her home, pounding into a fathomless oblivion, as rich and dark and endless as the sea that broke just beyond their windows.

As sweat covered their flushed bodies, a fresh wind blew up from the beach, ruffling the curtains and curling around a shredded pair of hot pink thong underwear and frayed old jeans.

When their fingers linked and they began to laugh, the wind carried the sound out over the balcony, down through the sunny courtyard, all the way through the olive trees along forty miles of rugged coast beneath a turquoise sky dotted with perfect clouds.

It might as well have been forever.

# about the author

Award-winning author Christina Skye lives on the western slope of the McDowell Mountains in Arizona. CODE NAME: PRINCESS is her nineteenth novel. She holds a doctorate in classical Chinese literature and has traveled ten times to the Orient. Her favorite things are desert wildflowers after a spring storm, lightning in the high country, and a good ghost story. Be sure to visit her online at www.christinaskye.com.

# AUTHOR'S NOTE

Thanks for joining me and Princess on a wild ride. Both Jess and Hawk were real fighters, but Princess was pretty amazing, too.

What unusual skills.

So unusual that she may be reappearing one of these days.

If you'd like to read more about the rugged Pacific Northwest, take a look at this informative guide: *Lonely Planet Pacific Northwest* by Daniel Schechter (Oakland: Lonely Planet Publications, 2002), which captures the grandeur and majesty of the region, along with its quirkier corners.

If you're fascinated by service dogs the way I am, you can get a glimpse into the canine working life in the wonderfully informative book *Dogs with Jobs* by Merrily Weisbord and Kim Kachanoff (New York: Pocket Books, 2000). Princess would be proud to serve in *this* company.

And now to Izzy.

What am I going to do with this tough charmer? The man has insinuated his way into five of my books already, starting with *The Perfect Gift*, followed by *Going Overboard, My Spy, Hot Pursuit,* and *Code Name: Nanny.* Will Izzy be back again?

Count on it.

Will he get a book of his own one day?

All I can say is that he's turning out to be very tough to pin down. Stay tuned to my web site (www.christinaskye.com) for breaking news on the Izzy front! All your letters keep telling me that you love this cool operator just as much as I do.

But before Izzy finds his match, I have a new Code Name book simmering.

A heroine who has come to the end of her rope.

A tough, lonely SEAL with skills he's just beginning to understand.

Get ready to travel west to one of my favorite places, high in the rugged mountains of Sante Fe.

Watch my web site for more details. . . .

Until then, happy reading,

*Christina*

*Look for*

# CHRISTINA SKYE'S
## Code Name: Nanny

*On sale now*

*Read on for a preview. . . .*

# CHRISTINA SKYE

NATIONALLY BESTSELLING
AUTHOR OF *HOT PURSUIT*

# CODE NAME:
## *Nanny*

She's an
FBI agent.
He's a Navy
SEAL. Together
they're igniting
enough heat
to blow both
their covers . . . .

# Code Name:
# Nanny
*On sale now*

The house was bare, white wall to white wall. Naked windows opened onto cold, rain-swept hills. Noises echoed, jarring in the empty space.

A young girl with brown hair walked through the silent rooms, her back ramrod straight. There was no reason to cry, Summer Mulcahey told herself. It was just a house now, not *their* house. The new family would be here any minute, backing up the drive in a shiny red station wagon packed with noise and children and dogs.

No, she wouldn't stay, not to watch strangers take over these rooms, trampling on her memories.

Shoulders rigid, Summer sat down on her battered suitcase, letting her mind touch the walls, searching through fifteen years of memories. She wanted the past carved into her mind, so she could always find it because the past would make her hard and strong.

She needed to be strong now.

There was a *thump* down the hall. Behind her the door swung open. "Aunt Sarah's down in the car." Her sister gestured impatiently, a brighter, rounder, more graceful version of Summer. "I want to go now."

"In a minute."

"You said you were ready." Jess's voice was strained. "You said you hated it here, Sum."

There was no fooling her twin, Summer thought ruefully. They had always read each other too well. "I do. But before I go, I want to remember the good parts." She took a deep breath. "Sneaking pancakes when Mom wasn't looking. Dad building our tree house." Her voice wavered. "You dancing in your red sneakers on that ugly picnic table that always rocked."

"I remember." Jess rubbed her cheeks sharply. "But they're gone now. Mom was . . . strange for a long time, if you ask me."

Both girls had suffered because of it, but neither mentioned that.

Summer's eyes stung, but no tears fell. "She couldn't forget Dad, Jess. She always called him her hero and said he would take care of her, no matter what." Summer glared out at the lawn sloping down to the river. "No man is *ever* going to take care of me. It's stupid to let anyone make you weak like that."

Jess hugged her arms to her chest. "How do you know? You're only fifteen."

"I just know." Summer leaned out the open window, the cold wind on her face. "Dad shouldn't have died, Jess. He wasn't even on duty. He was just going down the damned street for some damned milk."

Jess Mulcahey hated it when her twin cursed. Frowning, she crossed the bare floor and took her sister's hand. "I miss him, too. Sometimes I think I hear the front door open. I keep waiting for him to walk in, whistling Nat King Cole." Jess swallowed hard. " 'Unforgettable.' You know, the one he always sang to us at bedtime."

"I remember." *God help me, I'll always remember,* Summer thought. *But I'll be smart and I'll stay strong as the big trees along the river. No man is ever going to sweep me onto a white horse to make me feel safe.* Summer scowled at the room, repeating her silent vow. "Just remember, the world isn't safe, Jess. And no matter what they say, there aren't any more heroes."

"Maybe there are."

"Trust me, we wouldn't be here alone if I were wrong."

Silence fell. Down the lane the wind shook the poplars and the world seemed to condense, pressing down on Summer with iron fingers. The room was choked with the smell of loneliness.

First they had lost their father, then their mother. Now the two girls only had each other.

Jess broke the spell first, opening her neat blue coat and pulling out a fluffy white cat. Summer pressed the small, wriggling body to her cheek and felt as if she were waiting for something important to happen, some sign that it was over, finished, and they could finally leave.

But no sign came.

There should have been something more, Summer thought angrily. There should have been a chance for explanations and goodbyes. Already her parents felt distant and unreal.

Jess pressed her lips together hard, trying not to cry. "Look, Zza-Zza's ready to leave, and Aunt Sarah is waiting. She says we're going to get our own room with pink curtains."

Summer didn't answer. The woman downstairs wasn't their aunt, just a family friend, and the arrangement was temporary, but Summer wasn't cruel enough to point that out to her grieving sister. Jess wasn't strong like Summer was, and she needed to be protected from some things.

"I want to go, Sum." Jess's lips quivered. "Everything's sad and awful here now."

Things wouldn't ever be the same, Summer thought. No amount of pink curtains could change that. Her childhood was over, and she had to be strong now. For Jess and for herself.

Maybe for her dad, too.

Summer took a last look out the window. An old-fashioned wooden swing hugged the grassy slope to the river beside a crooked picnic table. Once there had been long walks and days of laughter here. There had been water fights and double dare and wild laughter.

Gone now. Almost forgotten, in fact. Two shattering deaths in the last year had done that, leaving the bone-deep emptiness that gripped Summer now.

A man from the Navy had come to the house one night. He had sat in the living room, speaking quietly, with care and concern. At first the two girls thought there had to be a mistake. They were certain their adored father would be coming back any second, whistling one of his favorite Nat King Cole songs.

But he hadn't come back, and they hadn't seen his body even at the funeral. Jess had cried for three straight days, but Summer couldn't seem to shed a tear.

*No more laughter.*

*No more Nat King Cole.*

*No more touch football by the river.*

One week ago their mother had stopped her constant coughing and slipped away. The doctors had called it pneumonia and complications, but Summer thought it was too many memories and a heart that just stopped trying.

Summer wished she could cry, but she couldn't. Maybe her heart was frozen, and it had just stopped trying, too. If so, she was glad. That would make her strong, and she didn't want to feel things.

Her sister shifted impatiently from foot to foot. "It's too quiet here. It's creepy, Sum. Let's just go."

"I'm ready." Summer tried to smile, holding out the struggling cat. "You take Zza-Zza while I get our suitcases."

Jess stuck out her lower lip. "No way. I'm going to carry my own stuff. You don't have to help me all the time."

"I'll do it, Jess. I'm stronger. Besides, you're better with Zza-Zza." Jess had always been the soft one, the easy communicator. Summer was all spunk and grit, the one who held off the bullies after school and fought the monsters hiding under their bed at night.

Since their father died, there had been too many monsters to count, and their mother hadn't seemed to notice.

Summer glanced at the window seat where she and Jess had dreamed about pirate ships and desert islands. Now the window looked small, and there were no dreams left.

Down below the house the river raced on, carrying leaves and small branches that bobbed and twisted in the fast currents. Her mother had always warned them not to get too close or they'd get carried away.

Instead she'd been the one carried off.

Summer shoved away the memories. She wasn't going to get all stupid and blubbery. Things changed, and you had to change with them. Besides, Jess needed her.

"You're right," she said ruthlessly. "Let's go. There's nothing here, anyway. This room is dumb. So is this house."

A bird sailed low over the cold river where December trees guarded a slate-gray sky. More leaves floated past, brown and twisted, long since dead.

Summer grabbed both suitcases. When she walked outside, she didn't look back.

S ummer wasn't frightened. Not exactly.

Anxious, maybe. Determined.

Okay, just a little frightened. Being around rich people always left her on edge, and these people were *very* rich.

She saw the house first, huge with gray stone walls and a broad wooden porch. An immaculate swath of grass sloped down to rugged boulders above a restless sea. As the taxi rounded the drive, Summer sat up straighter, feeling light-years away from the cement and sprawl of Philadelphia. She'd spent most of the last five years within fifteen miles of the Liberty Bell, but it was clear that Carmel was going to be a whole new planet.

The driver eyed her in the mirror. "Haven't seen you before."

Summer made a noncommittal sound, rolling down her window and nudging off one black high heel, which was pinching her toes badly.

"Got a nice family up there." The driver nodded up the cobblestone drive toward the big house. "Lookers, all of 'em. Even the little one, odd as she is."

Summer frowned at him. " 'Odd' how?"

"Guess you'll find out soon enough." His head swung around. "What are you, family, friend, or CNN bureau chief?"

"So you get a lot of reporters down here?"

"Buckets full all summer. Had that woman, Diane Sawyer, a few days back. Skinnier than she is on TV. Guess they all are." The driver's eyes narrowed. "Notice you didn't answer my question."

"That's right, I didn't." Summer looked away, mindful of the assignment that brought her here. Her carefully constructed story seemed almost real to her after the month of preparation she'd endured back in Philadelphia. The fact was, this was no vacation, and Summer was neither family nor friend. This was work with a capital W—FBI fieldwork.

She'd had tough assignments before, but never so close to big money and Washington power politics, and the situation left her edgy.

*Do the job,* she told herself sternly. *Forget about the nerves.*

The driver pulled to a halt near a wall of bougainvillaea flaming crimson against fieldstone walls. "Lotta people sniffing around lately. Brought up a bunch of Hol-ly-wood types last week." The man sniffed with disgust. "All Bel Air this and Ro-de-o Drive that." He stopped the taxi and twisted around to face Summer. "Outsiders. You can spot them a mile away."

Summer glanced at the meter and counted out the hefty fare, then added a fair tip. "Movie stars, you mean?"

"Those, too. Senator Winslow was here to meet them once or twice. Him, I'd recognize anywhere. A popular man with the ladies, and easy to see why, with that calm grin and the way he looks at you like he's really listening. Probably a big act. The way I see it, most politicians are rats looking for a hole." He took the money Summer held out. "You don't look like you're from Hol-ly-wood, though." As before, he tore the word into three disparaging syllables. "Don't sound much like one of those airheads from Washington, D.C., either. Too normal for a damned reporter." He studied her some more, putting some thought into it. "Odd thing is, I can't say *what* you look like."

*Which is part of the reason I'm so good at my job,* Summer thought. She opened her door and hefted her suitcase, which was full of navy suits and dark shoes just like the ones she was wearing. In her particular line of work, plain and inconspicuous were definite job assets.

She decided a little gossip wouldn't hurt her assignment. Bending close to the window, she nodded at the driver. "Sharp eyes."

"So what are you?"

Summer tucked her briefcase under her arm and smiled. "I'm the new nanny."

As she rolled her suitcase along the perfectly cut lawn, Summer scanned her base of operations for the next month. Her host, Cara O'Connor, wasn't on hand to greet her, but that had been expected since Cara was currently hard at work in San Francisco, where she was the city's youngest female assistant DA.

Summer quickly learned from a chatty housekeeper named Imelda that her two charges were upstairs finishing their homework over lemon bars and fruit drinks, awaiting her arrival. Praying she wouldn't be called to explain verb tenses or non-Euclidean geometry, Summer followed the housekeeper out to a Spanish-style guesthouse nearly hidden by towering oleander bushes. Imelda left so Summer could unpack and change before going to meet Cara O'Connor's two daughters.

Wiggling her feet, she kicked off her shoes and dropped her suitcase on the sofa, which was covered with fluffy pillows. Fresh roses filled the air with lush perfume. Summer trailed one finger along the wall of solid fieldstone that led to a six-foot fireplace.

Some digs. Not that she was going to get tied up in knots about it. No, she was going to treat the O'Connors like any other assignment.

Summer was about to start undressing when she heard a sound down the hall. Crossing the room quietly, she peered around a corner.

*There was a naked man in her shower.*

Six foot four inches of naked man, judging by the view she had from her location near the living room.

Summer took a sharp breath and forced herself to be calm. Granted, she had just staggered off two back-to-back flights and her eyes were burning with exhaustion, but that was definitely the outline of a male body behind the tall glass shower enclosure. She was pretty sure that ringing sound was water running, while that other sound, low and rumbling, was a dark male groan of satisfaction.

Her stomach clenched. Either there was a big mistake or this was another trick. She had suffered constant hazing on the job over the last months, from little things like papers taken off her desk to coffee spilled inside her locker. As the junior field officer, Summer had been prepared for a certain amount of hazing.

But this crossed the line.

She glared at the broad shoulders moving back and forth beneath a stream of hot water. No doubt this little surprise came courtesy of her fellow agents back in Philadelphia. With a few well-chosen questions, any one of them could have pinpointed her newest assignment.

Not all of them hated her, but most of them did, and words weren't going to change that. As Summer stood listening to the sound of the shower, something stabbed hard at the center of her chest. They wouldn't forget. They wanted payback, any way that would hurt her most.

Well, to hell with her pals back in Philadelphia and to hell with their crude tricks. Summer was staying right where she was. They weren't going to spook her.

Silently she checked the small desk near the sofa. A tan envelope lay on its side next to a painted Chinese vase. Across the middle of the envelope she saw her name written in small, elegant letters.

Her name. Her rooms. No mistakes there.

Exhausted and grimy from hours of travel, she stared at the cozy fruit basket on the lacquer dresser. The lush roses in crystal vases. No *way* was she leaving.

Summer set her briefcase down carefully on the thick rug. Her raincoat landed on a sleek leather ottoman nearby. Fighting her anger, she scanned the room again. There were no signs of someone living here—no dirty socks on the floor, no clean shirts hanging in the closet. The bed in the adjoining room was perfectly neat, with no dents in the pillows.

Beyond the living area, water continued to strike the glass walls of the shower. As Summer glared at her intruder, the towel hanging over the door slid free. Suddenly she had an unobstructed view of a narrow waist, sculpted thighs, and a world-class naked body.

A little voice whispered a warning.

Punchy with fury, she ignored it. Squaring her shoulders, she sat down in a velvet chair at the entrance to the bathroom, where she had a full view of the sunny shower enclosure.

He was singing an old Beatles song—low and very off-key—when the water hissed off.

The shower door slid open.

*Definitely* a world-class body. The man had the sculpted shoulders of an athlete in superb condition and abs to bounce a dime off. As he ran his hands over his face, drops of warm water clung to the dark hair on his chest, then slowly traveled lower.

An odd tingle shot through Summer's stomach. She hadn't planned to look, but she found herself looking anyway. There was no avoiding the fact that the man had *excellent* muscles.

Especially when he turned and saw her, his body locking hard.

"Don't tell me you're the maid." He had the hint of an accent, something smoky and rough that Summer couldn't trace.

"Guest," she countered flatly. "And unless you talk fast, you're spending the night as a guest of the local police, pal."

A smile played across his mouth. "Now you're terrifying

me." The roughness was there again, but there wasn't a hint of anxiety in his cool smile or the slow way he scooped up his towel and tossed it over his shoulder, where it concealed nothing.

Obviously, modesty was a foreign concept to the man.

Summer prayed to six patron saints for the ability to stay cool under his unrelenting stare, but the prayers weren't working. Heat rose in her face and fingers of awareness nudged a dozen sensitive nerve centers. Probably the result of the industrial-strength Dramamine she'd taken on the plane, dulling her normal edge.

Or maybe it was the man's cocky smile as he draped the towel low around his waist.

She was an expert in the Weaver stance and shotgun recoil. She knew about bomb dogs, wire fraud, and chain of custody for criminal evidence. But no one at Quantico had taught her the proper procedure for a naked smart-ass when said naked smart-ass was standing in your shower whistling "Penny Lane."

"Get out," she said tightly. "Otherwise you're going to be kissing the floor, and trust me I won't make it nice."

His brow rose. "You know judo?"

"Aikido."

Suddenly his eyes were dark and focused. "You're the new nanny?"

"That's right. And you are?"

"Gabe Morgan—landscape and general contracting. The girls told me you weren't coming until later tonight. My shower's been acting up, so I thought I'd sneak over and clean up before you arrived."

As an apology, it stunk. As an explanation, it was passable—assuming that Summer believed him.

Which she didn't.

" 'The girls'?"

"The two O'Connor kids. Audra and Sophy. They told me when you were to arrive."

Summer smiled tightly. "As you can see, they were wrong."

"In that case, sorry for the intrusion. No reason for things to get off on the wrong foot because of it."

"I'd say it's a perfect reason."

He crossed his arms, and Summer worked hard not to stare at the fine display. There was a small scar near the top of his shoulder that curved down in a tight hook. From a gardening tool?

"The old nanny let the girls run wild. Clearly, you're going to be a lot stricter."

"I'm not getting paid to let them run wild, Mr. Morgan."

"Call me Gabe."

Why was he standing there holding a conversation in his towel, for heaven's sake? Why didn't the man just *go*? "I doubt I'll call you anything until you get some clothes on."

"Too bad." Once again the grin teased his lips. "Clothes can be damned overrated, ma'am."

"Not by me."

Gabe Morgan shook his head. "Things were just starting to get interesting, too." He gave a two-finger wave as he crossed the living room. "I'll talk to Audra and Sophy about this. I'm pretty sure it's their harebrained idea of a joke on the new nanny. Meanwhile, enjoy the shower, now that I got things all warmed up for you." He tightened his towel, opening the front door. "By the way, they're good kids, but you should tan their hides for this little stunt. It's a war out there, and the kids are winning, from what I hear."

"Thank you for the astute advice, Mr. Morgan. I assure you, I know how to do my job," Summer said stiffly.

"Glad to hear it. Let me know if you need any help."

Summer crossed her arms. "I won't." She'd studied enough books on the subject in the last three weeks to tackle anything that was thrown at her.

So she hoped.

The towel slid lower on his lean hips. Summer was pretty sure her mouth was hanging open. She might drool any second.

"Whatever you say, 'Night, Ms. Mulvaney."

*She hadn't told him her name.*

The door closed. Summer sank back in the velvet chair outside the shower, feeling steam brush her face like a warm caress. She tried to forget his body and his grin—and failed at both.

During her FBI career she'd had her share of aggravating assignments. Some of them had been high profile and some of them had put her squarely in the path of grievous bodily harm.

Something told her *this* one was going to take the cake.

Gabe Morgan felt like shit.

Leave it to Cara O'Connor's kids to set up something low-down and sneaky like this. Not that he minded being caught buck naked, but the new nanny had looked angry enough to char steak.

As soon as the door to his guesthouse had closed, Gabe tossed down his towel and prowled through his living room. The woman didn't even look like a nanny, for God's sake. Since Gabe had only met one other nanny in his life, he didn't have a lot to compare by, but he was pretty sure nannies were starched and prim, expert at holding hands, defusing temper tantrums, and hiding any real, honest thoughts.

Not Summer Mulvaney. Beneath that dark suit she looked strong and surprisingly well-conditioned. Besides that, there was her kick-ass attitude. The woman was cool and confident, with an intensity that had caught him by surprise. She didn't mince words and he was pretty sure she didn't take crap from anyone.

It was a trait Gabe Morgan had always admired, whether in men or women.

But something about Summer Mulvaney bothered him. She didn't come across as your average, garden-variety nanny or nurturer. Then again, maybe he was crazy. There was no denying that this job was starting to get to him.

Frowning, Gabe shoved away thoughts of the new nanny as he rustled through his bureau, tugged on clothes, and located three fresh surgical bandages. He'd tackle fifty sit-ups and twenty squats, then see if he could push himself any further.

After that, he'd wrap his knee and take a short break, then start all over again.

He was so used to seeing the scars on his body that they might as well have been invisible. Even the memories had begun to blur, their grim details fading into a gray-green blur of jungle sky and blue-green water.

Followed by screaming pain.

But Gabe Morgan was an expert at pain. If a day went by without it, he worried that he was losing his edge. If a week went by, he started to feel bored.

Which was probably why he was so good at his current job.

But as he looked outside, he found himself remembering the nanny's eyes when he'd turned in the shower. They were more gray than blue, more angry than afraid. Strange mix.

Strange woman.

He shook his head, irritated. Summer Mulvaney had great legs—or she would have without that bland blue skirt covering them down to the knees. Not that he would get a chance to see her legs or any other interesting parts of her body up close.

A damned shame.

But Gabe didn't have time to waste on irrelevant things like his emotions or the new hired help.

It was time to get back to work, he thought grimly.